"You are too—"

"Nice. I know. I can't help my...

"Actually, I was going to say you are too good at this. Are you sure you've only been the uncle to one child?" J.R. wiggled her fingers at Hunter. "You give off a very strong fun-uncle vibe."

He was not expecting the compliment. "Really? Nico is only two, so I have to do very little to entertain him other than make goofy faces. Your Tessa is my first big-kid experience."

"Well, you're doing an excellent job of impressing her. First asking her to name the goat. Now steering the horses. You're a natural."

"Let's hope I'm as good at impressing her mom," he said, holding out his hand to help her get up into the wagon.

As soon as she placed her hand in his, he felt the spark. The way her blue eyes widened meant she must have, too. "You're doing a pretty good job of that, as well."

Dear Reader,

The Blackwells are back, and I couldn't be more excited! This time, Big E and Denny are teaming up to get Denny's estranged granddaughters back together, and if you've read the other Blackwell books, you know that when these two want something, they aren't giving up until they get it.

J.R. Blackwell is just like her grandma, stubborn as they come. Thankfully, this tough-as-nails Blackwell is about to meet her match. I loved bringing Mr. Sunshine, aka Hunter Robbins, to life. He's the ray of light in J.R.'s challenging world. He tries everything he can think of to make her smile. Who wouldn't want that in their life? Apparently, J.R. thinks she wouldn't...but maybe she'll change her mind once she gives the guy a chance!

I hope you enjoy this segment of The Blackwell Belles. Can Flora get one daughter closer to having all five of them at her Cowgirl Hall of Fame induction ceremony? This one might be a challenge. As Hunter learns, J.R. never makes anything easy!

Thanks for reading, and thank you for loving the Blackwells as much as we do!

Amy Vastine

A COWGIRL'S THANKSGIVING KISS

AMY VASTINE

If you purchased this book without a cover you should be aware that this book is stolen property. It was reported as "unsold and destroyed" to the publisher, and neither the author nor the publisher has received any payment for this "stripped book."

Recycling programs for this product may not exist in your area.

ISBN-13: 978-1-335-05125-7

A Cowgirl's Thanksgiving Kiss

Copyright © 2024 by Amy Vastine

All rights reserved. No part of this book may be used or reproduced in any manner whatsoever without written permission.

Without limiting the author's and publisher's exclusive rights, any unauthorized use of this publication to train generative artificial intelligence (AI) technologies is expressly prohibited.

This is a work of fiction. Names, characters, places and incidents are either the product of the author's imagination or are used fictitiously. Any resemblance to actual persons, living or dead, businesses, companies, events or locales is entirely coincidental.

For questions and comments about the quality of this book, please contact us at CustomerService@Harlequin.com.

TM and ® are trademarks of Harlequin Enterprises ULC.

Harlequin Enterprises ULC
22 Adelaide St. West, 41st Floor
Toronto, Ontario M5H 4E3, Canada
www.Harlequin.com

Printed in Lithuania

Amy Vastine has been plotting stories in her head for as long as she can remember. An eternal optimist, she studied social work, hoping to teach others how to find their silver lining. Now she enjoys creating happily-ever-afters for all to read. Amy lives outside Chicago with her high school–sweetheart husband, three teenagers who keep her on her toes and their two sweet but mischievous pups. Visit her at amyvastine.com.

Books by Amy Vastine

Harlequin Heartwarming

Stop the Wedding!

A Marriage of Inconvenience
The Sheriff's Valentine
The Christmas Wedding Crashers
His Texas Runaway Bride

Return of the Blackwell Brothers

The Rancher's Fake Fiancée

The Blackwell Sisters

Montana Wishes

The Blackwells of Eagle Springs

A Wyoming Secret Proposal

Visit the Author Profile page
at Harlequin.com for more titles.

To Lauren Olivia—the sunshine in my son's life.

Thank you for being you and
welcome to the family!

PROLOGUE

ELIAS BLACKWELL WAS ready to roll. His RV had a full tank of gas and a refrigerator stocked with plenty of snacks and drinks. He'd cleaned it up so his sister and niece had a comfortable place to sit for their next adventure. The only issue was getting these Blackwell women in the vehicle.

"You sure you don't want me to come along?" Barlow Blackwell had been saying goodbye to his wife, Flora, for fifteen minutes now. Big E was beginning to lose patience, something he never had much of to begin with and certainly was lacking these days.

"I appreciate the offer," Flora said, leaning into her husband. "But I've got this."

Barlow kissed her forehead. "I'm proud of you for figuring out how to make things right. Once you've reconciled with our daughters, maybe they could come visit us next time."

Big E caught Denny watching her son with a satisfied grin on her face. One of his sister's main goals was to see those two together again.

She had accomplished that, and he was happy for her.

Flora smiled up at her husband. "That sounds like an excellent plan. All this traveling has been wearing on me. It was nice to have some time with you. Makes me motivated to finish this so we can make up for lost time."

After visiting with Iris in Cottonwood Creek, Flora, Denny, and Big E had needed a break. It was time to check in with the families they had left behind to begin the mission of getting the Blackwell Belles back together. Denny had gone back to Eagle Springs to get an update from Corliss about the Flying Spur, Flora had asked for some time in Flame to help Barlow move into her place there, and Big E had returned to Falcon Creek so his wife and grandkids didn't think he had forgotten about them.

"Let's hit the road so we can get you two lovebirds back under the same roof again." They were already behind schedule. Flora wasn't much of an early riser and was never ready when she said she would be. The trip itinerary included a stop in Austin to meet with a friend before surprising J.R. in Brighton this evening.

"You'll be back by Thanksgiving?" Barlow asked Big E as his wife settled aboard the RV.

The old man shrugged from the vehicle's doorway. "Your daughters have yet to make things easy. We could be back in a couple days or a couple weeks. Who knows how long it will take to get J.R. to come back to the fold."

Barlow shoved his hands in his pockets. "Given how much my eldest is like her grandmother, what do you think?"

Big E hadn't been aware that he was heading toward Denny Jr. He took off his hat and shook his head solemnly. "Looks like you're going to be celebrating Thanksgiving alone. No way this is going to be easy if she's like my sister."

Denny harrumphed from behind him. "If she's like me, she'll be fair and wise. It won't be hard to get her to make a reasonable decision."

Barlow's eyebrows lifted as he rocked back on his heels. "Right, Ma. Exactly."

Her eyes narrowed and she pointed her finger. "You two think you're so funny. As if you both don't have the Blackwell stubbornness in spades."

Big E couldn't deny that. He put his hat back on and was about to swing the door shut.

"Maybe I'll drive down for Thanksgiving if you're still there," Barlow said. "Drive safe and stay in touch."

"We'll keep you posted," Big E said with a nod. Jasmine Rose Blackwell might be a carbon copy of her grandmother, but they were coming down there with the original. There was no way they would return empty-handed.

CHAPTER ONE

"TESSA! WE NEED to go...*right now!*"

J.R. Blackwell's day was not starting off the way she had hoped. She had hit Snooze one too many times and was forced to speed through her morning routine. After pouring cereal into bowls for a fast and easy breakfast, she realized they had no milk. The clothes she had put in the dryer last night, which included the outfit Tessa wanted to wear today, were still damp this morning because J.R. had apparently forgotten to push the start button.

The bus had left their street fifteen minutes ago. The ten-year-old who was supposed to be on it was still upstairs. It wasn't unusual to have to drive Tessa to school, but they weren't typically in such a rush. A quick glance at her watch told J.R. they should already be on the road if she was going to get to the ranch on time.

"I'm coming," Tessa replied as she skipped down the stairs with her head down. She pushed her hair in front of her face as she turned the corner, clearly hiding from her mother.

"Can you look at me please?" J.R. asked, trying to figure out what she didn't want her mother to see.

Tessa kept her back to her mom and sidestepped around the kitchen table to get her pink backpack off her chair. "We have to go, Mom. Come on."

"Show me your face, Tessa Jean."

Another heavy sigh made Tessa's shoulders lift and fall dramatically. She spun around and glared at J.R. It wasn't the way she used her eyes to express her displeasure, it was the massive amount of eye makeup that caused J.R. to gasp.

It had been a valiant attempt, but it was clear Tessa had never put on makeup before. Her eyeliner was too dark under one eye and barely there under the other. The mascara had been applied a tad thick and she must have accidentally swiped the wand against one of her eyelids. For some reason, unbeknownst to J.R., she had dabbed white eyeshadow in the inside corners of her eyes.

"Sweetheart..." J.R. started.

"Mom! We're going to be late. We need to go! I can't be late for school again."

"We are not going anywhere until you go wash that stuff off your face. You are ten. Ten-year-olds do not need to wear makeup. Plus, you are beautiful. You do not need to do anything to yourself to be prettier."

"Everyone in my class wears a little makeup. It's fine. I can't be late again or I'm going to lose recess."

A little was not the way to describe the amount of makeup on her daughter's face right now. "I have a feeling not everyone wears makeup, and I am not everyone's mom. I am your mom. I need you to go wash that off."

Tessa ran upstairs shouting something about J.R. being the worst mother in the world. Funny, that was what J.R. used to say about her own mother. Of course, she did that because Flora Blackwell used to force J.R. and her sisters to wear makeup even earlier than ten years old. The last time J.R. saw that much eyeshadow on a child was when she was doing tricks for the Blackwell Belles, something she wished she could scrub from her memory permanently. J.R. hated that she used to get paraded around rodeos like some kind of pink bubblegum princess more bedazzled than a rhinestone cowboy.

There was no way she was going to repeat her mother's mistakes. J.R. followed Tessa upstairs to help her get all that gunk off. There was probably little chance the girl knew waterproof mascara wouldn't wash off easily.

"Here, you need to use this to get that mascara off." J.R. handed Tessa some cotton pads and a bottle of eye makeup remover. "You don't have to scrub hard. Be gentle or you'll irritate your eyes."

Tessa's frown stayed firmly in place as she snatched the bottle of cleanser from her mother's hand. Time was moving too fast. J.R. wasn't ready for Tessa to grow up yet. It felt like yesterday she was rocking her to sleep and kissing her bald head. Suddenly, her baby girl had long blond hair and wanted to be a makeup artist.

"Where did you even learn about makeup?" J.R. asked.

"All you have to do is watch a couple makeup tutorials online. It's not that hard," she answered with a roll of her now bare eyes.

Online tutorials. Everything was online these days. Parenting was so much harder now than it was when she was growing up. J.R. and her four other sisters didn't have access to the internet. Their "influencers" were real-life people who they only saw in person. Their parents had known everyone they talked to, since they were constantly together on the road performing.

Being a single mom didn't make it easy. Tessa was more often out of J.R.'s sight than in. She knew the names of the girls in Tessa's fifth grade class, but she hadn't met them all. Tessa spent afternoons at her best friend's house next door. Addie was one year older than her *and* in middle school. Middle school was a scary place that J.R. was not ready to send Tessa to anytime soon. Throw in the internet and anyone could be telling Tessa what to do, what to wear, how to act.

Tessa finished the task of getting all that makeup off and stormed out of the bathroom like the perfect temperamental teenager-in-training she was becoming. J.R. followed her downstairs and out to the car. The sun was shining, but there was nothing bright and cheery about the day.

J.R. tried to ignore the fact that her grass needed to be cut and the vibrant, hot-pink Knock Out rose bushes she had planted last year were in desperate need of watering. Those chores would have to wait until the weekend. She had to stop at the grocery store after work or they'd have nothing to eat for dinner but the leftover Halloween candy from two weeks ago. The box sitting on the passenger's seat reminded her she also needed to go to the post office sooner rather than later.

"I might be a little late picking you up from the Langleys' today." The Langleys were the neighbors who took care of Tessa after school. Hilde Langley was a lifesaver. When J.R. moved into the neighborhood six years ago, Hilde had immediately volunteered to watch Tessa for her since she was a stay-at-home mom. The girls had grown up together and shared interest in the same things. They loved horses, played on the same soccer team, and always had a new TikTok dance to show J.R.

"I need to make a couple stops on my way home," J.R. explained.

Tessa said nothing in return. The cold shoulder must have been a trait she'd inherited from her father, who had been giving them both the cold shoulder since before Tessa was born. Getting involved with a rodeo cowboy while she was trying to finish college had not been one of J.R.'s better decisions. The only good thing that had come out of that relationship was Tessa. His lack of interest in his daughter was his loss, although that was sometimes a hard sell to a little girl who just wanted her dad to remember when it was her birthday.

When she pulled up in front of school, the makeupless child got out of the car and grumbled her goodbyes.

J.R. rolled down the passenger's side window and shouted, "I love you! Have a great day!" An impatient dad behind her honked. She gave him an apologetic wave of the hand and exited the drop-off lane, praying she didn't get to work too late.

Bucking Wonders Ranch was one of the largest bucking bull breeders in South Central Texas.

It was family owned by two brothers, Walter and Jed Wonders. Walter's son, Lou, was ranch manager. There were a couple ranch hands on staff, but the Wonders brothers liked to keep their staff small. Walter was the businessman and the face of the company, shaking hands and going to all the events while Jed did all the behind-the-scenes work. Bucking Wonders was one of the up-and-coming stock contractors in the country. They'd soon be number one if J.R. had anything to say about it. The bucking bull business was all about genetics, and J.R. knew a thing or two about that. Her dream was to one day make a real name for herself in the business like Jed and Walter. It was a man's world, though, and she would have to work harder and breed the best of the best to get the same attention.

She pulled into the dirt parking lot five minutes late. She gave herself a quick once-over in the rearview mirror. She hadn't had time to flat iron her hair so there was a little wave in her golden locks today. She slipped the hair tie she kept on her wrist off and swept her hair up in a ponytail. Stepping out of her car, she hoped no one would notice her tardiness.

"Well, there she is! Happy Thursday, Ms. Blackwell. I was starting to think you were planning on taking the day off." Hunter Robbins made sure no one was unaware of her late arrival. All six feet of him came moseying on over with two coffee cups in his hands. “I was worried I was going to have to drink both of these myself,” he said, holding out a cup and giving her that my-life-is-perfect smile.

“What makes you think I haven’t already had my caffeine for the day?”

“Well, something tells me if you had, you would have noticed that you skipped a button.” He nodded at her chest.

J.R. glanced down and quickly spun around while she fixed the buttons on her shirt. Must be nice to be Hunter. He didn’t live on only a few hours of sleep a night because there were bills to pay and dishes to wash and clothes to fold after the millions of other things that had to be done after putting in a full day’s work. He didn’t have to get a ten-going-on-twenty-year-old up and ready for school in the morning. He had enough time to stop at the coffee shop in town and make sure all of the buttons on his plaid button-down were properly fastened.

Turning back around to face him and his perfectly clean-shaven face, she took the cup from his hand. “Maybe I forgot to set the coffeepot timer last night. It happens.”

“It happens all the time,” he agreed. “Thankfully, you’ve got me around to help you out on days like this.” He winked and slid his now empty hand into the front pocket of his slim-fitting dark jeans.

"I need to find Jed to go over the schedule for today." She forced a small smile and tried to remember her manners. "Thanks for the coffee."

"Anytime, J.R. It's my pleasure." The dazzling smile he gave her in return made her almost forget where she said she was going.

Hunter Robbins was a nuisance, she told herself. How did he manage to be that positive and pleasant all the time? It was like the guy never had a bad day or a bad minute for that matter. For someone like J.R., who felt like she had bad years, it was a little much.

The two of them both worked under Jed. They were the team that managed the breeding, oversaw the training, and did the marketing and sales of the bulls. Hunter's strength was the training. As a former bull rider, he knew what it took to get these yearlings ready for competition. J.R.'s passion was the genetics. Her strength was finding the right bull and the right cow to create the next great champion.

Just as J.R. was about to go into the main office, Jed came out. Jed Wonders was as big as a bull. He had broad shoulders and a round belly. His salt-and-pepper hair was the only part of him thinning. "Oh, good, you're here. I need to talk to you and Hunter."

As if Hunter knew he was needed, he appeared at her side instantly, smiling ear to ear. "Team meeting?"

"I guess you could call it that. I have a big announcement and it impacts both of you." He ushered them inside.

The office space at the Bucking Wonders was small and a tad outdated. There were wood-paneled walls and industrial carpet that had more mystery stains than J.R. liked to think about. Off the main office area was a small bathroom and three smaller offices. Walter and Jed each had their own while Hunter and J.R. shared the third. When Hunter had joined the company, they had shoved a second desk into J.R.'s little space and forced her to have to look at his chiseled jaw five days a week.

Pam, Jed's wife and secretary, sat behind the desk in the reception area. Her hair was styled like she still lived in the nineties. Her bangs needed their own zip code, but she was the sweetest. Sweetest, not exactly the hardest working.

She paused the show she was streaming on her computer. "Did you tell them?"

"I'm bringing them in here to tell them."

"Well, tell them."

"I would if you could just shush."

Pam pushed her shoulders back, her tone indignant. "Did you just tell me to shush? I am the mother of your children."

Jed was a large and intimidating man. Neither J.R. nor Pam could wrap their arms all the way around his massive chest. But when Pam reminded him that she had birthed his children, he turned to putty in her hands. He bent down and rubbed his nose against hers. "I apologize, sweetheart. I didn't mean that."

"I figured as much," she cooed before shoving him away. "Now, tell them!"

Jed righted himself and straightened his shoulders. "As you know, I am not getting any younger. And even though Pam here still looks twenty-five, she is actually the same age as me. We've decided it is time to kick back and relax."

J.R. wasn't sure what he meant. Her brows pinched together as she looked between the two of them. "Are y'all going on vacation for the holidays?"

"No, silly. We're retiring!" Pam jumped out of her seat.

Retiring? J.R. was completely unprepared for this kind of news. Jed was her mentor, her boss. How would this place run without him? Hunter, on the other hand, responded just as one would assume. He immediately congratulated them and hugged Pam, lifting her off her feet and giving her a spin.

He set her down. "I am so happy for you guys.

How exciting! What's the big plan? Are you sticking around here or taking off on us?"

"We're leaving Brighton, Texas, and moving to Florida!" Pam clapped her hands. "I am spending the rest of my days staring at the ocean with a fruity drink in my hand."

J.R. blinked slowly. There was a faint ringing in her ears. "You're moving to Florida? Does Walter know?"

Jed chuckled. "Of course, he knows."

J.R. set her coffee down and pulled a tissue from the box on Pam's desk. "Who's going to handle everything you do? How can he possibly replace you?"

"Well, that's why I needed to talk to you two." Jed's expression turned serious, and J.R.'s stomach churned. She was not a fan of change. She liked stability and for things to stay the way she preferred them. As a child, she was always on the move, constantly learning new tricks, performing in front of new crowds. It made her, as an adult, seek out consistency. The Bucking Wonders Ranch had provided her that for the last six years. She didn't want things to change, but something told her change was coming.

CHAPTER TWO

HUNTER COULDN'T FIGURE out why J.R. had that crease between her eyebrows. Hating seeing her stressed, he wanted to take his thumb and smooth it out. Jed and Pam were clearly excited about their retirement. This was good news. If she was worried about who was going to take over for Jed when he left, she was wasting her time. There was no way that Walter and Jed weren't going to name J.R. as Jed's replacement.

"So, I've been talking to Walter. We both agree that I am irreplaceable."

Hunter chuckled at Jed's obvious joke while J.R. continued to stare at him with that anxious expression on her face. She had a tissue in her hand, not that she needed it to wipe away any tears. J.R. was not the crying type to his knowledge, but that thing was being torn into tiny bits and shoved back into her fist.

"But be replaced, I must," Jed continued. "Walter thought maybe we should look outside the ranch."

J.R. gasped, causing Jed to do the chuckling. If Hunter didn't know any better, he would have thought the woman was going to throw up. She was white as a ghost.

"Don't worry," he assured her. "I told him that you two have been doing the heavy lifting around here for a while now. I trust both of you completely, but I don't know that I can choose between you."

"But J.R. has been here longer," Hunter said, finding it impossible that there would even be a question as to who should take over. "I don't know why you'd—"

"Don't do that," J.R. snapped. "Don't act all humble like you're going to step aside for me. I don't need you to step aside."

"I wasn't stepping aside. I was just saying—"

"You don't need to say anything. Let's hear what Walter and Jed decided. So what did you decide?" she asked Jed, folding her arms across her chest.

"We're still debating, J.R. You have been here longer. I appreciate your animal sciences background and your understanding of the genetics behind all that we do. Hunter, you bring something equally important to the business. Your name recognition alone is valuable."

"I knew it," J.R. huffed.

Jed cocked his head. "I said we're still debating. It will be one of you, though. I thought you should know that. I didn't want y'all thinking we were going to overlook what you both mean to the business."

"I appreciate that, Jed." Hunter held out his hand and Jed shook it. Both men glanced in J.R.'s direction. It was clear she was still displeased.

She took a deep breath and smoothed her blond hair with her hand. Adjusting her expression, she said, "Congratulations on your retirement. Thank you for the update. Is that all? I have a lot of work ahead of me today."

Jed nodded. "That's it for me."

J.R. took off for their office, closing the door behind her.

"She took that well," Pam said, giving them a bemused smile.

Hunter picked up the coffee she had left behind. "I think she just needs to finish her morning caffeine."

Pam chuckled. "I love your optimism, sweetheart."

Hesitantly, Hunter reached for the doorknob, but the door opened before he grabbed it.

J.R. startled on the other side. "I forgot my coffee."

He held up his peace offering. "I was bringing it to you."

She snatched it and spun on her heels. He couldn't hide his shock. He knew her to have better manners than that. Hunter could tell she had a million things on her mind the second she stepped out of her car, but that didn't mean she got to be rude.

"You're welcome," he said as he stepped into the room after her.

"Sorry," she said with a sigh as she sat down at her desk. J.R.'s desk was covered in papers and colorful sticky notes. She could find anything she needed, but it looked a mess. Hunter, on the other hand, was a minimalist. His desk had a computer and desk calendar on it. He had one pen and one pencil that he kept in the drawer.

"Seems like a particularly bad day, huh?"

"Thank you for the coffee. I'm having a rough morning and it's not your fault. I shouldn't have made it seem that way."

Hunter considered making a joke to lighten the mood but simply gave her an understanding nod instead. Getting a laugh out of her was difficult on a good day and today was clearly not what she would consider good. He took a seat at his desk and checked his email, glancing over at J.R. every couple minutes to make sure she was okay.

"I guess we should be glad they aren't going to replace Jed with someone outside of the ranch.

They do that sometimes. Bring in 'fresh' perspectives," she said as she tapped on her keyboard a tad harder than needed.

"True."

"We should also remember it's a family business," she added. "They could have given it to someone in the family."

"Also true."

She stopped typing. "I don't even know if Lou has ever thought about working on this side of things."

"I'm fairly certain Lou doesn't want a different job. He likes what he does." Hunter and Lou had talked about the ranch many times over the last year. She had nothing to worry about.

"I think they have a cousin who has a couple of kids. I wonder if they've told the extended family. Someone could still come forward, looking to be part of the business."

"I don't think we need to worry about Jed handing over his job to some random cousin. He knows you are incredible at what you do here," he said, hoping that would calm her nerves.

Her frown somehow deepened. "Don't do that."

"What?"

"Act like you think I'm going to get the job."

"I do think you're going to get the job."

"They could very easily give the job to you. Do you not want the job? If you don't want it, you should say something to Jed." Before he could reply, she shook her head. "No, don't do that. Don't give me the job. I want to earn it. You want the job, don't you? Of course, you do. You'd be out of your mind if you turned down an opportunity like this. You want the job, right?"

Her words came out a million a minute. Hunter wasn't sure if it was safe to answer yet. Truth was, he had been waiting for someone to believe in him again.

Riding bulls had been his life. It had been the only thing he thought he was good at for as long as he could remember. He shifted in his seat as the pain in his shoulder acted up as if on cue. Two years ago, his dream of being the greatest bull rider in history had come crashing down. The bull he'd drawn that night in October had stomped on his head and shoulder after bucking him off. The helmet he had been wearing had saved his life, but the bull still fractured his skull. The incident left him with so much metal in his body that his oldest brother called him Robo Bro now. Doctors had told him that he was lucky to be alive. That had been all his parents needed to hear to beg him to retire.

If he couldn't ride bulls, he had to find a way to still be part of the sport. When Hunter left Austin to recover at his family's ranch on the outskirts of Brighton, Bucking Wonders was exactly the right place for him to do just that. It might not give him the same adrenaline rush, but breeding and brokering the sales of champion bulls was satisfying in a different way.

He cautiously began his reply, "I would never turn the opportunity down. If they think I am the right man—" J.R. grimaced. "I mean, the right *person* for the job, I would happily accept the responsibility."

J.R. tightened her ponytail. "Then don't sit there and tell me the job is mine. It could be yours." He swore he heard her mumble something about it should be hers under her breath.

She was a firecracker. No one worked harder to prove herself than J.R. Blackwell. Hunter wasn't sure why she constantly questioned herself. She was smarter than almost everyone he knew. Her ideas were always strong. Yet, she seemed to be ever prepared to be met with a lack of support.

"If Jed says it's between you and me, then I believe him. That's all I'm saying."

J.R. pondered that for a second before giving him a sharp nod. "You're right. That's what he said. That's what he meant."

J.R.'s phone rang and she dug through her bag to find it. When that didn't work, she dumped the entire contents onto her desk. Hunter stared wide-eyed as she pushed out the thousands of items that had magically been contained inside her purse. It was like seeing all those clowns climb out of a tiny VW bug at the circus.

She finally found her phone and was quick to answer. "Hello?" She paused to listen, becoming somehow more flustered by the second. "When did that form get sent home? I remember her talking about a field trip, but I don't remember seeing it. Can I just give my permission over the phone? I give my permission for her to go. Please let her go," she pleaded. J.R. pressed her hand to her forehead. "Yes, I understand there are rules. I get that there was a deadline for the form to come in. I'm sure I'm not the first person to forget to fill it out, though. Can't you make an exception? If you email me a copy, I can print it out, sign it, and send it back in a matter of minutes."

Hunter sensed she wasn't getting the answer she wanted based on the fact that her face was now red as a tomato, and she was holding a pen in her hand like it was a weapon instead of a writing tool.

"This is ridiculous! You're punishing a little girl because her mom didn't see a form in her backpack. I get it. I get it. I'm sure it has been mentioned in the class newsletter. I also get about nine hundred emails a day, so forgive me if I missed a newsletter here and there. I understand. Rules are rules. Your rules stink. No, I hope you have a good day." J.R. ended her call and dropped her phone in the pile of stuff on her desk.

"That didn't sound good. Anything I can do to help?"

"Not unless you have a time machine and can take me back to last Friday when my daughter's permission slip was due so that she can go on today's field trip instead of sitting in the principal's office crying." As she began putting everything back into her purse, her eyes glistened with unshed tears.

Hunter wasn't good with tears. He grew up in a house with all boys who only cried after getting beat up by one of the other ones. In those situations, teasing them relentlessly was the only appropriate response. That was not acceptable in this case.

"I'm sorry," he said, hoping that would do the trick.

"She's never going to forgive me for this." The tears started to fall, and Hunter felt like a failure. "She's been talking about this field trip and how they were going to get to milk a cow or something like that. I don't know how I forgot to sign the permission form. I mean, it was supposedly in the teacher's weekly newsletter for the last month. Don't people understand that working single mothers don't have the luxury of reading every online class newsletter?"

He tried to channel his mother. She was the one who took care of whoever was crying. "It's going to be okay. Like you said, you can't be the first person to forget."

"Oh, no. According to Principal Hudson, I am the first and only parent in all of Brighton, Texas, to forget to send in a field trip permission form. First one. The teacher didn't expect her to show up today and didn't know what to do with her, so Tessa is spending the day 'helping' in the office. That is if she stops crying."

"Do you want to go get her?"

It was amazing how quickly the tears stopped and the scorn was back in her tone. "Oh, yeah. It would look real good to leave work right when Walter is trying to decide who should take over for Jed. You'd like that, wouldn't you?"

Hunter stood up, hating to be misconstrued. "Listen, I have no agenda here. How about I go get her?"

She stopped throwing her possessions back into her purse. It was mind-boggling that all of it was going to fit. Her head fell into her hands. "I'm sure she'd forgive me in no time if I made her miss the class field trip and then had a complete stranger pick her up. I don't think there's a way for me to win today." The tears were back.

"I'm trying to help, but clearly, I'm only making things worse. I'm gonna head outside and check in with Lou." He didn't wait for her to say anything, choosing to hightail it to be with the bulls.

About an hour later, J.R. appeared in the training arena. She had put on a Bucking Wonders baseball cap, her ponytail sticking out the back. She often did that when she came outside to watch the bulls. Hunter liked it when she wore her hair up. He wondered what it would be like to run the backs of his fingers up her neck to her cheek. Would she lean into his touch?

She greeted Lou and the ranch hands before coming to stand next to Hunter.

"I'm sorry for taking my bad day out on you. That wasn't cool and you didn't deserve it," she said, staring straight ahead at the yearling with the bucking dummy on its back.

His gaze dropped to his boots. "Apology accepted."

"Tessa came home yesterday with a new bull joke. Want to hear it?"

He looked up and over at her. Hunter loved when she talked about her daughter. It was one subject that always brought a smile to her face. He felt like he knew the little girl without even meeting her yet. "Lay it on me."

"What do you call a sleeping bull?"

"I don't know, what do you call a sleeping bull?"

"A bulldozer."

Hunter shook his head and gave a little chuckle. "That's a good one."

J.R. rested her arms on the railing in front of them, smiling like he had expected. "I laughed when she told me. She then claimed it wasn't that funny. Ten-year-olds are interesting creatures. If I hadn't laughed, she would have been mad at me, but laughing too hard was embarrassing."

"She sounds like a hoot. I hope to get to meet her one day. I think we'd get along perfectly."

She sighed. "She probably would love you, and I would probably be annoyed."

He laughed, knowing she didn't dislike him as much as she wanted to. "It wouldn't even win me any points to get along with your daughter?"

Taking a step back, J.R. threw her thumb over her shoulder. "I'm going to go back to the office. The only one you and I should be worried about winning points from is Walter."

Hunter could picture her as a ten-year-old. She would have been one of those girls at recess who raced the boys and won. Her competitiveness only made her more attractive. "You forget that there's nothing I love more than a good ol'-fashioned competition," he said as she walked away.

"I'm betting on it!" she shouted in return, giving him a wave goodbye without turning around.

J.R. Blackwell was rough and tough and good at bucking him off, but Hunter wasn't giving up on her just yet.

CHAPTER THREE

"I'M SORRY. I'll be sorry for the rest of my life, okay?"

Tessa pulled a french fry from the pile in front of her and dipped it in the ketchup before stuffing it in her mouth. She was a master at the silent treatment. Not even a surprise trip to her favorite restaurant for dinner was winning her over after the field trip debacle.

"I will take you to that same farm. You will get to see and do all the same things the other kids did today. I promise."

Rain pelted the window they were sitting near and there was a rumble of thunder. The weather was mirroring Tessa's mood. The angry little girl had picked up another fry, but it didn't make it to her mouth this time. She tossed it down next to her half-eaten cheeseburger. "I don't want to go to the farm by myself. I wanted to go with my friends."

J.R. knew that was the real issue but had hoped a private trip would appease her. Clearly, that wasn't the case. Time was the only thing that would heal this wound, which meant J.R. would have to suffer the consequences of being a forgetful mother for a bit longer. That realization was all it took to lose what little appetite she'd had.

The walk to the car was just as painfully silent as dinner had been. This was some kind of bad karma for all the times J.R. had been upset with her mother and tried to pull the same exact thing. Of course, Flora Blackwell had never respected what her daughters wanted and could be relentless when someone attempted to shut her out. J.R. was not going to be like her mother. If Tessa needed some time to sulk, she could have it. Even if the quiet was a killer.

The box meant for the post office still sat in the passenger seat. J.R. had opted to pick Tessa up straight away after work, leaving the errands she needed to run for a day when her daughter didn't hate her guts. She checked the rearview mirror to make sure Tessa was buckled in before driving away. The little girl stared solemnly out the window; her forehead rested on the glass. Did Flora ever feel this kind of guilt? Was that why she hadn't allowed J.R. to be mad when she had been a child? If that was why, it sure did backfire because once J.R. broke away, she never looked back. Freezing her mother out was much easier when they didn't live under the same roof.

J.R. was determined to prevent repeating those mistakes. She didn't want Tessa to tolerate her until she was eighteen and then rarely ever talk to her again.

When they got home, Tessa ran right upstairs to her room. Deflated, J.R. sat down at the kitchen table and rubbed her aching temples. The dishes needed to be done and there was still no milk in the fridge for tomorrow's breakfast. She'd have to wake up early tomorrow to make some pancakes. The mix she had in the pantry only needed water. She had water.

Today had been a wakeup call in more ways than one. She needed to get on her A-game—at home and at work. If there was one thing she had learned being a Blackwell Belle, it was that you don't get first place handed to you, you have to work for it day and night. If she wanted to be the best mom she could be and the one who earned Jed's position at the ranch, she was going to have to work for it day and night. Even though she was bone-tired, she was going to spend some time tonight reading all the old classroom newsletters to make sure there was nothing else she'd missed.

A text came through about an hour later from Hunter.

Hope your night has been better than your day.

He was such a good guy, but that was the same thing J.R. had believed about her ex. They all started out nice guys until they decided it wasn't worth the hassle to be nice anymore. Hunter no longer rode bulls anymore, but J.R. knew guys like him, guys who had been lavished with attention when they were riding. She was sure Hunter had plenty of rodeo groupies who would love to be on the receiving end of his charm. J.R. had a job to earn and a daughter to raise. Swooning over Hunter was not going to help her accomplish either of those things.

It hasn't been great but didn't do anything to make it worse.

At least she had that going for her. She hadn't gained any ground but hadn't lost any either. Maybe after a good night's sleep, Tessa would realize that missing the field trip wasn't the worst thing in life.

Maybe I can help. One of the goats at my family's ranch had a kid today.

The Robbins family owned a popular guest ranch on the outskirts of town called the R&R Dude Ranch. She had never been there but knew people who had hosted their family reunions there. J.R. often wondered why Hunter didn't work for his family instead of Bucking Wonders but never had the nerve to ask. She knew he moved back there after the accident that ended his riding career.

How is that going to help me? she texted back.

Here are some pictures for you to show Tessa.

Hunter sent three photos of the adorable baby goat. It was black with a white stripe on its head, white legs, and had a little white on its tail as well. Tessa was sure to fall in love.

He's pretty cute. I think you're right. These could earn me a few points.

Happy to help :)

J.R. shook her head and couldn't stop herself from smiling. Did this grown man just send her a smiley face? He was even Mr. Sunshine via text. She went upstairs to show Tessa the pictures. There was no response when she knocked on the little girl's door that was decorated with drawings of horses.

"Tessa, can I come in please?" she asked, turning the doorknob but not pushing open the door.

No response came from the other side. The child was a champion at the silent treatment. She had incredible self-restraint.

"I'm coming in. I want to show you something."

Hopefully, this wasn't the same as what her mother used to do to her. It wasn't like she had said don't come in. J.R. pushed the door open to find Tessa sitting on the floor, playing with the flocked horse figurines her grandparents had gotten her for Christmas last year. J.R. had quickly surmised that her mother had purposely chosen horses that looked exactly like the ones the Belles had ridden over the years to torture her. As much as she didn't want to remember that time in her life, her mother wasn't going to let her forget. She would have thrown them in the garbage if they hadn't been Tessa's favorite gift.

"My co-worker sent me some pictures of a baby goat that was born on his family's ranch today. Want to see?"

Tessa paused, her brow furrowed. She must have been contemplating whether this was a trick to get her to talk to her or not. When her face relaxed, J.R. knew she was about to give in.

"A baby goat?"

J.R. took a seat on the floor next to her daughter and held out her phone. "Yeah, it's super cute. Check it out."

Tessa swiped through the pictures. "Is it a boy or a girl?"

"Let me ask. I think it's a boy, but I'll text him to be sure." J.R. took the phone back and sent

Hunter the question. He was quick to reply. "He said it's a boy."

"What's his name?"

J.R. asked Hunter, who again got back to her right away. "He said he doesn't have a name yet. He wants to know if *you* want to name him."

The light in Tessa's eyes was back. She sat up a little straighter. "Me? For real?"

"For real. He said his brothers are really bad at naming goats. They need your help."

Tessa grinned. She was charmed by this man even though the mother she was angry with was acting as his messenger. "Well, I need to meet him before I can name him. I have to know him better to pick the perfect name for him."

"I don't know if we can do that, sweetheart. Mr. Robbins is my co-worker. I'm not sure if I can just ask him to invite us to his family's ranch."

Tessa's face fell and the scowl reappeared. As quickly as J.R. had begun to win her back, she lost her again. "Of course, you can't."

As if he could hear the conversation going on in the room, Hunter sent a text.

You two should come out to the R&R sometime and meet the little guy. Maybe it would help make up for missing the farm field trip. We've got a lot going on here that's way more fun than any farm!

J.R. was conflicted. She could say yes and let Hunter save the day, but that would leave her in his debt. She didn't need to be in Hunter Robbins's debt. They were in the middle of a competition for a job that she wanted more than anything. It was one thing to accept a cup of coffee, it was another to accept an outing at his family's guest ranch.

"What did he say?" Tessa asked, trying to look at J.R.'s phone. Reflexively, J.R. tipped the screen away, causing Tessa to fold her arms and turn her body away. "Fine, don't tell me. I don't want to talk anymore anyway."

Not wanting to lose ground, J.R. relented. "He just invited us to the ranch so you can meet the baby goat and see some other things on his ranch. He said it's way cooler than a farm. They have tons of real horses for you to play with," J.R. said, lifting up the toy horse that most closely resembled the Andalusian she used to ride as a kid.

It was as if the rest of the day had never happened. Tessa jumped up, beaming. She wrapped her arms around her mom and hugged her like she hadn't iced her out for the last few hours. "Yes! Can we go tomorrow?"

"I don't know if I can make that happen as quickly as tomorrow. Maybe on the weekend when you don't have school. I'll set something up with Mr. Robbins when I see him at work in the morning."

Tessa let go and hopped up and down. "Text him back. Quick!"

J.R. typed a reply, thanking Hunter for his offer and that they could talk about it at work.

"Okay, all set. We will work out the details tomorrow. I think we need to start getting ready for bed, what do you think?"

Now that Hunter had saved the day, Tessa was completely compliant. She cleaned up her horses and took a shower. They made sure that she had the perfect outfit ready to go for the morning. There would be no more damp shirts to worry about. Tessa let J.R. brush her hair and read a couple chapters with her from the book she was reading for her upcoming book report.

The storm outside sounded like it was getting worse instead of easing like the tension inside the house thankfully had. The wind howled and the rain hit the house like it was rocks instead of water. J.R. pulled the blanket on Tessa's bed up higher to keep her daughter warm.

"Is there going to be a tornado?" Tessa asked after J.R. gave her a kiss good-night.

"November isn't usually tornado time. This is probably just a bad rainstorm. I'm sure it'll blow over by the time we get up in the morning," J.R. reassured her.

Tessa grabbed hold of her stuffed cupcake that she always slept with and snuggled into her bed. "Good night, Mom."

"Good night, sweetheart."

The contentment J.R. felt as she slipped out of the room was a million times better than any other emotion she'd experienced all day. It was a heavy dose of relief with a side of joy. She had beat herself up for hours, focused too much on what she wasn't doing right instead of showing herself a little grace. Tessa was a resilient kid. She was sensitive but also so very sweet. If J.R.'s parenting had to be judged by the kind of person her daughter was, she would be top of the class because Tessa was an amazing kid.

J.R. returned downstairs a new woman, ready to conquer whatever the next day would bring her. She washed the dishes that had been left from breakfast and finished reading through all those newsletters, making sure to write things down on the calendar in the kitchen. She even set a few reminders on her phone. She was just about to head to bed herself when the phone rang. Hunter was calling.

"I know I owe you big-time for saving me from a whole evening of the silent treatment, but do you know what time it is?" she asked as she plopped back down on the couch.

"I know, sorry. I just wasn't sure when Tessa

went to bed, and I didn't want to call while you two were still hanging out."

Clearly, he was not familiar with ten-year-olds at all. "It's after ten o'clock, Hunter. Tessa has been in bed since eight thirty."

"Oh, right. It's been a long time since I was ten. I don't remember what time my parents used to make us go to bed. Of course, with four boys only a couple years apart in age who shared two rooms next to each other, we were rarely asleep when we were supposed to be."

"Yeah, well, as one of five girls all a few years apart, I know a thing or two about sharing space and somebody always talking when they were supposed to be sleeping." J.R. had shared a room with at least one of her sisters until everything fell apart and they disbanded. Sadly, they barely spoke to one another anymore. If it weren't for Tessa, she probably wouldn't hear from any of them. She emailed school pictures and sent Christmas cards. Maybe she would get a text from Violet or Willow here and there. She had sent Iris a congratulatory email when she was featured in a magazine for her interior design. She'd seen Maggie once or twice when she was in town for a rodeo, but other than that, they didn't reach out much. J.R. blamed their mom for that.

"Funny that we both come from families of

either all boys or all girls. You don't know what it's like to have a brother and I can't even begin to imagine what a sister would be like."

"I'm sure it's not that much different. Did your brothers generally annoy you when you were growing up, tease you, and hog the bathroom when you needed it?"

Hunter chuckled. "That describes them pretty well. Did your sisters keep your secrets yet threaten to tell on you if you didn't do what they said?"

"Only one of them did that. Did your brothers borrow your stuff without asking and then swear they didn't ruin it when they finally gave it back? My sister Maggie was famous for that."

"No, but my brother Cody always raced me to the stable so he could pick first from the horses and even though he knew I wanted to ride Spot, he would pick him more than half the time."

"We never fought over horses surprisingly, probably because it wasn't up to us which horse we got to ride. That was always up to my mom."

"Why did your mom decide?" he asked innocently.

J.R. was not about to go down the deep, dark rabbit hole that was her relationship with her mother. "First, can we talk about your horse named Spot? No wonder you want to give my daughter the chance to name this new goat. Who gave a horse a name clearly meant for a dog?"

There was laughter again from the other side of the call. "I wasn't lying when I said we were bad at naming animals. Spot was an Appaloosa as you might have guessed. I was seven when he was born and I got to name him. We took turns naming the horses like we took turns riding them. Being trail riding horses meant my dad wanted them to be used to different riders, so we never got to call any of them 'our' horse, but I felt a special connection to Spot since I had named him."

It was interesting the difference between them. In J.R.'s family business, it was imperative that the rider and the horse have a connection. Without that trust, the tricks could be dangerous. She couldn't imagine riding Maggie's horse or doing her tricks on Violet's horse. She was not going to mention any of that to Hunter, however. J.R. did not talk about the Blackwell Belles. Ever. She did not want anyone to connect her back to that if she could help it.

"Okay. Since you were a child, I can forgive you for sticking some poor, beautiful stallion with the name Spot."

"Let's hope Tessa is more creative than I was at her age. I'm glad that we can show you around over here. I think she'll really enjoy it."

J.R. couldn't deny that he was right. "She was absolutely thrilled when I told her you invited us. She wanted to come tomorrow, but I told her we needed to wait until a weekend that works for all of us. Please don't think you need to fit this in anytime soon."

"Don't worry about it. We could have you come tomorrow if you wanted to, but I do think a weekend day would give her more time to explore the ranch. You two could come on Saturday. There's a hayride and a pumpkin pie eating contest. I don't know about you, but I love a good pumpkin pie."

This was moving very fast. J.R. bit down on her lip. Why did she suddenly feel excited about spending time with Hunter outside of work? They were both going after the same job. They couldn't be friends. That just wouldn't work. "I'll have to look at our calendar. We can figure it out tomorrow." She pretended to yawn. "I am too exhausted tonight to think clearly."

"Right. Of course. I'm sorry about calling so late. I just wanted to make sure things were better and to let you know that the invitation was totally sincere."

Sincere seemed to be this man's middle name. She hated that she doubted him yet feared believing it to be true at the same time. "I appreciate that, Hunter. I really do."

Before they could say good-night, the storm outside raged. A loud cracking noise was soon followed by a crash, the house going dark, and then screams from Tessa. J.R. didn't bother with goodbyes, she flew up the stairs.

CHAPTER FOUR

NOTHING PREPARED HUNTER for the fear that would course through his body when he heard the noises on the other end of his call with J.R. and then the line going dead. It only grew when she didn't answer his calls when he tried to reconnect with her to make sure everything was okay. That had to mean everything was *not* okay. There was only one thing to do.

He ran out of the house and to his truck, getting soaking wet in the process since he hadn't bothered to grab a coat or hat. He had to get to J.R.'s and make sure everyone was safe. Heart thumping in his chest, he started his truck, turned on his windshield wipers, and put it in Drive.

His phone rang before he made it off the property. Only it wasn't J.R., it was his brother Cody.

"Where are you headed in the middle of the night in a storm this bad?" his brother asked once he connected his phone to the truck's Bluetooth.

"I was on the phone with J.R. Blackwell when something happened and we got disconnected. There was a real loud bang and then someone, probably her daughter, was screaming. She's not answering me when I call her back. I am not going to be able to sleep if I don't know they are okay."

"I should have figured you were putting on your white hat and going to rescue someone in distress. So very Hunter of you."

Cody always liked to give Hunter a hard time about being "the nice guy" because nice guys never get the girl according to him. Hunter didn't believe that, though. Their brother Everett was a perfectly nice guy and he was married to a lovely woman. Hunter would be happy with someone like Savannah. He'd be happier with someone like J.R., but first, he had to make sure she was still alive.

"I'll be back soon. Don't wait up."

"Oh, I'm waiting up to hear what all this is about. This is like one of those 9-1-1 shows but real life. Maybe a robber broke in and you're gonna have to make a citizen's arrest. You got any weapons in that truck of yours?"

The only time Hunter had a gun was when he was hunting. He wasn't about to knock on J.R.'s door with a rifle in hand. "I don't think I'm going to need to arrest anyone tonight. I'm more worried something fell and someone got hurt. That's what it sounded like."

"Boring. Maybe I won't stay up."

"Sorry to disappoint. Do whatever you need to do, man. Bye." Hunter knew the way to J.R.'s house because he once had to drive her to and from work when her car broke down. She only let him do it once even though her car was in the shop for three days because she lied and said she had a neighbor help her out. Only, she didn't have a neighbor in this case. He figured it out later that she paid a rideshare driver to drive her instead.

She was as independent as they came. J.R. never wanted to ask anyone for anything that she thought she could do on her own. He admired her self-determination, but he wished the woman would see that there was no shame in asking for help once in a while.

Tonight, she had no say. He was going to check on her whether she liked it or not. That was what she got for not answering his calls.

Fifteen minutes later, Hunter turned onto J.R.'s street. There was a firetruck outside as well as an ambulance and police car parked in front of her house. Hunter's heart went from beating out of control to a dead stop. Was Tessa hurt? Was that why she was screaming? He hadn't even had a chance to meet the little girl and yet, the thought of something happening to her made him feel sick.

The truck's windshield wipers were working overtime. It wasn't only the rain making it difficult to see what was going on, but the whole street was dark as if the electricity had been knocked out. If it wasn't for the emergency vehicles and their red-and-blue lights, it would have been pitch-black.

Hunter pulled up behind the sheriff's SUV. He reached in the back seat for a sweatshirt he had left there the other night. It would have to play the part of umbrella in this mess. The only way he was going to be sure J.R. and her daughter were okay was to see her, talk to her. He braced himself for the impact of the wind and the rain and pushed open his door, jumping out and making a mad dash toward the people huddled behind the ambulance. They fortunately had umbrellas and flashlights.

"J.R.? Is J.R. Blackwell out here?" he called out as he approached.

At least three flashlights shone in his direction, and he quickly looked away. The sweatshirt over his head was already soaked through and he was getting just as wet as he would be without it.

"Hunter?" J.R.'s voice cut through the din of the storm. "What are you doing here?"

The flashlights dipped and Hunter was able

to see again. There was J.R., sitting in the back of the ambulance with a little girl wrapped in a blanket next to her. It took everything he had to resist running to her and holding her in his arms. Seeing J.R. safe and sound was all he had wanted and there she was, dripping wet but in one piece.

"You hung up after all that noise and then didn't answer when I called back. I was worried something terrible had happened. Looks like I was right."

Even in the dark, Hunter could now see that a huge tree had been uprooted and had fallen right on J.R.'s house. Another one had fallen on the power lines, which the fire fighters seemed most concerned about at the moment.

"Are you Hunter Robbins? *The* Hunter Robbins?" one of the first responders asked.

Even though his career as a bull rider had died, Hunter's celebrity somehow lived on. Every once in a while, someone would recognize him from the circuit.

"Guilty as charged."

"I saw you ride in Dallas back in 2019. You were amazing and my friends and I were so excited to tell people in the crowd that you were our hometown guy," the man said.

Hunter forced a smile. It should have felt good to know he evoked a feeling of pride in others, but the disappointment of not being able to do that anymore took all the joy out of it.

"Get under this umbrella," a female EMT offered. "You're getting drenched."

He thanked them for the temporary shelter from the storm. "Was Tessa hurt? Were you?" he asked J.R.

She shook her head. "We're fine. Shook up, soaking wet, and homeless, but fine."

"Thank God no one was hurt. I was praying everything was okay the whole drive over here."

"We're fine," J.R. assured him. "You didn't have to come all this way and you definitely don't need to stand in the rain. Please, go home. Have a good night."

"Why don't you come back to the R&R with me? We can get you a place to stay at the ranch."

"Sounds like you've got a friend to take you in after all," the sheriff said. He turned to Hunter. "She's been telling us there was no one to take them in and she would go to a hotel."

J.R. looked pained instead of relieved. "I don't want to impose on anyone. A hotel is perfectly fine for the two of us."

Typical. Her refusal to lean on anyone was extremely frustrating. "I live on a guest ranch, J.R. It's literally a hotel on a ranch. We have guest rooms just like they do at that place off the highway, which I heard hasn't been updated since 1980."

Tessa perked up. "Are you the man with the baby goat?"

"I am, and he's so excited to meet you."

J.R. gave him a look that accused him of not playing fair. If Tessa wanted to come to the guest ranch, they were going to come to the guest ranch. All he had to do was convince the little girl and J.R. would have to give in.

"You know, you could meet the goat tomorrow morning if you come to the ranch tonight."

"Really? *Please*, Mom, please can we go to the ranch?" Tessa begged. There was no way she could say no now. Hunter fought not to smirk triumphantly.

"You were planning to come on Saturday anyway," Hunter reminded J.R. "Now, you'll get the full experience."

"Fine." J.R.'s voice was full of defeat. "We will *rent* a room at the ranch. Insurance is going to be paying for this, so we might as well support a local business run by someone I know."

Hunter kept his mouth shut. They could argue about what she would or would not have to pay for later. He was simply going to enjoy that she had agreed to come back with him. Knowing he could provide her and her daughter with a warm, dry, safe place to stay was very satisfying.

The authorities escorted J.R. back into her house to grab a few things. The tree had collapsed a section of the roof, making that part of the upstairs unsafe to enter. Hunter waited with Tessa in the garage. J.R. came out with two small duffle bags and Tessa's backpack.

"I couldn't get in your room, baby. It'll probably be a couple days before we can get some more of your stuff. There was a basket of clean laundry in my room waiting to be folded. I shoved it all in here." J.R. opened the trunk of her car and threw her bags in. She slammed it shut.

Hunter stepped out of her way. "Follow me to the R&R?"

"You promise this won't be a problem for your parents? You have some vacancies?"

"I promise. My mother would wring my neck if she found out that I let a..." He stopped himself from calling her his friend. He wouldn't mind if they were friends. He'd actually love it if she'd consider being more than friends. "...a co-worker in need stay at that rundown hotel on the outskirts of town instead of one of our lodging options."

"I don't drive fast in the rain. I have precious cargo, you know." She nodded to the little girl in the back seat.

He gave her a reassuring smile. "I know. I'll make sure to get you there safely."

Hunter must have checked his rearview mirror a thousand times on the drive back to the R&R to be certain they were right behind him. He ran over to J.R.'s car when they got there to let her know to wait for him there. "I have to go in the main house to get the keys to one of the open rooms since the lodge is closed for the night."

"I have no idea how long we need a place to stay. It could be until Thanksgiving for all I know. Make sure we're not taking someone's rental in a couple weeks."

"I got you. Don't worry." He winked and ran into the house.

Immediately, he was greeted by Cody. "You're back. What happened, Mr. Wannabe Texas Ranger?"

"Storm knocked over a tree that collapsed her roof. They need to stay on the ranch for a bit while things get cleaned up and repaired. Do we have a space that isn't going to be used for a couple weeks?"

Cody popped up out of his chair. He walked over to the rack with all the lodging keys that they kept in the main house in case they needed to get into one that was rented out. There were several rooms in the main lodge as well as a variety of cabins scattered around the property for families to rent. "Oh, man. I didn't think it was going to be something serious. I thought you'd return with a story about scaring the poor woman half to death by showing up to her house after she gave you a clear signal she didn't want to talk to you tonight."

"You're hilarious. It was serious. Please tell me we have a cabin for them. I don't want them cramped in a guest room at the lodge if they need to stay here awhile."

Cody opened the oversized ledger that his parents used as a copy of the reservations. Hunter's dad didn't trust computers, so he had everything written on a good old-fashioned reservation book to keep track of who was coming to stay with them, when and where they would sleep. He left the electronic stuff to the younger generation in the main lodge. "Looks like the Branding Iron is open until after the holidays."

"Does that one give her and her daughter enough room?" Hunter lived on the property, but he didn't have anything to do with the day-to-day operations. The ranch had gone through a couple renovations since he was a kid. He didn't have all the new accommodations in the guesthouses memorized like his brother did.

"It's got two queen beds, a bathroom, and a kitchenette, which she might appreciate if she has to stay awhile. Do you want me to look at the bigger spaces? I forgot you said she had a daughter. Heck, the Grand Dixie Private Lodge is open."

That one Hunter did know about. That was their most deluxe accommodation. J.R. could have a six-bedroom, six-bath lodge with the great room, full kitchen, and washer and dryer. It even had a pool table. They only rented it out when they had a wedding or some big family reunion booked.

"If she found out I upgraded her to something like that, she'd be mad." Hunter ran his fingers through his wet hair. He wasn't sure if it was the angel on his shoulder or the devil, but one of them was very adamant about what he should do. "So, let's make sure she doesn't find out. As far as anyone is concerned, the Grand Dixie was all we had available for the time she needs a place to stay. You got me?"

Cody chuckled as he turned to pull the keys from the hook on the wall behind him. "Whatever you say, brother."

This time on his way out, Hunter grabbed a hat. He stopped by J.R.'s car and she rolled down her window. The rain was practically coming down sideways, so she only opened it a crack. "Follow me. We only had one place available, so don't give me a hard time about it."

He ran off to his truck before she could argue with him. She would have to accept his kindness. It was the right thing to do if she had any manners. Plus, Tessa had to be exhausted and there wasn't a better place for her to get a good night's sleep than the Grand Dixie.

J.R. followed him to the private lodge and refused to let him help her with her bags. "Why do I feel like I'm going to be mad even though you asked me not to be?" she asked, walking with him to the door.

Hunter prepared for her wrath. He unlocked the door and held it open for J.R. and Tessa.

Once inside, J.R. gasped. "What in the world? No way, Hunter. What kind of hotel room is this? This is not a hotel room."

The Grand Dixie was one enormous space divided into different sections.

"Look at how big the TV is, Mom!" Tessa ran over to the entertainment area right where they had walked in. There was a brown leather sectional and two cowhide easy chairs sitting in front of a wall with a seventy-five-inch flat-screen TV hanging in the middle of it. "And we get a pool table! Can you teach me how to play pool, Mr. Robbins?"

"Please call me Hunter because tomorrow you're going to meet four other guys with that last name and it will get real confusing real fast, and I'd be happy to teach you to play pool."

J.R. pushed her wet hair off her forehead. She

stepped closer to Hunter and lowered her voice. "We cannot stay here. This is like some presidential suite or something. This cannot be your only open room."

"It's actually a private lodge. There are six bedrooms with their own bathroom." He pointed to the three doors that lined the west wall and the three doors on the east wall. "We only have families rent it out one or two times a year. It's the only place my brother said we could give you," he lied.

"Six bedrooms?" J.R.'s eyes bulged. "Are you kidding me? We're going to go to the outdated, 1980s hotel. We cannot stay here."

Tessa skipped through the dining room area, which housed the banquet table that sat ten, straight to the kitchen that took up the other end of the lodge with its giant island, wall of cabinets, and a walk-in pantry.

"Mom! Come look at this kitchen. They have two refrigerators, a big one and a little one."

Hunter held his hand over his mouth and whispered to J.R., "Wine fridge, aka small one. You will have to stock it yourself. Food and beverages are not included."

Tessa ran from the kitchen back to where J.R. was still frozen by the front door. Pure excitement shone in her eyes. "And look at all the movies they have over there." She pointed to the cabinet under the television that was filled with DVDs and various board games. “This place is so cool! Can I invite my friends for a sleepover?”

“There’s plenty of room for you to have friends over. Six rooms to be exact,” Hunter chimed in.

“Six rooms? This place is awesome!” Tessa took off, opening each bedroom door and flipping on the lights. She was more impressed with each room she entered.

“Tessa. Tessa, honey.” J.R.’s attempts to rein her in were fruitless.

“She will never forget what a cool mom you are if you let her stay here instead of some rinky-dink hotel room. Come on, J.R. Will you please take advantage of your good fortune on a night when you’ve had so much go wrong?”

Tessa burst out of the last room. “Mom, can I have this room? It has horses everywhere. I love it so much. Please?”

Hunter watched as J.R. accepted her fate. She had to let him spoil her. She had no other choice.

She sighed and dropped the bags she was carrying. “The horse room is all yours, sweetheart.”

Hunter had to turn away because he didn’t dare push her buttons and there was no hiding the smile of victory on his face.

CHAPTER FIVE

MAYBE IT WAS the lack of sleep, but J.R. still wanted to wipe that smirk off Hunter's face. Not only had he driven across town to convince her to stay at his family's guest ranch, but he forced her to stay in a luxury private lodge like they were some kind of royalty. J.R. and Tessa were not royalty. They were simple people. At least that was how J.R. was raising Tessa—to be humble and content with what she had. The Robbins family was making that a little challenging.

Hunter had texted her first thing in the morning that he would meet them in the main lodge to finish getting signed in. The lodge was the gathering space for guests at the ranch. There was a desk where people checked in and checked out, a seating area with a fireplace and comfy-looking couches, and a dining hall where the guests could get breakfast, lunch, and dinner. Rows of picnic-like rectangular tables with bench seating filled the space. Colorful centerpieces of orange, white, and green pumpkins surrounded by silk autumn leaves decorated each table.

Instead of a quick two-minute exchange, they were greeted by Hunter's whole family and an invitation to join them for a full breakfast complete with scrambled eggs, sausage, bacon, and Texas toast.

Hunter had three older brothers who worked at the family ranch. Jack Jr. was the oldest. He was married to Cora, and they had a son named Nico and were expecting their second child in a few months. Everett was the second oldest. He was also married and his wife, Savannah, worked at the ranch as their event manager. Last but not least, there was Cody. He wasn't married and was supposedly the one J.R. had to blame for her over-the-top accommodations.

The Robbinses already knew all about the disaster that brought J.R. and Tessa to the R&R Dude Ranch. Hunter's dad, Jackson, volunteered to take a look at the tree and find a way to remove it. He also said he'd share a list of people who could do the work on the house and roof.

The rest of the family showered Tessa with attention as she sat among them at the table that had been reserved for the family. Hunter and his brother Everett fought about who would be the better one to teach her how to play pool. Cody offered to take her to meet the baby goat after breakfast. Jackson let her know how excited they were that she agreed to name the little guy.

J.R. checked her watch. They had gotten up much earlier today, but they were still on a tight schedule. She would not be late to work today.

"We're not going to have enough time to go to the barn this morning, sweetheart. We've got to make sure we get to school on time and we have a little bit more of a drive from out here than from home."

Hunter's eyebrows pinched together. "You're sending her to school today?"

"Of course."

"You aren't going to work, are you?"

J.R. matched his quizzical expression with one of her own. "Why wouldn't I?"

"Your house has a tree sitting on top of it," he said as if she might have forgotten. "I think Jed will understand that you need to take the day off."

J.R. let out a humorless chuckle. She could not afford to take a day off work right now. Walter and Jed had a difficult decision to make and she planned to make sure to give them no reason to write her off as someone who had too much going on in her personal life to be able to handle the increase in work responsibilities.

Since she hadn't been able to sleep in her over-the-top private lodge even with its incredibly comfortable beds, she had taken advantage of the extra hours to take care of several things on her ever-growing to-do list. "I already emailed my insurance agent, googled a few tree removal service places, and started a list of everything I know needs to be replaced."

"Hunter said you couldn't get much of Tessa's stuff because that's where the tree crashed through the roof. I'm running into town later today. I can stop and pick up whatever essentials you need," Cora offered. "If you give me Tessa's size, I can pick up a few outfits for her, some underwear, socks, whatever you need."

These people had known her for a total of ten minutes and they were already doing too much. She could not bring herself to let practical strangers go out of their way for her like that. "That's so sweet of you, but you don't need to do that. I can go after work."

"I insist."

Jack Jr. interrupted before J.R. could refuse again. "We're expecting a girl this time around and Cora's been buying up everything pink ever since she found out. You'd be doing me a mighty favor by letting her shop for someone else's little girl because the nursery's closet can't hold any more outfits."

"Cora used to work as a buyer for a fancy department store in Dallas," Savannah said to Tessa.

"She'll pick out stuff that'll not only be comfortable but totally cool. Your friends will be so jealous."

"Please let Cora pick out some outfits for me, Mom. Please." Tessa intertwined her fingers as if she was praying and begging for a yes at the same time.

It was so unfair to use her daughter against her twice now. Hunter did it last night with the private lodge and now his sisters-in-law were doing the same thing. There was no way to say no when Tessa had been through so much trauma last night. "Fine, I'll write down your sizes and a budget amount. Some of your clothes back home will be salvageable." At least she hoped so. "You don't need an entire new wardrobe." J.R. turned to Cora. "Thank you very much for helping us out."

"No worries. I can also pick Tessa up from school and bring her back here this afternoon. That way we can show her around the ranch before dark and you can run some errands after work without worrying about her. I know shopping trips can go much quicker when you're shopping alone."

J.R. was so caught off guard. Cora got how hard it was. She might not be a single mother, but she was a mother whose husband probably worked way more than an eight-hour day. J.R. had never had this level of support even when she was married. Chad, her ex, hadn't been a very hands-on parent before they got divorced and Tessa had only been two years old when that happened. On top of that, J.R. had no family in the area to help out and her relationships with her mom and her sisters were so strained, she couldn't bring herself to ask them for help even temporarily. If she couldn't accept help from her own family, how could she accept it from Hunter's?

"I hate to burden you with watching her until I get home. I have after-school care set up for her. She's used to the routine of going to our neighbors."

Hunter decided to rejoin the conversation. "Who knows if they even got the power up and running yet. Your neighbor might appreciate that you can make other arrangements."

J.R. hadn't considered that possibility. She really needed to call Hilde and see how things were going. Hilde and her husband were the ones who had called for the fire truck and ambulance last night. They had offered up their guest bedroom, but J.R. had opted not to stay at their house because of the power outage and because insurance would reimburse her for the cost of a hotel room. Hilde was going to be very surprised when she found out where they actually ended up.

J.R. decided to defer to Tessa, assuming she would want to go to her best friend's house. The Robbinses wouldn't argue with a child. "What do you want to do, Tessa? Go to the Langleys' or come here after school?"

Tessa tipped her head to the side ever so slightly as she considered her options. She straightened up when the decision was made. "I've been waiting to meet the baby goat since last night. I want to come here."

Well, that settled that. J.R. had to roll with it and let the Robbinses help her with Tessa. She would need to remember to tell the school that Tessa would not be taking the bus home today.

"How long have you worked at Bucking Wonders?" Hunter's mom, Julie, asked as she spooned some breakfast potatoes onto Tessa's plate. Tessa smiled, gobbling everything up like she'd never been fed before today.

"Six years. I've been so lucky to learn the business under someone like Jed."

"Hunter speaks well of everyone he works with." Julie's smile was exactly like her son's, big and seemingly permanent. She looked younger than J.R. expected her to be. "We've been so happy that he's found a home there. This job makes me much less worried about him than his former profession."

"Mom…" Hunter said from the other side of the table.

"What? Nothing tries to kill you at your new job. Can't I be happy about that?"

"Nothing *tries* to kill him, but has anyone ever been in a small space with this man for an extended period of time when he is chewing gum?" J.R. asked, looking to his brothers.

Everett chuckled and slammed his hand on the table, making the plates and silverware rattle. "It's so annoying, isn't it? I don't even know how he manages to make so much noise. It's like he blows ten bubbles and pops them in his mouth at the same time."

"Exactly!" J.R. threw her hands up. "All day it's chomp-chomp and then pop, pop, pop."

"Oh, he is such a gum smacker. It's bad," Cody agreed.

"I try my best to block it out," J.R. continued with her roast. "There's just so much smacking and cracking. I haven't attempted murder, but, not gonna lie, I've thought about it."

All three Robbins siblings erupted in laughter. Hunter took the teasing like a pro. Unfazed by her jibes, he still grinned at J.R. from across the table.

"Note to self, no more gum in the office. I'll save it for when I go out to check on the bulls."

"You must have brothers," Savannah guessed incorrectly.

"Four younger sisters actually."

"Oh goodness, God bless your parents," Julie said. "I had one sister and my dad always joked that was why he lost all his hair and my mom used to say it's why they couldn't afford to retire."

J.R. probably didn't give her parents enough credit for managing their large family of females. At the same time, she could not imagine her mother having boys. "My mom would be in awe of you for surviving in a house full of all this testosterone."

Julie tipped her head back and laughed. "It definitely has been an adventure. I'm sure I've taken a few more trips to the ER, but she's probably wiped way more tears."

"You'd be surprised how many times we had to see a doctor." Trick riding was a dangerous sport. There were a million ways the girls could hurt themselves during practice while learning a new trick or during a performance even though they had successfully done a certain move a million times. She couldn't elaborate for Mrs. Robbins because she never mentioned her past with the Belles. Ever.

"Between all four boys, I don't think there is a body part that hasn't been examined by a doctor because of a fall, a fight, a work-related injury, or a sport," Julie said.

Jack Jr. jabbed Hunter with his elbow. "Robo Bro practically took care of that statistic in one fell swoop."

Hunter's gaze dropped to the food on his plate but the hand holding his fork stilled. He didn't talk about his injury, but everyone at Bucking Wonders knew about it. Anyone with anything to do with bull riding knew about Hunter's accident.

"There's been too much yapping at this table and not enough eating," Hunter's dad said, breaking the awkward silence that had ensued. "Everyone's got work to do today and the sooner we finish eating, the sooner y'all can get busy doing what needs to be done."

No one argued with the patriarch. Jackson Robbins was a large, fit man with a thick, dark beard that had flecks of gray. The chitchat ended and everyone got to eating until they were full. Hunter's brothers and Savannah took off as soon as they were finished, saying their goodbyes and each making their own promise to show Tessa the best parts of the ranch when she got back from school.

Hunter swallowed down the rest of his orange juice and glanced over at J.R. "Do you want to drive to work together or separately?"

The thought of everyone at work seeing them pull up together in the same truck was enough to make her want to run back to her private lodge, pack up what little they came with, and check with Hilde about her offer to stay in her guest bedroom.

"She has errands to run after work, Hunter," Cora reminded him.

Wiping his mouth with his napkin, his cheeks reddened just a bit. "Right. We need to ride separately." He got up from his seat. "I guess I'll see you at work. Have a good day at school, Tessa, and don't have too much fun before I get home from work. Remember, I get the first game of pool, okay?"

Tessa continued to eat up all the attention. "Okay, but don't be too late. If Mr. Everett asks me really nice, it's going to be hard to say no."

"Do not give in to Mr. Everett. I'll be home before he finishes all his chores around this place. He can't play until all his chores are done. Got it?"

"Got it," she replied with a giggle. J.R. loved that sound. She certainly didn't hear it enough.

Checking her watch again, J.R. tossed her napkin on her plate. "We need to get going, Tessa. I don't want you to be late. Thank you so much for inviting us to breakfast, Mrs. Robbins."

"I expect you two to join us whenever you

can while you're staying here. Does Tessa need a lunch for school? I could throw something together while you get packed up to leave?"

"Oh, that's so kind of you." J.R. hadn't thought about lunch. "I can give her lunch money and she can buy a lunch at school today."

"Nonsense. I'll have something ready before you leave." Just like her son, she did not take no thank you for an answer.

"You all have been so generous. I don't know what to say other than thank you very much."

Julie stood up from the table and placed a hand on J.R.'s shoulder. "You're very welcome. It's nice to finally meet the woman from work who Hunter speaks so fondly of."

"Mom..." Hunter said with a groan.

"What? You share an office. You two spend a lot of time together at work, so of course you've mentioned her before and that you think she's a smart cookie. Why wouldn't she want to know that?"

J.R. would have been more embarrassed if she hadn't been enjoying Hunter's utter mortification. It was interesting to learn that Hunter talked about her to his family before she arrived. She tried to imagine what it would be like to have other adults at home to talk to about work. Would she have mentioned Hunter to them if she did? Something told her it would have only been to complain about how nice he was. She needed to be nicer. Hunter came from good people. Maybe he really was a genuinely good guy.

She and Tessa hustled back to the Grand Dixie to grab what they needed for school and work. J.R.'s head was spinning with a million thoughts. The last twenty-four hours had proved to be mind-boggling. She needed no more surprises today.

Just then, her phone rang. Her mother's face stared back at her from the screen. A sudden dread filled J.R.'s entire body and soul. There was never a good reason for her mother to be calling. It was much too early in the morning for this to be a social call. Her mom was known to take her sweet time in the morning since they had retired from touring.

J.R. answered, needing to get whatever bad news was attached to this call out in the open, so she could go back to worrying about the five million other things on her plate. "Hi, Mom."

"Jasmine Rose, do you know that there is a tree sitting on top of your house?"

CHAPTER SIX

HUNTER WAS SURPRISED when he pulled into work and saw that he had beaten J.R. there. She had left right after breakfast to run Tessa to school. She should have made it to Bucking Wonders before he did. The dark cloud of worry quickly lifted. As soon as he stepped out of his truck, she drove into the usually dusty parking lot. Today, after last night's rain, it was more of a mud puddle.

"I was worried you got lost on your new drive to work," he said when she got out of her car.

She gave him an unamused glance as she stepped right into a puddle that engulfed her whole foot. Her frustration overflowed like the dirty water in the hole and she let out a growl.

Instinctively, Hunter picked her up and set her down on dry ground. Instead of pulling away, as he expected, she leaned into his embrace for a moment like she needed a hug. Hunter was happy to oblige.

"It's not a good day. Why can't I just have one good day?" she grumbled against his chest.

"It's going to be a great day." He gently ran his hands up and down her back. "You'll see."

J.R. pulled back, clearly coming to her senses. "Always Mr. Glass-is-half-full. What you fail to realize is that my glass has been empty from the beginning!" She marched toward the office muttering about her muddy boot and this no-good day.

Hunter thought the morning had started out well. J.R. had accepted some help from his family without much of a fight. All he wanted to do was ease some of her worries and help Tessa have the time of her life while she was at the ranch. He had left for work feeling like he was moving in that direction. What could have happened on the ride to school that would have dampened her spirits this much?

"Good morning, sunshine," Pam greeted Hunter when he entered the main office.

"Happy Friday to you, Miss Pam."

"The weekend cannot start soon enough," she quipped.

"You got some big plans this weekend?"

"It's the second Saturday of the month tomorrow!"

It took him a second but then it came to him. Once a month Pam and her friends had brunch at their favorite restaurant in Austin and went to see a matinee at the big multiplex. She always came to work on the Monday after a brunch and matinee weekend ready with her movie review.

Hunter sat on the edge of her desk. “What movie are you seeing this time?”

Pam sighed and rolled her eyes. “Oh, I have no idea. It’s Dolly’s turn to choose and she is the most indecisive one of the bunch. She probably won’t pick one until we’re standing in line for the tickets. She drives me batty. Who am I kidding, they all do. Barb always picks some artsy movie that no one likes but her. Joanne refuses to buy herself a bag of popcorn because she claims she’s too full from brunch but then asks whoever she sits next to if she can have some of theirs. Lois, without fail, falls asleep halfway through whatever we’re watching and wakes up right at the climax and whispers ‘what have I missed’ loudly to whoever gets stuck next to her.”

Her descriptions of her friends made him laugh. “You know you’re going to miss your Saturday brunch and matinee when you move to Florida.”

She frowned and looked up at him over the rim of her glasses that had slipped down her nose. “I’m going to have to fly back to Texas once a month so I don’t miss it.”

"That or you'll have to find some Florida snowbirds to go to the movies with."

"You act like making friends is so easy. I've had the same friends for the last thirty years. I'm not sure I know how to make a friend—I haven't had to do it in so long!"

Hunter flashed her a smile. "I have a feeling it will come back to you real quick. You have nothing to worry about."

He stood up just as J.R. came out of the bathroom, holding her boot and hurrying into their office.

"Heads-up—she's not having a good day," Pam warned. "You might want to join Lou in the arena if you can. You'd think the world was ending the way she's on edge some days."

"The storm knocked a tree over onto her house last night. She and Tessa had to be displaced until repairs to their roof can be done."

"What? She didn't tell me that. She said she stepped in a puddle!"

"Well, that happened, too."

"What can we do to help? Does she need to take the day off? I'm sure Jed will let her go handle her business."

"Don't say anything to Jed. You know J.R., she keeps her personal life private. If she wants him to know, she'll tell him."

"How did you find out?" Pam asked, narrowing her eyes.

Hunter had probably shared more than J.R. would be happy with, so he decided to keep the details vague. "She's renting a room at my family's ranch. Someone must have told her we could give her more room than a hotel."

Pam pressed her lips together and tapped her pen on the desk. "Mmm-hmm. *Someone*, huh?"

Hunter shrugged and began to back away. He really wanted to check on J.R. and find out what else happened to put her in this mood. "People in this town know what's what. She, like you, has a lot of friends."

"Mmm-hmm."

"Better get to work before your husband fires me for chatting up his wife." He gave her a wink before turning toward his office. He ducked inside and closed the door behind him. "I may have accidentally told Pam about your house issues."

J.R. was already on her computer. She stopped typing and rubbed her forehead with her eyes closed.

Hunter tried to explain, "I'm sorry. I wanted her to understand why today was a difficult day for you."

She dropped her hand and glared at him. "So telling our boss's wife I'm distracted by personal issues was the way to make my day less difficult? The boss who is trying to decide which one of us gets his job?"

Hunter could see why she would feel that way. "There was no intent to make you look bad, J.R. Pam could tell you were in a bad mood and I thought she should know that it was more than a soggy boot."

"I'm not allowed to be in a bad mood because my boot got muddy? I need a better excuse?"

He'd somehow gone from giving her a hug a few minutes ago to giving her a headache. That was not how he was supposed to help her turn her day around. "You have a right to be in a bad mood over whatever put you in a bad mood. I shouldn't have said anything. I asked her not to tell Jed. I'm sorry I overstepped, but we both know this isn't about a boot or even your house. What happened between breakfast and getting to work? I promise it'll stay between me and you."

She let out a hard chuckle. "You want me to trust you after you just admitted that you gossiped about me immediately upon entering the office?"

Hunter had made it a bit harder to defend himself. "I wasn't gossiping. I was..." He struggled to find another word for it. "I was gossiping, but for the right reasons, not the mean ones. I was trying to garner you a little sympathy."

"I don't need sympathy. I need to do my work

without everyone wondering if I'm okay or able to do a good job because of everything going on in my life right now."

"That's fair. I didn't think about it like that, but I do want you to know that there's nothing wrong with being human. You have a lot going on in your life. That's not a weakness, it's reality. You also get to show Jed and Walter that you persevere through the hard times. You do your job despite the disaster at your house."

J.R. moved the stapler on her desk a smidgen to the right and straightened the framed picture of Tessa. "That was actually a very good pep talk." She glanced over at him. "You're right. I don't have to hide the fact that I can overcome adversity. I should embrace it and prove I can overcome it."

Hunter imagined himself doing a celebration dance like football players did in the end zone after a touchdown. He had successfully helped turn her attitude around. "Exactly. Now, can you tell me what other adversity you encountered today? Because I know something happened."

"Ugh." J.R. covered her face with her hands. "My mother is in town."

It had been made clear over the last few conversations they'd had that her relationship with her mom was a tad strained. Hunter knew better than to try to find the bright side of this surprise visit.

There was a sharp knock at the door, and Jed and Walter walked in. J.R. and Hunter both startled and then attempted to look casual.

"Good morning," Hunter managed to get out first.

"Good morning, you two," Jed replied before cutting right to the chase. "We're here to talk about the job, my job, the one that needs to be filled by one of you sooner rather than later."

Hunter leaned back in his chair. He needed to appear calm and cool even though his mind was whirling with all the questions he had for J.R. about her mom's arrival and his anxiety over what Jed and Walter were about to say.

J.R. folded her hands in her lap and swallowed hard. "I hope we're going to be given a chance to state our case for why we should be the one you choose before you make a decision," she said, sounding much more confident than Hunter felt.

"That's not necessary," Walter cut in. "We already know how we're going to make the decision."

How? Did that mean they hadn't decided yet?

"What my brother means is that there's no doubt you both are good for this company, but only one of you can take over for me. The bottom line is that there's nothing more important than our company's bottom line. You need to show us who is going to make sure we continue to be a profitable business, that Bucking Wonders maintains its reputation as an elite bucking bull breeder."

"How do we do that?" Hunter asked.

Jed walked over to the calendar J.R. had pinned to the wall. He pointed to November 30. "We all know the weekend after Thanksgiving is the annual Bred to Win Yearling Bucking Bull Sale. Each of you is going to choose one of our yearlings. Whoever chooses the bull that goes for the most money, wins the job."

"We want to see if buyers agree with how you think, what you believe makes a champion bull," Walter added. "If you can convince buyers, you can convince us."

"What if we both think the same bull is going to be the one to sell for the most? How do we decide who gets to claim that bull?" Hunter thought that was a reasonable question. It had been a team effort to decide which cows would be bred with which bulls. For months, Hunter and J.R. worked with Jed on the marketing brochure for the sale and made group decisions about which ones would be featured first. It was likely they would be choosing from a small pool of the elite.

Jed shook his head and smiled. "You won't. You two see things differently. I know you have your favorites in this lot. That's why I know this is a good way to choose."

J.R. had yet to say anything. Hunter couldn't read her expression. Her brow was slightly furrowed and she nibbled on her bottom lip. She had her hair down today and she tucked some behind her ear.

"So, it all boils down to one sale?" she finally asked. "Nothing else we've contributed thus far matters?"

"You don't trust your science? His instincts?" Walter challenged her.

J.R.'s jaw ticked. Hunter knew if there was anything in this world that she trusted, it was her science and her knowledge of bulls. She also respected Hunter's experience based on the questions she often asked him when she was reviewing data.

"I have no doubt that I made excellent choices with the breeding this time around. I know I can pick the calf that will sell for top dollar."

Jed knew J.R. better than Walter did, and that his questions would teeter on offensive to her. "We've considered everything you bring to the company, J.R. It's why we aren't looking outside the company and want to promote one of you. I know you've been here longer than Hunter, but you both provide insights that are invaluable. You're not the same, but it's your differences that make it challenging to choose one over the other."

She sat with that for a minute. "I assume you're giving us these two weeks to do some additional marketing on the one we choose."

Jed's smile broadened. "If you want to win, you'll market the heck out of your choice starting today."

That was all J.R. needed. She picked up a pen and started jotting notes. Hunter felt a step behind. He wasn't sure which bull he wanted to choose yet. He knew who his favorites were, but he hadn't been thinking in terms of how much they'd get for them at auction. His focus was more on the bull they were going to be in a few years. He saw the potential in them to be prize-winning.

"I personally can't wait to see what you do with this challenge," Walter said.

"We'll let you two get to work." Jed put his hand on his brother's shoulder and guided him out.

J.R. hadn't needed that prompt. She was already working. Hunter wasn't sure where to begin. How was it that she could shift her attention to the task at hand when the rest of her world was seemingly falling apart around her?

"Well, I didn't think that was how this was going to go down." Hunter had assumed the promotion was hers. That they were taking their time and giving him a little consideration to be nice. This new arrangement made him feel like he had a legitimate chance at earning the position. Hunter knew what people were looking for in a bucking bull. Back when he was a rider, if he didn't get paired with a bull that scored high enough, he didn't score high enough no matter how well he rode that bull. Staying on a bull that should have bucked him off after two seconds was the dream for a rider. Hunter knew what that bull looked like.

She didn't look up from her notebook. "It changes things but not by much."

"I guess it all comes down to who's the better salesperson. Will you convince buyers to part with more money than I can?"

"It will depend on our sales pitch," she said, finally glancing up at him. "I'm confident that my data will trump your gut feeling."

Hunter pressed a hand against his chest. "Ouch. Those are fighting words, Ms. Blackwell. Is that all you think I bring to the table? A gut feeling?"

She set her pen down. "I wish, but we both know you've got a few more tricks up your sleeve."

He was going to take that as a compliment even if it wasn't. Her phone rang and she silenced it as soon as she looked at who was calling. She pinched the bridge of her nose.

"Let me guess—my gut tells me that was your surprise visitor."

J.R. raked her fingers through her long blond hair. "My mother, my grandmother, and my... I don't even know what he is, my great-uncle, I think, decided to make a stop here in Brighton. They were supposed to surprise me last night, but I guess the storm kept them in Austin. I don't know what they want, but I can promise you they want something that I surely won't want to give them, and everyone will be unhappy in the end."

"There's no chance they simply missed you and wanted to check in?"

"First of all, my grandmother is my father's mother. She owns a ranch in Wyoming and, last I heard, was sicker than sick with some kidney disease. But that's not even as fishy as the fact that I don't even think she likes my mom all that much. For them to choose to spend time together is very strange. Then there's my great-uncle. He's my grandmother's estranged brother who she didn't see for like sixty years until a couple years ago when he helped her save her ranch and basically the whole town where she lives. He owns a ranch up in Montana or was it South Dakota?" She closed her eyes and tapped her temple as if that would jar loose the correct answer in her brain. "I think it's Montana. Regardless, the fact that the three of them are parked outside my house right now is bizarre and destined to be nothing but trouble for me."

"And I thought my family was complicated."

J.R.'s phone rang again. "Complicated doesn't begin to describe my family," she said as she pressed the button to answer the call.

CHAPTER SEVEN

FLORA WOULD END up at Bucking Wonders if J.R. didn't answer the phone, and the last thing she needed right now was for her mother to show up at her place of employment.

"Mom, I'm at work. Is there a dire emergency or can I talk to you when I am done working like we agreed when I spoke to you earlier?"

Flora ignored her question as expected. "Big E wants to know if you own a chainsaw and if we can have the code to your garage so we can get it if you have one."

"I can only imagine why he's asking for a chainsaw. I do not need him to do any work on the tree that is sitting on top of my house right now, Mother. I am waiting to hear back from my insurance agent and then I am going to call a company whose job is to clear fallen trees. I don't need Grandma Denny's eighty-whatever-year-old brother to do it."

J.R. made eye contact with Hunter to say, *see*

what I'm dealing with? He didn't hold back his laughter.

"I tried to tell him that you probably had people for that, but he asked me to ask you. I'm worried he's going to go knock on your neighbor's door and ask them for one if you don't have one, though."

J.R.'s blood pressure skyrocketed. "Mom, for the love of all that is good in this world, please do not let Big E ask anyone for a chainsaw. Do not let him go to a store and purchase a chainsaw. Please tell him that I do not give him permission to do anything to the tree on my house right now. Do you understand?"

"She doesn't want you to help with the tree. She said she's hiring a company."

"Tell him I already hired a company, and they are on their way," J.R. quickly interrupted. She didn't care if it was a lie. She would call someone as soon as she got off the phone. She would do anything to stop this man from trying to take care of it himself.

"She said someone is on their way." There was a pause and J.R. could tell someone else was speaking in the background, but she couldn't make out what they were saying. "He said he just wants to start cutting up the bigger branches that fell in the yard. He's not much for sitting still.

He's a rancher, sweetheart. He can't just sit here when there's work to be done."

J.R. didn't care if Big E needed to be active. He could be active all he wanted anywhere but her property. "Why don't y'all go into town and get some food? Or you could drive into Austin. There's plenty to do downtown."

"I don't think I can convince them to go to Austin." There was a voice in the background again. This time, J.R. could tell it was her grandmother asking for the phone.

"Jasmine?" Grandma Denny's voice was gruff. It made her just as intimidating over the phone as she was in person.

"Hi, Gran."

"What time are you expecting the workers to come get this tree taken care of? Hopefully your father has taught you that you should never have someone come do work on your property without having someone present. We can stay here and oversee it for you."

J.R. rested her forehead on her hand. These three were somehow making things even more difficult than she thought possible. "Gran, that is so sweet of you. I need to follow up with them to find out what time they're exactly coming, but I don't want to bother y'all with any of that. I think you should go enjoy yourself in the city or go check out the town of Brighton. There's plenty to do right here if you don't want to drive far."

Grandma Denny must have covered the phone with her hand. Everything was muffled. "I'm talking to her, Elias. I don't need you to talk to her for me. She's my granddaughter." Her voice became clear again. "Sorry about that, Jasmine. My brother thinks he has to be in charge of everything. He forgets I'm a grown woman who hasn't needed him to tell me what to do for sixty years and still don't." She went back to bickering with Big E.

"Send them to the R&R," Hunter whispered. "I'll have my family keep them busy until we're done with work."

As much as J.R. did not want to rely on Hunter and his family any more than she already was, this was possibly the only solution to her problem.

"Gran," J.R. said, trying to get the woman's attention. "Gran, why don't you three head over to the place where Tessa and I are staying. My friend from work set me up at his family's guest ranch. If Big E needs something to do, I am sure he could find something to do there. Doesn't he run a guest ranch in Montana?"

"He does. He thinks it's the best in the world even though his grandchildren are the ones doing all the work. Yeah, you heard me. You know your ranch is doing so well because those boys and their wives are working their tushes off." She was back to arguing with her brother.

J.R. muted herself. "I don't know if I want to do this to your family," she said to Hunter. "They seem to like me right now, but once they meet these three, they might ask you to ask me to leave."

His shoulders shook with silent laughter. His smile was so wide it made the corners of his eyes wrinkle. "They can handle it. I promise."

"You think that, but you are not listening to the other side of this conversation. If you were, you might not be so quick to promise anything."

Hunter pulled out his own phone, undeterred. "I'm texting Cody right now. He'll take care of them."

J.R. unmuted her phone. "Gran, I'm going to send my mom a text with the address to the ranch where I'm staying. Y'all should go there and wait for me, okay?"

"You need to talk to your mom? Here she is."

"No, I—"

It was too late, Flora was back on the phone. "These two fight like cats and dogs. It's a wonder I have lasted this long."

"I'm going to send you a text with the address for the ranch where Tessa and I are staying. Can you please make sure they drive you there? I don't need Big E to do anything at my house."

"Oh, he's excited about checking out this guest ranch. Is this a nice place or is it a dump? I hate to think you and Tessa are staying in a bunkhouse or something."

Little did she know they were living in the lap of luxury. J.R. wanted to keep it that way, too. If her mother knew she was staying in a six-bedroom private lodge, she might try to stay with them and possibly never leave.

"It's okay. I know you have very high standards, but Tessa and I just needed a safe, dry place to stay for a few days. We aren't picky."

"Oh, Jasmine Rose. You haven't changed one bit, have you? You need to embrace being pampered once in a while. You deserve it, raising that little girl on your own because her father is a good-for-nothing."

There she went. J.R. was not about to listen to her mother bash Chad, even though he totally deserved it. "Mom, stop. Please don't talk about Chad. Especially in front of Tessa. Promise me."

"Fine. But I'm sure that child knows what a deadbeat her daddy is. I don't need to tell her."

"Tessa loves her dad. She does not need to hear anyone else's opinion on him."

"Fine, fine. We will see you at the ranch, sweetheart."

"Bye, Mom." J.R. hung up and rubbed her temples. One phone call and she already had a headache. She pleaded with Hunter, "Please tell your brother to not show my mom where I am staying. I do not want her to make herself comfortable at the Grand Dixie, okay?"

"You have a six-bedroom private lodge and you aren't going to let your mom, your grandmother, or your great-uncle stay with you?" Hunter's eyes were wide and his tone was completely judgmental.

"You do not understand because you do not know them. You would not be judging me so hard if you did. Please text your brother to keep them in the main lodge. Please."

"I'm gonna have to tell my whole family because they'll probably all meet them and everyone will assume they're staying with you. This is going to be difficult for my mom."

"See, they're going to think I'm a terrible person. My mother is already working her magic." Flora had a way of bringing out the worst in J.R. At the same time, if she didn't create some boundaries without Flora knowing, her mother would not allow her to have any. J.R. needed them to tell her what they were doing there and then go back where they came from. She did not want to entice them to extend their stay any longer than necessary.

"You're not a terrible person. My mom is just all about *togetherness*. She assumes all families are like ours."

"You mean big and happy?"

He nodded as he typed up the message to his family.

"Well, the Blackwells are big but happy isn't the way any of us would describe our family." J.R. wished it wasn't true, but it had been a very long time since she could characterize her family as happy. Maybe in the very beginning, when they first started the trick riding and performing at small venues. J.R. had some memories that included them having fun and getting along. She also had memories of the fighting, the exhaustion, the refusal to acknowledge they were growing up and perhaps wanted something else out of life than being the Blackwell Belles.

"I'm sorry it was like that for you," Hunter said, looking up from his phone. "I can't imagine not thinking of family as my safe place. The only thing I wanted after I got injured was to come home."

"Don't ever take that for granted." What she wouldn't do to have that kind of support. Maybe that was why she was so quick to refuse help from others, she didn't know how to accept it because she never felt like she got it from the people who were supposed to give it.

He nodded and finished his text. He waited for some replies to come in. "You're all set. They've either given me the thumbs-up or told me they've got your back."

"Oh, can you ask Cora to tell Tessa not to tell Grandma about our lodge. Tell her that I want to surprise Grandma, so I need her to keep it a secret until I get there. Tessa will want to show them her horse room if we don't tell her it's a secret."

Hunter sent the text to his sister-in-law. J.R. would figure out how to keep the secret a secret before she got back to the ranch. Tessa's desire to learn how to play pool might become a problem.

With that out of the way, J.R. and Hunter needed to get back to work. She didn't want to be the reason he could say he didn't do everything he wanted to because he was distracted by her family drama.

"No more worrying about me. You better start thinking about which bull you're going to put up against mine. You'll need all the time we've been given if you want your bids to come close to what I'm expecting. I wouldn't want it to be a complete blowout."

Hunter was on his feet. "You have no idea how much I love a good competition. I'm going to talk to Lou. I think I know who I want to pick, but if Lou doesn't agree, I'm gonna need to think about it some more."

"You go consult your resources, I'm going to consult mine," she said, clicking on the file that listed all the calves and their heritage. J.R. had two calves in mind, but she wanted to make sure the one she chose was perfect.

J.R. worked nonstop until lunchtime. Hunter offered to run out and pick something up while she made her calls to her insurance agent and to the tree removal services.

Hunter had spent the rest of the morning with Lou and the calves. They probably agreed on which one they thought was going to win. Hunter and Lou were very like-minded. It sometimes made J.R. jealous. Lou had always been nice to her, but it was clear that he loved Hunter the moment they met. Lou had been a fan of Hunter's and had followed his career since they were both from Brighton. They had a camaraderie that J.R. didn't have with anyone.

After lunch, it was J.R.'s turn to go watch some training. The calf she chose was named Buckwild. His lineage was the one she had most carefully considered in this group. His father was Wild-n-Out, who historically sired calves that went on to win derby and classic events and were big earners. His calves were always big and athletic, able to get off the ground and kick with the best of them. Buckwild's mom, Pearl, was from a very special line. Her mom was the daughter of Kingston, one of the best bulls to come out of Texas. Her dad was a championship bull named Knocker Rocker. Pearl had produced more than five big earners over the few years. They all tended to be skilled at twisting and turning. That, combined with the kicking power of Wild-n-Out's offspring, made them a perfect match.

"Who do you want to see today?" Lou asked as J.R. entered the arena.

She wondered if he would tell her who Hunter had chosen. She had to admit she was curious. There were ten calves to choose from, but only about half had the potential to make the big bucks, literally and figuratively.

"When I tell you, are you going to text Hunter right away?"

Lou was the quintessential cowboy. He had deep lines in his tanned face and a raspy voice from smoking cigarettes for too many years. She'd never seen him in anything other than jeans and a button-down shirt in all the years she'd worked with him.

He flicked the brim of his hat up, smiling like the cat that caught the canary. "No, not right away. I'll wait until you leave and then I'll text him."

"Who did he want to see today? And has he chosen the one he thinks is going to win yet?"

"You're worried about how quickly I'm gonna spill the beans to him, but you want me to tell you everything about his choice?" Lou chuckled and shook his head.

"Tell me who he picked so I know he didn't pick the one I picked."

Lou decided to be as difficult as her family had been today. "Tell me who you picked and I'll tell you if he picked that one or not."

J.R. frowned but knew better than to argue with him. "I picked Buckwild."

"Oh, really?" He feigned surprise. "You picked the one you've been favoriting this whole time? Big surprise."

"It's the best choice and I dare you to deny it. Is that who Hunter chose? Your uncle said there was no way we would pick the same one."

"Huh, my uncle was…correct. He did not pick Buckwild. Although, we did have a brief conversation about him."

She wondered what that conversation had been about but was more interested in who he did choose. "So, who is Buckwild going up against?"

"Hunter chose Sweetwater's Revenge."

"Sweetwater's Revenge? He wasn't even in my top three."

Lou shrugged his shoulders. "What can I say? You two focus on different stuff. Hunter thinks Sweetwater will be a champion someday."

J.R. was intrigued by his decision. She wanted to run back into the office and pick his brain as well as pull up the heredity spreadsheet and examine Sweetwater's lineage.

"Maybe he'll be champion of something, but it won't be of this sale, because that's going to be Buckwild."

"Maybe, maybe not," Lou teased with a smirk. He left her there to go get Buckwild ready for some bucking practice.

J.R. believed in her science and the science told her she should shout it from the rooftops—Buckwild was the bull with the most earning potential.

CHAPTER EIGHT

"ARE YOU SURE these people are related to the woman we met at breakfast this morning?"

Hunter got up and closed his office door all the way shut, so no one else could hear this conversation. "She warned me that they were kind of a handful."

Cody had called because he said there was no way he could type everything that had been going on all day via text. "Besides going on and on about how he does things at his ranch in comparison to what we do here, her great-uncle asked Dad who did his online marketing for him because the internet is where it's at and they get all these hits on their social media platforms. Dad proceeded to tell him that he hated computers and that all the problems in the world are due to our reliance on electronic devices. I think they're still talking about it and that was over an hour ago."

Hunter knew all too well that no one should get his dad started on the dangers of technology. "If that's the worst of it, it doesn't sound too bad."

Cody barked a laugh. "Oh, that's just the beginning of the fun. Jack Jr. found her grandmother mucking one of the horse stalls. He had to wrestle the shovel out of the woman's hand, explaining that we prefer guests not to do the work we hire ranch hands to do or else the ranch hands will be bored. The best part is her mother. I don't have enough time to tell you about this dog that she has with her. I will instead share that she broke a fingernail and has been complaining about it like it is some sort of chronic illness that she will never recover from."

J.R.'s family proved to be as interesting as she had led him to believe. "You guys haven't told them she's staying in the private lodge, have you?"

"Well, when the nail broke, Mrs. Blackwell could not find her emery board in their RV, so she asked if she could go to J.R.'s room to look for one. By the way, she calls J.R. by her full name—Jasmine Rose. It's a mouthful. Anyway, I had no idea what an emery board was, so I texted Savannah and, luckily, she knew and brought her one before I had to divulge J.R.'s living arrangements. An emery board is a nail file, in case you were wondering."

"Good to know. Thank goodness for Savannah."

Cody hummed in agreement. "Tessa's here now, so she's getting all their attention for the time being. The four of them went to check out the goats and kid. That should keep them busy for a little bit, but I sure hope y'all are leaving work soon because these three are more work than all the other guests here combined."

Hunter scrubbed his face with his hand. Everything about J.R.'s mood this morning made more sense. "We should be leaving soon. At least, I will be. I'll do my best to make sure she comes with me. I'm actually surprised she hasn't asked to leave a little earlier today. I know she has so much to do between her family dropping in and the tree dropping on her house."

"My guess is she is avoiding these people for as long as she can. Don't let her work overtime, that's all I'm asking."

Hunter let his brother go, promising to get J.R. out of the office on time. She was supposed to run errands after work, but that might have to wait now that her family was in town.

J.R. returned to the office, a satisfied grin on her face. She sat down at her desk and stretched her arms out in front of her before she started typing something on her keyboard. She looked more comfortable than she had in a long time.

"Things must have gone well in the training arena," Hunter guessed.

Her smugness could not be hidden. "Knowing Lou, he already texted you all about it."

"Buckwild is a solid choice. He's champion material for sure." Hunter wasn't surprised by her choice. He was an excellent kicker, he had good spin. His lineage was impressive, and was what J.R. was sure to focus on with prospective buyers.

"So is Sweetwater's Revenge," J.R. replied. "His father's line is top-notch."

"I can't explain it, he just speaks to me. If I was riding, I would want to draw him."

She pulled some sticky notes out of her desk drawer. "Hopefully, you can figure out how to put whatever you're feeling into words, so you can sell him to someone else."

Hunter didn't want to start obsessing about his shortcomings. The marketing lingo was more J.R.'s thing than his. He didn't doubt his gut, but explaining what his gut was telling him was something he needed to work on. Buyers weren't gut readers. They were going to require more than his word that Sweetwater's Revenge was the best.

"Good thing we have these two weeks to figure it out," he said, making a mental note to review old sale brochures for some examples of selling points.

J.R. scribbled something on the sticky note and tugged it off the pad. She stuck it on her computer and started writing another.

It was intimidating but also refreshing to see her so self-assured. He didn't want to dampen her spirits, but Cody was right, she couldn't avoid her mother any longer. "My brother called. He said it's probably a good idea if you get back to the ranch as quick as you can. Maybe I can run those errands you needed running?"

She pulled the sticky note off the pad and pressed it somewhere on her desk calendar. The relaxed expression evaporated off her face. She closed her eyes and took a deep breath. When she opened them, her gaze zeroed in on him.

"Your brother already sent out an SOS?"

"It's not that bad. They're anxious to see you."

She cocked her head slightly, unconvinced. "What kind of trouble have they gotten themselves into so soon? Just tell me. You know I'll find out when I get there."

"Your grandma may have decided to muck the stalls in the horse barn and your mom broke a nail."

Her eyes went wide. "My mom broke a nail mucking the stalls?"

"I don't know how your mom broke her nail, but

I don't think it was mucking with your grandma. It sounded like she was in the lodge with Cody, your grandma was out and about with Jack Jr., and my dad has been getting an earful from your great-uncle. They're all meeting the baby goat with Tessa right now."

J.R. sighed. "My errands can wait until tomorrow. I've got the whole weekend to get my huge to-do list completed."

"I can help you this weekend. Whatever you need. I have no plans, so I'm at your service."

"You're too nice. You know that, right?"

"Why do you make too nice sound like a bad thing?"

She took a moment to perhaps collect her thoughts. "I am constantly struggling to keep my head above water, and I am painfully aware that it causes me to be gruff with you sometimes. The fact that you haven't gotten tired of being so nice to someone who's such a hot mess makes me feel like an even bigger jerk."

All this vulnerability was new, and Hunter liked it. He knew she didn't, however. He rested his elbows on his desk and leaned forward. "I'm not going to stop being nice to you. I like you, J.R. Do you have your moments? Sure. All people do. You're also the one person here who remembers everyone's birthday. You kindly share your knowledge about the genetics side of this business with me whenever I ask. I've learned more in the last year from you than anyone else here. And even when life isn't being kind to you, you still find time to make me laugh by sharing Tessa's bull jokes. I hate to break it to you, but you're also a nice person."

Hunter more than liked her. She was everything he found attractive in a woman. Her physical beauty might have been what first caught his eye, but there were beautiful women everywhere. J.R. was more than a pretty face. It was what was beneath the surface that he fell hard for. She was smart, and not in a generic way. She knew stuff that interested him. She had knowledge of the things that were his passion as well as hers.

He also admired the way she had never let the hurdles in her life deter her from moving forward. She held her own in a business that few women were able to break into. Professionally, she was impressive. Yet, there was still more that drew him to her. It was obvious that Tessa was a great kid, and Hunter knew J.R. was raising her daughter alone, which meant she deserved all the credit.

She was the kind of woman he not only wanted in his life but needed.

"Someday, I will pay you back for all this kindness. As much as I've tried to refuse your help, it's truly the only thing getting me through this."

She had no idea how that simple sentiment made his whole day. "Happy to do it."

She shook her head and went back to whatever she was doing on her computer. "Of course, you are. Too nice, way too nice."

HUNTER MANAGED TO convince J.R. to leave a few minutes early. Jed and Walter had already left; there was no reason not to let the weekend begin. She followed him back to the ranch and they found her family waiting in the dining hall in the main lodge. The three new guests were casually sitting at a table like it was completely normal that they had driven down to visit J.R. without any warning and certainly without an invite.

"Mom!" Tessa lit up as soon as J.R. walked in the room. She ran over and gave her mom a hug. "I met the baby goat, and I named him. Want to know his name?"

"I need to know his name. Tell me," J.R. said as Tessa led her over to the table where the rest of the Blackwells sat.

"He's so cute, Mom, and smart. He's only one day old, and he can already walk and hop. Mr. Everett said he's got really big ears for a baby. He also makes the funniest noise. What's it called again, Great-gran?"

"He bleats."

"That's right. He bleats and you can see his little pink tongue when he does it. It's so hilarious. It looks like he's got bubble gum in his mouth."

Hunter loved how animated she was. She was a carbon copy of her mother not just in looks but in personality. The way she talked about the goat was exactly how J.R. got when she talked about the science behind breeding bulls.

"So, what did you name him?" J.R. asked.

"I decided to call him Bubba. Like the gum Hubba Bubba. What do you think?"

"I love it. I can't wait to meet him." J.R. turned her attention to the rest of her family. "Hi, Gran, Uncle Elias, Mom."

While J.R. and Tessa resembled each other in every way, J.R.'s mom was very much not like her daughter. Flora Blackwell looked highly polished, as if hours had gone into making sure her appearance was perfect from her styled head to her fashionable footwear. She stood up and gave J.R. a hug that seemed to come as a surprise. "It's good to see you, sweetheart. I realized over the last couple months that I've missed you girls more than I was willing to admit."

The look of shock on J.R.'s face was priceless. "It's not like Brighton is on the other side of the world. Guess we could both make a better effort to check in more often."

Her mom pulled back. "I'd like that." She scanned J.R. from head to toe and back again.

"You look tired, Jasmine Rose, and pale. Why aren't you getting enough sun? Don't they let you go outside at that job of yours?"

"I get plenty of sun, Mom. It's called sunscreen. In today's world, pale is in."

Her grandmother stood up from the table next. "If you're gonna hug Flora, you better hug me, too."

J.R. gave the old woman a warm smile and hugged her tightly. "It's so good to see you, Gran. You look amazing. I don't know what those doctors in Wyoming are doing, but I hope they keep doing it. Corliss had us all super worried not too long ago."

"Your cousin has a flair for the dramatics. What can I say? It's not that easy to take down someone like me. I might just outlive you all."

"Lord help us," her great-uncle said from his spot at the table.

J.R. let go of her grandma and stuck a hand out. "I finally get to meet the infamous Great-uncle Elias. Corliss has also had a lot to say about you as well over the last year."

"Call me Big E," he said, shaking her hand. "We missed you at the family reunion a few months ago. Your lack of attendance forced us to come to you."

"August was a busy time. I promise to make an effort for the next big Blackwell gathering."

"Did you hear that, Flora?" Big E said, waggling his overgrown eyebrows. "She just promised to come to the next Blackwell gathering."

Flora smoothed her hands over her blouse and fidgeted with her purse. Hunter noticed a furry little head sticking out of it.

"Who's this little guy?" he asked, reaching to pet the puppy's head.

Flora turned and focused her attention on him. Hunter's cheeks heated under her stare. Her voice changed and she fluttered her eyelashes. "This is Zinni, but I think the real question is who are you, big guy?" She poked his chest with her finger as if to check for muscles. "Jasmine Rose, you need to introduce us to your friend."

J.R. looked as mortified as he felt. "Mom, please don't touch my co-worker. Everybody, this is Hunter. He's the man I work with, who so graciously offered his family's ranch for Tessa and me to stay at while our roof is getting repaired. Hunter, this is my mom, Flora, my grandmother, Denny, and her brother, Big E."

"It's so nice to meet y'all. J.R.'s told me a lot about you."

"Oh, boy. And you still wanted to meet us? That's impressive," her grandmother joked.

"You're single, Hunter?" Flora asked.

"Mom..." J.R.'s tone was similar to his own

when his mother was embarrassing him this morning.

"I'm simply asking. I'm not implying anything. I was also wondering what his stance was on dating women who have been married before and who have young children or maybe just one child."

"Mom!" J.R.'s face was flush with fury. "We're not going to bother Hunter with nonsense. He's had a long day and I'm sure he wants to go have dinner with his family."

Hunter could take a hint unlike J.R.'s mother. "I should let you all catch up. I'm sure I'll see you again before you leave."

"We're not leaving until J.R.'s roof is repaired and the other damage is fixed," Big E said. "Who else is going to oversee the construction on the house when J.R. has to work?"

J.R.'s red face somehow blanched white as a ghost when her great-uncle announced this wouldn't be a short visit. "Y'all do not have to do that. I assure you that I have hired a very reputable company and they will not need any overseeing."

"You have clearly not been talking to any of your sisters, have you?" Denny asked, shaking her head. "We didn't drive all the way to see you to only stay a couple days. Violet and Iris have learned that the hard way."

"I was going to say what about Maggie, but then I remembered we didn't drive *to* her," Big E said, stroking his chin. "We drove *with* her. She didn't realize we weren't going to leave as soon as we got her where she was headed." He chuckled and gave them all a wink.

J.R. folded her arms across her chest. "Someone needs to tell me what's going on and they need to start doing it right away."

Hunter took that as his cue to hightail it out of there.

CHAPTER NINE

J.R. COULD ALMOST hear Aunt Dandy from heaven, telling her to breathe in and breathe out. Getting all riled up wasn't going to make things any easier. Aunt Dandy, or Aunt Dandelion, was her mother's sister. She and Flora had been the first incarnation of the Belles before Flora became a Blackwell and the troupe changed into one featuring J.R. and her sisters.

Once Hunter excused himself, J.R. got Tessa settled at one end of the table with the coloring app on her phone while she sat the three elders on the other end to tell her what they were really doing there.

"Why are you visiting all of us? Is someone dying?" She lowered her voice when she mentioned death, so Tessa wouldn't overhear if that was it.

"No, no one is dying," her mother answered as if that was an absurd guess.

"Then what is it all about?"

"I'm being inducted into the Cowgirl Hall of

Fame at the end of the year. We've been coming to see each of you girls to let you know about the ceremony."

There had to be more to it. It was an amazing honor, but this kind of news could have easily been shared over the phone. "Congratulations, Mom. That's very exciting. You must be thrilled."

"I am. Your aunt is also being inducted, posthumously. She would have truly been over the moon about it."

Aunt Dandy loved the spotlight as much as Flora did. The two of them constantly attempted to outdo one another. It was always a competition of which one of them could be flashier, who could do the bigger trick.

"That's true. What else? I know there's something else."

"You girls are all the same! Aren't they?" Flora looked to Gran for validation.

"They're Blackwells. They got your looks and my brains." Gran always called it like she saw it.

Flora took a calming breath of her own. "I've been trying to learn a thing or two on this reunion trip. I'm going to be transparent with you, Jasmine Rose. I have nothing to hide. You and your sisters have all been invited to perform at my induction ceremony. I would like it if you would agree to come. Maggie, Violet, and Iris are all willing to perform."

J.R. immediately wished her mom had come to tell her anything other than that. She started shaking her head before the words could come out.

"Don't say no before you hear me out," Flora pleaded.

There was absolutely nothing that her mother could say that would change her mind. J.R. had left the Belles behind and had no intention of bringing them back from the dead. It would put her career at risk. Being a member of the Blackwell Belles would make it that much harder for some in the business of bull breeding to take her seriously. It was why she went by J.R. instead of Jasmine Rose. She didn't want anyone to connect her to her past.

"I can't do it, Mom. I haven't done tricks on a horse since I left to go to college. If I tried to do tricks next month, I would probably seriously injure myself. My answer is no. Tessa and I will happily cheer you on from the audience, but I will not perform."

"Sweetheart, please. They want all of you. Your sisters have agreed."

"Well..." Gran interrupted.

Of course, Flora was manipulating the truth to get what she wanted. This was what she did. "They haven't all agreed, have they?"

"They have, but they all have conditions. Maggie wanted Ferdinand from Violet, who wanted Aunt Dandy's saddle from Iris. Everyone has agreed to give their sisters what they're asking for."

J.R. glanced at her grandmother and back to her mother. "You need something from me in order for Iris to perform. Don't you?"

"You say it like I'm going to ask you to give up a kidney or something. All she wants is Aunt Dandy's charm bracelet. She said that if she can have that, she'll give Dandy's saddle to Violet and perform one last time."

J.R. hadn't thought about Aunt Dandy's charm bracelet in forever. She wasn't sure where it even was. It was probably in her room somewhere, but none of that mattered because she was not going to agree to perform even if the other three got what they wanted and were in.

"Mom," she said with a heavy sigh. "I am in the midst of one of the worst twenty-four hours of my life. I don't have the emotional stamina to have this argument with you anymore tonight."

"Maybe what we need is some food in our bellies and a good night's sleep. We can revisit all this induction ceremony stuff tomorrow," Gran interjected. "The Robbinses have been kind enough to offer us a spot to park our RV on their property."

"What if I stayed with you and Tessa, so I can

get some more time with my granddaughter?" her mom asked.

This was what J.R. had been trying to avoid but should have figured would be inevitable. "You're all in luck. The only space that was open was a private lodge. I have six bedrooms. You all are welcome to stay with me and Tessa."

"Private lodge?" Gran was ecstatic. "Woo-hee, Elias, did you hear that? You don't have a private lodge with six bedrooms at your guest ranch, do ya?"

"What are you talking about, Denny? We have family cabins. Don't you start comparing my ranch to this one. We know the Blackwell Guest Ranch is superior."

"You're telling me not to compare this place to yours? That's all you been doing all day!" Gran nudged J.R. with her elbow. "All that's come out of my brother's mouth has been, 'At *my* ranch, we do it this way.' Or, 'At *my* ranch, we would never do this, that, or the other.' He's been commenting on every single difference between this place and his since we got here."

"I am allowed to comment because I know what kind of operation we run up there in Falcon Creek. You, on the other hand, have yet to visit me, so you don't know what it's like and therefore cannot comment."

Bickering Blackwells. So predictable. J.R. was

going to regret this invitation, but it was too late to take it back now.

"I have one condition," she announced over the arguing.

"What would that be?" Gran asked.

"No talk about the Belles."

"Jasmine—" her mom started.

"Mom, that's my condition. Take it or leave it. Otherwise, you're welcome to sleep in the RV another night."

Flora sighed. "Fine. I won't say a word unless you bring it up."

J.R. turned her attention to Denny and Big E. "Agreed?"

"Whatever you say," Gran replied. "We won't breathe a word about it."

Thankfully, the Grand Dixie was huge. They could all stay there and not be on top of one another. It would have been the perfect place for the whole family when they were growing up. Each girl would have had her own bathroom. J.R. couldn't imagine what that would have been like.

The three older Blackwells had not had the luxury of a private bathroom in a bit and all disappeared to take showers while J.R. ordered pizza. The kitchen came fully stocked with plates, cups, and silverware. There were more pots and pans than J.R. had back at her house as well as plenty of gadgets and gizmos.

"We should ask Mr. Hunter if he wants to have pizza with us so after dinner he can teach me to play pool," Tessa said as she helped her mom set the table.

"I don't know if you're going to be able to get that lesson in tonight, honey. Mr. Hunter has had a long day." And Flora had definitely scared him a little bit. Hunter probably wanted nothing to do with them.

"We could at least ask him. It's the nice thing to do, isn't it?" Tessa stared at her with those big, innocent eyes. Being nice was on the list of things J.R. wanted to be.

"I'll text him, but don't be surprised if he says he can't come." J.R. wasn't sure if she wanted him to say yes or no. Why was there part of her that already felt disappointed by the possibility of him turning her down? She sent her invitation and couldn't bear to stare at her phone, waiting for his reply. She set the phone down and continued to set the table for five.

Her phone chimed with a text.

"What did he say?" Tessa bounced up and down.

J.R.'s stomach was in knots. Yes meant the potential of more embarrassing conversation and no meant she would have to wait until tomorrow to see him again. Why did that feel like a long time? She picked up her phone and read his text back to her.

I would love to. Can I bring dessert? Or maybe a bottle of wine?

The knots disappeared and her stomach did a flip. Of course, he didn't simply agree to come but had to offer to do something for her as well. J.R. was learning that accepting help wasn't so bad.

Both, she typed in reply.

"He said he would love to join us. That was very nice of you to think of him, Tessa."

"Did you tell him I still want to learn to play pool? I didn't let Mr. Everett show me."

"I'll let him know. I'm sure he'll be real glad you saved the lesson for him to teach." It wasn't surprising that Tessa was already charmed by Hunter. He was handsome and charismatic. He had those warm brown eyes that held her gaze and a smile that could set a weaker woman on fire.

J.R. shook her head in an attempt at shaking those thoughts out of her mind. What in the world was happening to her? A tree fell on her house, her mother had made an unannounced visit to convince her to perform with the Belles one last time, and she was in a battle with this man for the job she wanted more than anything, but here she was thinking about how perfect he was and how nice it felt when he held her in his arms this morning after she stepped in that puddle. That had been the best hug she'd gotten in a very long time.

She was clearly delirious. Everything that was going on in her life had obviously broken her brain. Hunter was a great guy, but he wasn't the guy for her. She didn't need a guy. Guys did nothing but complicate her life, and J.R.'s life was complicated enough.

A knock on the door pulled her out of her mixed-up thoughts. Tessa ran to the door and jerked it open. There on the other side, looking like he was there to pick her up for a date, was Hunter. In one hand, he had a bottle of wine and in the other, he was holding a pie. How did he know that she loved pie more than any dessert in the world?

"Hi, Mr. Hunter! Can you teach me to play pool before the pizza comes?" Tessa was halfway to the pool table before Hunter even stepped inside.

J.R. mouthed *sorry* and held the door open for him. "Let's give Mr. Hunter a minute before we start demanding lessons, Tessa." J.R. took the pie and Hunter carried the wine into the kitchen.

"She's a little eager to learn, if you hadn't noticed."

"Oh, I noticed. The Blackwells are sometimes very clear about their thoughts and feelings."

She knew he was referring to the things her mother had said earlier. How she wished she could go back in time and stop Flora from speaking to him at all. "Filters are things that only a few of us were given."

"If only you were as transparent," he said with a smirk.

J.R. tried to hide her own smile but failed. She turned away and dug through the kitchen drawer for a corkscrew to distract herself. She would not be charmed by this man. They were co-workers. Come the new year, either she was going to be his boss or he hers. They couldn't think about being anything more.

Hunter came up behind her and his proximity made it difficult for her to keep that rational thought in her head. He opened the cabinet next to her and took out two wineglasses.

"It was really nice of you to invite me for dinner. I wasn't expecting to hear from you until tomorrow."

"It was Tessa's idea actually." J.R. found the corkscrew and spun around to face the island. "She's the nice one."

"She learned it from someone."

"They teach all that stuff at school now," she said, refusing to give in. "Social emotional learning, they call it. I read about it in the class newsletters. They are very serious about educating the whole child."

She tried to get the cork out of the wine but she couldn't get the corkscrew to go in. Hunter put his hands over hers and her breathing hitched while her heart took off, beating faster by the second. He took the corkscrew from her and opened the bottle.

"Those kinds of concepts have to be reinforced at home or they don't stick. Parents have a much bigger influence over children than anyone else."

"You've met my mother and you still believe in me?"

Hunter chuckled as he poured her a glass of wine. "I believe even more in your resilience. That's for sure."

J.R. snorted, she laughed so hard. Sometimes she felt like it was a miracle she had survived her childhood and her mother.

Tessa popped up out of nowhere. "Now can he teach me to play?"

Hunter set the glass he'd poured for himself back on the counter and clapped his hands together. "Let's do this."

The two of them went over to the pool table while J.R. tried to get a grip. She was falling under some kind of spell and she needed to be careful or she was destined to be the one hurt in the end of it all.

Big E was the first to finish showering and dressing for dinner. He came out of his room and immediately began throwing in his two cents about the rules of pool. Gran came out next and joined them around the pool table, correcting Big E whenever she got the chance. Before she knew it, Gran and Big E were playing while Tessa looked on and Hunter was back in the kitchen enjoying his wine.

"Sorry. They have a tendency to take over pretty much everything."

"Don't be sorry. They're giving me more time to hang out with you. Nothing wrong with that." He held up his glass and she clinked hers against it. "I like this version of you."

J.R. felt her face scrunch up. "What version is that?"

"Comfortable and chill."

J.R. had changed out of her work clothes and into a sweatshirt and leggings. Hunter had definitely never seen her like this.

"I don't know how those words could describe me when I've been made homeless by a storm, my estranged mom is staying with me, and I only got a couple hours of sleep last night."

He gave her a crooked smile. "I don't know, but you're pulling it off."

It was because of him. That was the thought that popped in her head, but she would never admit out loud. He had taken her in when she needed a place to stay. He had made it okay to be not okay about her mother's arrival this morning. He exuded a calmness that she couldn't help but absorb.

There was another knock at the door. The pizza had arrived. J.R. took the interruption as a chance to pull herself back together and once again remind herself to be smart.

Flora came out of her room as if on cue. "Hunter's here and he's brought wine. Marry this man immediately, Jasmine Rose," she said as she searched the cabinets for a wineglass for herself.

Every time her mother opened her mouth, she reaffirmed that J.R. was right to be cautious. If her mother thought it was a good idea to be with Hunter, then it had to be a terrible one.

CHAPTER TEN

HUNTER WAS SMITTEN. He was obviously smitten by J.R., but it didn't end there. Her daughter was adorable. She talked a mile a minute and had so many questions about the ranch, the horses, and her new best friend, Bubba. J.R.'s mother was a riot. He could tell that she rubbed J.R. wrong sometimes, but there was something about her spirit that made Hunter smile. Grandma Denny was his favorite, though. J.R. and Denny had been cut from the same cloth. She had raised twins as a single mom while running her own ranch. She had helped build the town where she lived and recently saved it from being turned into a lake. That resiliency that Hunter admired in J.R. must have been passed down from Denny.

Then, there was Big E. The old man was a hoot. He certainly had no qualms about sharing the knowledge and experience his over eighty-plus years on this planet had provided him. The guy had an opinion about everything, not to mention personality to spare.

The best part? Her family seemed to like Hunter, too. The worst part? The more they enjoyed his company, the quieter J.R. got. By the end of the night, she wouldn't even look at him. It didn't make any sense.

J.R. stretched and let out an exaggerated yawn. "Tessa, I think it's time to get ready for bed."

"I'm not tired. Not even a bit," the little girl protested.

"If I'm tired, you have to be tired. Let's go get your pajamas on."

That was Hunter's cue to go back to the main house. "I should be heading home to my pajamas as well." He stood up from the table and pushed his chair back in. "I'd be happy to come by tomorrow, help you knock off some of those things on your massive to-do list."

"You don't have to do that. I've got it all under control," she replied, not making any eye contact. "Tessa, move it."

"We should get all the muscle we can over to the house," Big E said. "Hunter, can we borrow a chainsaw? J.R. doesn't have one."

"We do not need a chainsaw. The tree removal service will have the tree out of there tomorrow. I'm meeting a contractor to get an estimate on the cost to fix the damage."

Hunter didn't want to step on her toes. He wanted to help, not stress her out. "You can text me if you need anything. Even if it's just setting Tessa up with a hayride or getting Big E in the pie eating contest."

"Can I invite Addie over to meet Bubba and go on a hayride?" Tessa asked her mom.

J.R. put her hands on Tessa's shoulders and turned her in the direction of her bedroom. "Not unless you go get ready for bed like I asked you more than once already."

To Hunter's surprise, Tessa made a quick detour to give him a hug goodbye. "Bye, Mr. Hunter. Thanks for letting me name Bubba and thanks for letting us stay here."

He gave her a little squeeze. "You're welcome, honey. I'll make sure to reserve you and your friend a spot on the hayride tomorrow."

"Mom was right, this place is way better than the farm," she said as she skipped off to her room.

Hunter gave a wave goodbye to Flora, Denny, and Big E. "Thank you for having me for dinner. Have a good night."

"Good night, Hunter," Flora said, getting up from the table as well. "Walk him out, Jasmine Rose. I'll make sure Tessa brushes her teeth."

J.R. pushed her shoulders back and pressed her lips together. Without a word she walked toward the door. Denny and Big E gave Hunter a smile and wave. He turned and followed her out.

"Did I do something wrong?" he asked when they stepped outside.

J.R. tipped her face up to the night sky. After all the rain last night, the sky was clear now and filled with stars. A full moon glowed bright. "It's not you, it's me."

That was clear as mud. "I know this is all really overwhelming. I don't want to add to your plate. Just promise me that you'll let me help if there's something I can do to make things easier for you, and I promise to wait for you to ask."

She took a deep breath and lowered her gaze. "Thank you. I promise to let you know if I need something."

His fingers twitched with the need to touch her, to reach out and pull her in for a hug. He lifted his hand and she didn't flinch or move away. He took that as a sign that it was okay to embrace her. "Everything is going to be alright, J.R. Things will seem more manageable after a good night's sleep."

J.R stiffened for a second but let her arms slide around his neck. She rested her cheek against his chest. "You're too nice."

"We decided that's not a bad thing, remember?"

She let out a tiny laugh and pulled back. "Good night, Hunter."

"Good night."

She went back inside and he made the trek across the property to the main house. Hunter had moved to Austin after high school to ride for Team Texas Grit. He had come home to visit when he wasn't on tour, but moving back to the ranch permanently after his injury had been harder than he imagined. He had gotten used to the travel and the change of scenery. He was often around other people, but also alone quite a bit. At home, he was never alone. Sometimes that was annoying and sometimes it was nice.

Tonight, he was happy to find his mom in the kitchen when he got home.

"How are our guests at the Grand Dixie?" she asked as she folded and put away dish towels.

"They're settling in. I really owe everyone for their help with J.R.'s family today. I heard Dad got an earful from her great-uncle."

His mom smiled. "Oh, I think he got a hundred earfuls today. You know everyone was happy to help. J.R. seems…nice."

Hunter let out a breathy laugh. "Interesting choice of words. She thinks I'm *too* nice, and for some reason that makes her put up a wall sometimes."

"And you would prefer there to be no walls between you and the lovely Miss Blackwell, is that it?"

His mom knew him too well. "I have a huge

crush. That's probably why she thinks I'm too nice. I want her to like me back, so of course I'm going to be nice. I need to figure out how to rein it in so it's not too much. Otherwise, it's going to make her not like me."

His mom folded the last dish towel and patted his arm. "Oh, sweetheart. You've always been my sensitive one. If she is worthy of your affection, she will relish all of it. You shouldn't have to hold back who you are for someone else. You are one of the kindest, sweetest souls on this planet. She should be thanking her lucky stars to have someone like you showering her with love."

"I get the sense that she's not used to having love be unconditional. She's been hurt before, making trusting me impossible."

"Difficult but not impossible," his mom corrected. "That's why you need to stay true to yourself. Show her that you're genuinely a good guy and that when she's ready, you'd be willing to be *her* good guy."

"You're right, as usual." Hunter gave his mom a kiss on the cheek. His stomach growled loud enough to be part of the conversation. It wasn't unusual for him to get hungry when he was busy overthinking. He opened the fridge and searched for a quick snack. One other major benefit of living at home besides free relationship advice was a stocked refrigerator.

There was leftover mac 'n' cheese in there from the family dinner. It was his lucky night.

"I hid some of that in there for you. I knew you'd want some later tonight."

He put it in the microwave and hit the reheat button. "You're the best."

Her expression turned serious. "*You're* the best. Don't let anyone ever make you feel different."

Julie Robbins was a mama bear. Whether it was his heart or his overall well-being, she was always fiercely protective. She had been the one to nurse him back to health after all the surgeries. She had driven him to physical therapy and had gone to all the follow-up doctor appointments. She had been the one to beg him not to ever get back on a bull. She couldn't bear to watch him risk his life. When it came to his heart, she would not be happy if pursuing J.R. was the relationship equivalent of bull riding.

THE NEXT MORNING, Hunter woke up determined to keep his promise not to do anything until J.R. asked him to. It was harder than he expected it to be. There was so much she needed to do, and he knew she was going to attempt to do it all on her own.

Grocery shopping seemed like one task he could handle that would allow her to focus on the things that she had to do herself. It would also allow her to be more independent while she was at the ranch. With her family here, she wouldn't have to always be the one to cook, if they didn't feel like going to the lodge for meals.

He began to doubt the wisdom of this decision the moment he knocked on the door of the Grand Dixie with a load of grocery bags in his arms. She was going to be annoyed. She had asked him to do one thing—nothing—and he couldn't even do that. He almost took off but then Denny answered the door.

"Well, look who's here. Good morning, Mr. Robbins."

"Good morning. I woke up and had to do my weekly grocery shopping and ended up throwing a few extra things into my cart that I thought y'all might enjoy. I did not go out of my way or anything. I was already at the store for myself, so hopefully J.R. will accept these groceries and not be mad."

Denny chuckled. "That girl has you tied in knots! Stop being so worried about doing nice things for people. It's the right thing to do and she'll get over it. Believe me, I was just like her at her age. Stubborn, independent to my core, and determined to make it in a man's world by proving I didn't need anyone to help me. Truth is, I should have accepted help long before my health forced me to. She needs to learn from my mistakes. Come on in and put those bags down in the kitchen for me."

Big E was sitting on a stool at the island, drinking a coffee. "Thank goodness someone did some shopping. We had to use the coffee we had in the RV and there was only enough to make one pot. Something tells me J.R. drinks a whole pot herself."

Hunter set the groceries down and found the one bag that had the can of coffee inside. "I had a feeling this would come in handy."

Denny rummaged through a few bags. "All this is for us?"

He nodded, knowing that it was a tough sell to say he didn't go to the store for them.

"She'll be mad, but then she'll get over it. Remember that," she said as she began putting the groceries away.

"Who was at the—" J.R. came out of her bedroom with a towel wrapped around her head. "Hunter, I thought we had a deal."

"I went to the store to get myself some groceries this morning and since I was there for me, it didn't seem like a very big deal if I picked up a couple things for you."

"You went grocery shopping for yourself on a Saturday morning before 9:00 a.m.?"

He nodded.

"You do know that I know you live in the house with your parents and your brother, right?"

He nodded again.

"Did you do the shopping for the whole family this morning? Was it your turn to do the shopping?"

"I was just picking up a few things for myself. My mom does the shopping for the whole family."

She went back into her room and came out with her purse in hand. "How much do I owe you? I can write you a check."

There was no way she would let him leave this lodge without a check. He made up an amount. "Thirty-seven dollars and fifteen cents."

She put a hand on her hip and tilted her head ever so slightly to the side. "Thirty-seven dollars and fifteen cents for five bags of groceries?"

Hunter went back to nodding.

She took her checkbook out of her purse and set it on the island while she dug in there for a pen, mumbling the whole time about promises and there being no way he used coupons, and thirty-seven fifteen being baloney. She wrote him the check, tore it out of the book, and handed it to him.

"Thank you for thinking of us while you were shopping for yourself this morning. You *didn't*—" she eyeballed him so hard, making it clear that she did not believe one word or one nod of his head "—have to do that. I will text you if we need any other help today."

There was no way she believed him and she was clearly steamed about it, but he believed that once she had that first cup of coffee and enjoyed a toasted bagel that she could slather with cream cheese, she would forgive him.

Hunter ran straight to his truck and drove it to the main house. He sat there with a satisfied grin on his face. Like his mama said, he needed to stay true to who he was, and hopefully J.R. would come to accept the love and kindness he wanted to shower her with.

His phone rang as he stepped out of the truck. A familiar face popped up on his screen. "Randy Wilder, what's going on, my friend?"

Randy was a bull rider from Team Texas Grit. They had known each other since they were kids in junior rodeoing but had gotten close when they both made it to the pro tours. He was one of the few riders from the circuit who continued to stay in touch.

"I'm just checking in with the guy who lasted eight seconds on a bull named Hot Tamale because that bull kicked my butt last night in Albany. You're not even competing and I can't beat you."

"You were in Albany last night? How did you

do? I'm assuming not as well as you wanted if you drew Hot Tamale."

"Dude, I held on for five seconds. That animal is a beast, I thought he was going to throw me out of the stadium."

It was like a shot of adrenaline to talk about riding. Just thinking about it made his body tingle with excitement. There was nothing quite like the thrill he experienced on the back of a bull.

"I wish I could have seen that."

"I'm headed back to Austin and I was hoping to get you to come to the training facility. Maybe you could give me some pointers."

Hunter stayed by his truck. If his mother overheard any of this conversation, she'd be on him for the rest of the day. He was so paranoid that he glanced around to make sure no one was outside and could eavesdrop.

"You want pointers from me? Did you hit your head when you fell off Hot Tamale that you'd be seeking out advice from a retired nobody?"

"Hey, now. You are Hunter Robbins, 2011 Rookie of the Year, World Champion three different times. If I had been smart, I would have asked for your advice a long time ago."

"Now I'm sure you hit your head because the Randy I know doesn't do nice. He's a smart aleck who loves to give witty commentary and comebacks."

Laughter rang out from the other end of the line. "Can't a guy turn a leaf?"

"It's more like a leopard can't change his spots."

"For real, though. Last time we talked, you told me you were working on your flexibility and strength training. You still doing that?"

"I am. Not like I used to when I was seeing a physical therapist. I would say I've recovered ninety percent. Thanks to all this metal in my arm, I don't think I'll ever be a hundred percent."

"You been doing any work on a drop barrel?"

Drop barrels were a training device used by riders to work on their technique in a safer environment than the back of a two-thousand-pound bull. Hunter wasn't working out to get back on a bull. There was no reason to have one of those.

"I'm not riding anymore. I don't need to practice on anything."

"We could change that. Lionel and I were talking, and he said he's still got people asking about you."

Lionel Fullerton was Hunter's former agent. He had helped him secure some lucrative endorsements back in the day. "I'm sure Lionel misses his cut of my deals."

"Of course, he does, but the truth is we miss you on the tour, man. It's been two years. Are you sure I can't convince you to just practice with me? Retirement has to be so boring."

Retirement was giving his parents peace of mind, so they didn't worry about anything serious happening to their child. On the other hand, retirement did lack those feelings he could only get on the back of a bull. There was the one he got when he was preparing for a ride, the one he got when he was in the chute, and the one that only lasted about eight seconds. Those feelings were like a drug. Hard to give up, for sure.

"You call me when you're back in Austin. Maybe I'll stop by one day and I'll critique you on a barrel drop. We can see if you have more core strength than I did back in the day." Hunter wasn't too worried about Randy following through. He would remember to check in, but then get caught back up in his own life and forget about Hunter for another couple months. "I don't even need to watch you ride to tell you that's your problem. You never want to spend enough time building your core, buddy."

"You and your obsession with my abs. I'm going to hold you to that promise to come out. We miss you on the tour and I bet you miss us."

As much as he knew he should say he didn't, he did. Instead of speaking the truth, he kept quiet. He wasn't ready to admit there was a part of him that didn't care about the risks.

CHAPTER ELEVEN

"IT'S GOING TO be about eighteen grand just to rebuild and put on a new roof. You also have some pretty major water damage in the bedroom. I sure hope you have good insurance. This isn't going to be cheap," the contractor said as they finished their walk of J.R.'s house.

She was completely overwhelmed by the amount of damage that had been done not only by the tree but the rainwater. Tessa's room took the brunt of it, but the water that came in from the gaping hole had nowhere to go but down, so the room under hers didn't fare much better. The ceilings, the walls, the carpet, the electrical. This was a nightmare that J.R. couldn't wake up from.

"What if we did the demo ourselves?" Big E interjected. "Would that reduce some of the cost?"

J.R. put her foot down immediately. "I am not doing the demo myself or letting you do it, Big E. That's not happening."

"What if Hunter and his brothers helped? They would probably knock it out in no time."

When had Hunter become her white knight in shining armor? Her family was under the impression that Hunter and his brothers were at her beck and call. They were not. Nor did she want them to be.

"I have very good insurance. They are going to pay someone to do this for me. I have a deductible that isn't going to change regardless of whether I do some of the work or they do it all."

"Let her handle this, Elias," Gran said, attempting to keep him out of the conversation with the contractor. "She knows what she's doing. When she tells you to stay out of it, she means stay out of it."

"That's not what you told Hunter to do this morning."

That little tidbit caught J.R.'s attention. "What did you tell Hunter this morning, Gran?"

Grandma Denny waved her off. "Don't listen to anything my brother says."

She wasn't going to get a straight answer, so she decided to focus on what she could control. She directed the contractor to write up his quote and send it to her claims adjuster. She'd wait to hear back from him if things were approved by insurance.

The next thing on her list was to find Aunt Dandy's silver charm bracelet. The sooner she gave that to her mother, perhaps the sooner they would leave. J.R. wasn't going to perform, but she could give Iris the bracelet. It wasn't with her other jewelry nor was it in her dresser. She checked her closet but came up empty-handed.

She sat on her bed and tried to remember the last time she saw it but couldn't. She knew it came with her to this house after the divorce. She remembered showing it to Tessa once and explaining what each of the charms meant. The bracelet was the physical representation of Aunt Dandy's life and J.R. and her sister's involvement in it. There were flower charms for each girl, a few that marked important accomplishments by the Belles, several that simply reminded her of riding and performing.

J.R. never wore the bracelet, but having it gave her a chance to visit with the memory of her aunt whenever she needed to. Apparently she hadn't needed to in a while. She didn't know what she was going to tell her mother. Maybe Iris would still perform even without the bracelet.

The last task was to gather up some of Tessa's things from her room. Unfortunately, the walk-through made it painfully clear that Tessa's room was pretty much a complete loss. She was going to have to replace almost everything in there. That meant she needed to do some shopping.

Hilde was chatting with Denny and Elias when J.R. came back outside. Her sweet friend opened her arms when she saw her. Hilde was good at mothering everyone. She wrapped J.R. in a warm embrace. "I am so sorry you guys are going through all this."

"Well, in my life, when it rains, it doesn't just pour. It knocks the trees right onto my house."

Hilde gave her one more squeeze. "At least you have some family here to help you out. I was just talking to your grandparents. How nice that they're here."

"Uh, grandmother and great-uncle," Gran clarified. "We didn't get a chance to finish introductions. I wouldn't spend time with this man unless we were blood related."

"Oh, yeah?" Big E put his hands on his hips. "When we were kids, you used to follow me around like a lost puppy."

"That was eighty years ago! Now, *I* can't shake *you* off."

"Ignore them," J.R. said to Hilde as she slowly pulled her away from the two old folk, who kept up their bickering. "They'll go back and forth like this for another ten minutes before they notice we're not standing there anymore."

"I don't think I've ever met anyone from your family in all the years you've lived here."

"Lucky me that the first time anyone comes to visit, my house is uninhabitable." J.R. found the timing of it comical.

"Where is Tessa? Addie's been asking about her constantly."

J.R. hadn't had the chance to fill Hilde in on all the goings-on. It had only been a day and a half ago when her world flipped upside down. She hadn't had a second to come up for air. She had texted Hilde briefly, but she hadn't shared that much information with her friend.

"She stayed back with my mom." Flora was at the ranch with Tessa. Big E had asserted that someone should go with J.R. to see the house, so he and Gran volunteered for that job. "My mom also came with those two to surprise me."

"That's nice! I can't wait to meet your mom." Hilde had no clue about J.R.'s complicated relationship with her mother.

"I don't think they'll be here very long. With the holidays coming up, I'm sure they need to be getting back home soon."

"Sure. Well, I just wanted to come out and make sure there wasn't anything Ken and I can be doing to help. Are you set up somewhere decent? Do you want me to take Tessa?"

"We are staying in this massive private lodge on the R&R Dude Ranch. Hunter hooked us up. We're literally living like rock stars in our private suite. Tessa is having the time of her life. She wants Addie to come over and spend the night, that's how much she loves it."

Hilde and her husband, Ken, were big rodeo fans. Ken used to barrel race when he was younger. He had freaked out when he found out Hunter was working with J.R. at Bucking Wonders.

"Hunter Robbins is hosting you on his family's ranch and set you up in a private lodge? Ken is going to flip. No wonder you didn't take us up on our offer to stay here."

"Let's not get too excited. It's not like he asked me to marry him or something. He's just being a nice friend like you."

"Ken would never recover if you married Hunter Robbins. It would be like you marrying Texas royalty," Hilde said, not letting it go. She talked like Ken had the man-crush, but she was practically swooning.

"Okay, okay, no one is getting married to anyone. Least of all me to Hunter. Please stop referring to him by his first and last name. It's weird. He's my co-worker. I will call you later to set something up so Addie can come hang out with Tessa. Can you guys just watch over the house for me? Let's hope we'll be neighbors again soon."

Hilde pulled her in for another hug. "We will watch over the house. I can give you updates once you get some people out here to start cleaning up."

J.R. thanked her for being a good neighbor.

She didn't have any more time to waste. What she needed to do next was trade the two old people for Tessa. Mother and daughter would shop more efficiently without the opinions of these two cantankerous octogenarians.

On the drive back to the ranch, J.R. brought back the question of what was said to Hunter this morning. "Just tell me because I will ask him and he's not a good enough liar and will have to tell me."

Grandma Denny sat in the passenger's seat while Big E acted as backseat driver from the actual back seat. "I told him not to worry so much. That you need to learn to accept kindness from others. Don't be a fool like me and fight it until you're too sick to have anything to say about it."

That explained why Hunter had dared to drop off all those groceries this morning. As much as she wanted to be mad at him for not honoring their agreement from the night before, it was extremely helpful to have some food at the private lodge. She had texted him another thank-you after she'd finished her second cup of coffee.

"I'm a working single mom. I need to ask people to help me all the time. Is it wrong to want to do the things that I can do for myself without someone feeling like they have to jump in and come to my aid?"

"I've learned that just because I can do a million

things on my own, doesn't mean I should. I understand wanting to be self-sufficient, which you are, by the way. Just don't use that as an excuse to push good people away. That man, who brought you groceries on a Saturday morning when he could have slept in, is good people."

Gran's opinion held so much more weight than Flora's. J.R.'s mother was a creature of comfort. She loved being pampered. She was all about special treatment. Of course, she'd encourage J.R. to throw herself at a guy like Hunter, who was nice to look at and supersweet.

Gran, on the other hand, had worked hard her whole life. There was nothing glamorous about running a ranch. She lost her husband so young, but persevered and made a life for herself and her children. She was someone J.R. completely looked up to, strove to be like. She would never push any of her grandchildren toward someone simply because they were good-looking or charming. If Gran saw something in Hunter, it was deeper than the things on the surface.

"You never needed a man," J.R. pointed out because J.R. didn't need one either. However, she'd always wondered why Gran never remarried or even dated for that matter. Was it a conscious decision or was she never interested in anyone else? J.R. wasn't desperate for a relationship, but sometimes she worried she'd spend the rest of her life alone because no one wanted her when there were less complicated women out there.

"I was isolated. Eagle Springs isn't like Brighton. Not to mention the men I've hung around weren't like Hunter Robbins."

J.R. slid on her sunglasses. She hadn't met a lot of men like Hunter either. He wasn't put off by the fact that she had a daughter. He showed an interest in Tessa and thought about her and her needs like a real caregiver, not someone trying to impress a single mom. Yet, there were still plenty of reasons she shouldn't entertain the thought of getting closer to him.

"Should I start giving you all the reasons it doesn't matter how great he is? Because there are lots of reasons I should keep things professional with Hunter."

Gran chuckled. "There always are, sweetheart."

"There's no perfect man out there." Big E finally joined the conversation. "But some of us are worth the trouble we cause. That's what my wife would tell you."

"The fact that your wife believed that about you twice in one lifetime is beyond me," Gran teased. "You are one of those guys who's nothing but trouble."

"Oh, yeah? Hey, if it weren't for troublesome me, your ranch would be at the bottom of a lake."

"You just love to take all the credit, don't you?"

"I have to take it because you never want to give any up."

"That's because I spent my entire childhood listening to you thinking you were king of the world. Someone needs to keep you humble."

If this was what it was like to be brother and sister, maybe J.R. was glad she'd only had sisters. She turned up the radio as a hint. Gran had given her a lot to think about and she had too much to still do today. She couldn't let their bickering distract her.

BACK AT THE RANCH, J.R. walked into the Grand Dixie expecting to find Tessa and her mother watching television or giving each other manicures or something like that. However, neither one of them was anywhere to be found.

She called Flora, but her mom's phone rang from where it sat on the dining room table. J.R. ended the call and slipped her phone in her back pocket, trying not to let her imagination get out of control. They probably went to visit Bubba. That was all Tessa could talk about during breakfast.

"How do I get to the barn where they keep the goats?"

"It's the one south of the horse stables," Gran replied, setting down her purse on the island. "I'd walk you over there, but I have a couple missed calls from Corliss. I should call her back."

"You could call Hunter. I bet he knows where the goats are kept," Big E said, opening the refrigerator to get one of the sodas Hunter had bought for them.

"Seriously? A few minutes ago, you were ready to start construction on my house, but directing me to the goat barn so I can find my daughter is suddenly too much to ask?"

The old man shrugged. "I'm nothing but trouble, remember?"

J.R. pulled her phone back out and called Hunter. He answered as if he was waiting for her call.

"Is this for real? Are you reaching out to me because you're going to let me do something for you?"

J.R. rolled her eyes. "I need something very simple. Can you tell me how to get to the barn where Bubba is kept? I've lost my mom and my daughter."

"I will happily tell you how to get to Bubba's barn, but that will not solve your problem if you are trying to find your lost mother and daughter."

She leaned against the island, amused. "And how would you know that?"

"Because they are standing here with me, waiting to get on the next hayride."

She should have known their disappearance had his name written all over it. "Tell me where to find you and don't get on that hayride without me."

She could hear the smile in his voice. "Yes, ma'am."

Hunter directed her to meet them behind the main lodge. The ranch was full of life today. There were several activities scheduled and guests were moving about the property going from one to the other. J.R. spotted her mother first. Flora was wearing her bedazzled jeans and her white leather jacket with the fringe. Her hands flailed as she held court in line. Hunter and Tessa gave her their rapt attention.

Tessa had a taffy apple in one hand and Hunter's hand in the other. Her heart skipped a beat at the sight. They both laughed at something Flora said and Tessa glanced up at Hunter as if to make sure he thought it was funny, too. Tessa's happiness was everything, which made it very difficult to be mad that they were off having fun without J.R.

"We're eating taffy apples before lunch?" she asked, sneaking up behind them.

"Mom, did you know that Grandma could stand on a horse while it was running?"

J.R. nodded. She should have figured Flora was regaling them with stories of her riding days. "I did."

"She could also hang off the side with one of her feet in the air," Tessa continued.

Flora used to do a lot of the same tricks that J.R. did when she performed. J.R. was the best at the strap and vault tricks. She was the first to master a Suicide Drag, where she hung upside down on the side of the galloping horse and her hands touched the ground. It looked pretty, but it was very dangerous.

"That's why Grandma is getting inducted into the Cowgirl Hall of Fame. She was awesome back in the day."

"Back in the day?" Flora put her hand on her chest. "I am still awesome."

J.R. lifted one eyebrow. "Please tell me you aren't going to do any drag tricks at this ceremony."

"I am not performing at my induction. I am the guest of honor. Although, I have thought about entering the arena doing a Hippodrome."

"Mom, when was the last time you stood on a horse?"

"My horse doesn't have to be doing a full-out gallop. Maybe we could trot in." J.R. hadn't meant to make her feel defensive, but Flora's tone told her that was exactly what happened.

"I think you should just enjoy being the princess at the ball instead of worrying about being entertainment."

Her mom adjusted the collar of her jacket. "You're probably right. That's what you girls are for."

J.R. did not want to start a conversation about the performance that she and Tessa would most definitely be watching from the stands. There was no need to bring up anything having to do with the Blackwell Belles.

"I'm sure they're going to show lots of videos of you in action. I can't wait to see it," she said, shifting the focus back on Flora. She prayed Hunter didn't pick up on the comment about the tricks being for her and her sisters.

"I hope they let me have some say in which clips they show. I want to make sure they have my best stuff. Dandelion's best, too. My sister would never forgive me if I let them show anything but her greatest moments."

"Aunt Dandy will be smiling down on you no matter what they show, Mom."

Just then, the horses pulling the wagon full of the first batch of hayriders came around the corner. Tessa bounced on the balls of her feet. J.R. took the taffy apple from her.

"I don't think you're going to be able to eat this on the hayride."

"I'll take it," Flora offered. "You're here now to go on the ride with her. I'm going to go back to the lodge. I think I left my phone there."

"It's sitting on the table in the dining room." J.R. handed her the taffy apple that had one tiny bite taken out of it. Flora held the stick with two fingers like she was afraid it would get her messy. "I'll see you later, Hunter. Thank you for helping me entertain Tessa."

"No problem. It's my pleasure," Hunter said. He scratched the back of his neck and fixed his gaze on J.R. "Is it okay if I join you on the hayride or did you want some mother/daughter time?"

It was cute that he thought to ask. She had already decided she was going to take her grandmother's advice. "I'm hoping that if we're accompanied by the boss's son, we'll get the primo seats in the wagon."

A relieved smile spread across his face. "Oh, I can get you the primo seats. Don't you worry."

CHAPTER TWELVE

EVERETT WAS MANNING the hayride this morning. He brought the horses to a stop and one of the ranch hands took the reins. Everett hopped off the wagon to help unload the guests.

Hunter stepped around the other guests waiting for the next ride to get his brother's attention. "Can I take the next group out?"

"You want to run the hayride for me?"

"Well, not for the rest of the day, only for this one ride." As soon as he shared that tidbit, Everett frowned. "I have some special guests on this one and I want to give Tessa a front row seat," Hunter explained.

Everett leaned back to get a good look at the whole line of guests until he spotted Tessa and J.R. "Oh, I see. You want to impress your little friend and her pretty mother."

"Go ahead, give me a hard time." Hunter didn't care what kind of grief he would have to take as long as he got his way. "Say what you need to say and then let me take this bunch out."

"Do you even know where to go?"

"I assume you take the main trail."

"Yes, but you aren't going to take it to the end. You're going to turn around by the old willow tree. Mom has a bunch of pumpkins under the tree. You let all the kids off to pick a pumpkin and then come back."

Hunter gave him a thumbs-up. "Got it. Thanks, brother." He jogged back to Tessa and J.R. "I have secured us the best spot. How do you feel about helping me drive?"

Tessa's face lit up. Her eyes got wide and her mouth fell open. "For real? I get to steer the horses?"

"You can help *me* steer the horses."

"Yes!" Thankfully, she was still excited about it. He feared she didn't understand that he would not be letting go of the reins at all, but he took her hand and led them around the other guests so they could get settled in the front before they loaded everyone else on.

J.R. shook her head. He knew what she was thinking before she said it. "You are too—"

"Nice. I know. I can't help myself."

"Actually, I was going to say you are too good at this. Are you sure you've only been the uncle to one child?" She wiggled her fingers at him. "You give off a very strong fun uncle vibe."

He was not expecting the compliment. "Really? Nico is only two, I have to do very little to entertain him other than make goofy faces that seem to crack him up. Tessa is my first big kid experience."

"Well, you're doing an excellent job of impressing her. First, naming the goat. Now, steering the horses. You're a natural."

"Let's hope I'm as good at impressing her mom," he said, holding out his hand to help her get up into the wagon.

As soon as she placed her hand in his, he felt the spark. The way her blue eyes widened meant she must have, too. "You're doing a pretty good job of that as well."

Hunter got them situated on the small bench seat at the front of the wagon. It was just big enough for the three of them to sit together. Hunter sat in the middle with J.R. to his right and Tessa to his left. The two draft horses were ready to lead them along the trail.

Everett took a seat directly behind them. "I'm assuming you don't know the hayride script."

Hunter turned his head. "The script?"

"Looks like I must ride along so I can tell everyone the history of the ranch and point out all the interesting scenery. Hi, J.R. Hi, Tessa. Make sure this guy doesn't crash the wagon, okay?"

Tessa nodded as if he was being serious.

Hunter leaned over to Tessa. "I'm a very good wagon driver. I promise not to crash."

He could feel J.R. shake with quiet laughter. Getting J.R. to laugh wasn't easy, so when it happened, it felt like a major win.

During the hayride, Everett enlightened the guests about the R&R's history and how their great-great-grandparents bought the land back in the early 1900s, using it to raise horses and goats. In the 1930s, their daughter and her husband, Hunter's great-grandparents, had convinced them to convert the ranch into a dude ranch and open it up to guests. They took over running the R&R right around the start of World War II. It was because they were located between Austin and San Antonio, that they were able to attract some of the servicemen who were training to be pilots in San Antonio or stationed at Camp Mabry in Austin. After the war, those servicemen returned with their families, and thanks to their loyalty and referrals, the ranch continued to flourish. Hunter's grandfather took it over in the 1960s and he passed it on to their dad in the '90s, who had done his best to keep the tradition of true Texas hospitality alive.

"Your great-great-grandparents raised goats like Bubba?" Tessa asked after listening to everything.

"I guess they did. I didn't even know that until today. Pretty cool, huh?"

"Are we all learning things on this hayride?" J.R. asked as they approached the willow tree.

"I knew the ranch has been in my family for many generations. I guess I thought it's always been a dude ranch. I didn't realize that it started out just a regular ranch. I should pay better attention when my parents talk about this stuff."

Hunter had forgotten how beautiful it was out here, away from the main house. They were in the heart of Texas Hill Country. The rolling green hills, the enormous oak trees, and the natural spring-fed creek made for a gorgeous backdrop to the trails. There were a lot of things he should have paid more attention to since he'd been back.

"Don't feel bad." J.R. placed her hand on his, causing him to lose all train of thought. "My family history is wild. I don't think I even know all of it. I should ask my gran more questions about how the Blackwells started out in Montana and how she ended up in Wyoming. My entire life, up until a little over a year ago, I had no idea that she was actually engaged to marry my grandfather's brother but ran off to elope with my grandpa. We learned a lot about Gran after all that stuff went down in Eagle Springs."

Hunter's jaw dropped. "Grandma Denny ran off to be with her fiancé's brother?"

"It was quite the scandal and the reason she hadn't talked to her brother for decades. Big E and Gran have only been in contact for a couple of years, if you can believe it."

"That's probably a good thing. The way those two bicker."

He earned more of her laughter. "So true."

Hunter stopped the horses and Everett unloaded all the children to go gather up a pumpkin from under the tree. Tessa was so excited. She ran full speed toward the pumpkins as soon as her feet touched the ground.

"She's having so much fun," J.R. said with a contented sigh. "Who would have thought a tree falling through her bedroom ceiling would have been the best thing to happen to her in a long time?"

"I'm glad we've been able to make this a positive experience for her. I'm sure she was terrified the night of the storm." Hunter returned the earlier gesture and placed his hand over hers. When she didn't pull away, he silently celebrated in his head. "How did it go with the contractor this morning? Did you get things sorted out?"

"It's going to cost a lot of money to fix everything, but at least almost everything can be fixed. I need to take Tessa shopping because nothing in that room is going to come out unscathed. She'll need all new everything."

He shouldn't have brought it up. The burden of all that had to be done seemed to settle back on her shoulders. He gave her hand a squeeze. "It's going to be okay. I think she's at that age where shopping is one of her favorite things to do."

J.R. gave him a half smile. "Isn't that the truth? I'm going to need that promotion at work just to cover all of this."

Hunter didn't want her worrying about work any more than he wanted her worrying about her house. "Maybe I should rejoin the circuit and I can donate all my winnings to you and Tessa."

She gave him a playful shove. "Yeah, right. Your mom would hate me. She told me you're never allowed back on a bull. At least not as long as she's alive."

His mom had very strong feelings about bull riding. None of them were good. "Maybe I can convince Big E to invest in Sweetwater's Revenge and he can use all that money that bull is going to win to get you back on your feet."

"Oh, you want *my* great-uncle to buy your bull? Maybe I'll suggest he get in on the sale of Buckwild because he's going to be the highest earning bull to ever come out of Bucking Wonders."

Hunter put his hands up like he was surrendering. "Whatever you say. I'm just trying to look out for you Blackwells. I'm sure Buckwild will make some money. I just don't know if he'll make as much as Sweetwater's Revenge, but you do you."

"Time will tell. That's my new motto," she replied. "I am not making assumptions about how things are going to go. I'll be patient and see where things go." He got the sense that she was talking about more than the bulls.

"That's a good motto."

If she didn't jump to conclusions about him, he had a better shot at making a good impression. More than being right about which bull would bring in the most money, Hunter wanted to be right about what a good couple they would make. He wanted to prove to her that he would be worth her time and patience. She could trust him to be loving and caring today and every day. He was going to take his mother's advice and stay the course. He would be himself and time would tell her that he was the person for her.

Thinking about his mom reminded him that there was something he had to tell J.R. "I forgot to mention that my mom and your mom talked when we were visiting Bubba before the hayride. My mom invited y'all to Thanksgiving and your mom accepted on your behalf."

J.R. pinched the bridge of her nose. "Why

does my mother think she can make decisions for me like I'm a child? Did she forget she is my guest?"

"I would tell you that you can back out if you had other plans, but my mom would be so disappointed. Any chance you can make it work?"

"We usually go to my neighbor's house for Thanksgiving. I guess my mom thinks she's still going to be here. Hilde couldn't host all five of us." She blew out a breath. "If they're still here, your mom would actually be saving the day. I have no idea how to cook a turkey."

"Perfect. Knowing that is going to make her so happy. It makes me happy."

J.R. side-eyed him. "You have no idea what you've asked for. Your mom might regret asking us to come."

"Your family isn't nearly as bad as you make them out to be." In fact, Hunter thought they were hilarious most of the time.

Tessa climbed back onto the wagon with her pumpkin. "I love this one. It's cute and fat."

"Fat pumpkins are my favorite," Hunter said, helping her onto the bench.

"Can I steer the horses on the way back to the lodge?" Tessa looked up at him with the same blue eyes as her mom. It was hard to say no.

"You can definitely help me on the way back."

"Do you think that Grandma could stand on

these horses? They're big but they walk pretty slow."

J.R. leaned forward. "These aren't the kind of horses that Grandma rode in the show. These guys are work horses not rodeo horses. Grandma rode quarter horses, or her favorite were paint horses. She had this one white-and-brown Tovero paint horse that had these amazing blue eyes."

"Is it still alive? Can I see it?" Tessa asked.

"Probably not. She rode that one when I was a teenager. I bet Grandma has some pictures or videos of it she could show you, though. Remind me to ask her when we get back to our lodge."

Hunter was impressed with her knowledge of the different breeds. She obviously grew up around horses if her mom was a famous trick rider. She just never talked about riding or raising horses. "Did you ever learn to ride like your mom and your aunt?" he asked.

Her entire disposition changed in an instant. She sat ramrod straight and her complexion paled. The smile on her face faded fast. "I don't ride," she answered.

"You never even tried?" It seemed reasonable that she and her sisters would have followed in their mother's footsteps. "Did any of your sisters?"

"No one wants to be like my mother." She

glanced over her shoulder. "I think everyone is back. Everett, are we ready to go?"

"We're ready. All the pumpkins have been secured."

Hunter wasn't sure what he had said that caused him to hit a nerve, but J.R. was quiet the rest of the way back to the lodge. When they got off the wagon, she was quick to have Tessa thank him and say her goodbyes.

He caught her hand before she could walk away. "Are you okay? Did I do something? Say something?"

"No. You were great. We had fun." It was obvious that she was trying hard to keep her tone light, but it came off as forced. "Tessa and I need to get that shopping in after lunch. I don't want to put it off until tomorrow. If I don't keep checking things off my list, I'll never get it all done."

Hunter nodded like that made sense even though nothing about her running off like this made any. "Maybe we can get together later tonight. There's a bonfire after dinner. You and the rest of the family could come hang out."

"Can we do the bonfire, Mom?" Tessa asked, giving her mom those puppy dog eyes.

"We'll see. We might be tired from all the activity today. I'll text you, Hunter. Thanks again for the hayride." She pulled her hand from his grasp. The loss of contact pained him. She took Tessa by the hand and practically ran away.

"Yeah. You're welcome," he said to their retreating figures.

Everett slapped a hand down on his shoulder. "What did you say to scare her away like that?"

Hunter would have loved to know. "I have no idea. One minute, everything was great. We were laughing, we were joking. She was talking about her mom and horses. Next minute, she totally shut down. Couldn't wait to get away from me. It makes no sense."

"You must have said something. Did you make a bad joke? Sometimes you tell really bad jokes and it makes me want to get as far away from you as possible because I fear your horrible sense of humor might rub off on me."

Hunter gave Everett a brotherly shove. "I wasn't trying to be funny. I asked her if she and her sisters ever did the same kind of riding as their mom. That's it."

"That's it? Maybe she can't ride a horse. Wouldn't it be embarrassing to have a mom who's a famous trick rider and you can't ride at all." Everett slapped him on the back. "See? You did offend her."

Was that it? Earlier today, Tessa had mentioned she'd never been on a horse. Flora had nearly lost her mind when she heard that. She had told Hunter that they needed to get Tessa on a horse as soon as possible. Maybe that was it. J.R. didn't like riding or maybe had a bad experience on a horse. That would be a good reason to not put her daughter on one. Hunter would probably have a hard time allowing his son or daughter to take up bull riding after everything he went through.

Not knowing was the hard part. Maybe he'd suggest they go horseback riding on Sunday and see what she had to say about it. Hopefully, she would trust him enough if there was some kind of story to tell. Maybe he could even help her get over a fear, if that was the issue. He also felt the need to warn her that Flora was bound and determined to get Tessa on a horse. If there was one thing he knew about J.R. for certain, it was that no one made decisions about Tessa without going through her first.

CHAPTER THIRTEEN

WHY WAS SHE so foolish? J.R. should have known better than to get herself into a conversation about trick riding around Hunter. She didn't want to lie to him, but she also didn't want to tell him the truth. She wasn't ready to divulge that part of her history just yet.

"How was the hayride?" Gran asked when they got back to the Grand Dixie.

"So fun. Look at the pumpkin I picked when we got to the old willow tree." Tessa showed off her cute fat pumpkin that she had already named Plumpkin.

"Where is Flora?" J.R. asked, needing to tell her mom that she couldn't find Aunt Dandy's bracelet so if she was sticking around to get the piece of jewelry, it was pointless. Maybe it was time for them to move on to wherever they were headed next.

"She's in her room, resting."

Flora rested more than a newborn baby. J.R.

knocked on the door to see if she was possibly awake.

"Come in," Flora called out from the other side.

J.R. turned the knob and pushed the door open. Zinni, her mother's little dog, was zooming around the room like it was doing parkour. As soon as she spotted the open door, she yipped and took off, running into the main living area.

"Oh, now you've done it! You let her out. Make sure no one opens the door to the outside or we'll be spending the rest of the day looking for her."

"Tessa?" J.R. called out. "Can you catch Grandma's dog for me? And can we make sure no one opens any doors to the outside so she doesn't run away."

"Do not let that dog outside," Big E said. "She is not used to having all this freedom and she does not handle it well."

J.R. went to sit on the bed next to her mom. "I think we need to talk."

Flora sat up. The annoyed look on her face changed to one of glee. "Yes, let's talk. How did things go? Did you two make plans to get together later? You know you really should put a little more effort into your makeup routine. A little blush and some mascara go a long way."

J.R. blinked, trying to make sense of what her mother was talking about. Had they just entered the Twilight Zone or something? What was happening?

"Mom, I want to talk about the performance and the bracelet. What are you talking about?"

"Ohhhh! I thought you wanted to talk about Hunter." She frowned. "Here I was all excited to get to have girl-talk with you. I don't think you ever wanted to do that with me when you were a teenager."

One hundred percent. J.R. never wanted to do "girl-talk" with her mother growing up. She certainly didn't want to do it now.

Flora brightened a bit. "But I'm glad you want to talk about performing. I'm glad you've reconsidered."

"I haven't reconsidered, Mom. I will not perform at your ceremony."

Flora's face changed once again. "I don't understand why you are being so stubborn about this. Everyone else has agreed."

"Have they, though? It sounds like everything is contingent on Iris getting the bracelet, Violet getting the saddle, Maggie getting Ferdinand. It doesn't sound like anyone has agreed to get back on a horse without something in return, and I am not giving you the bracelet."

"What do you mean you aren't giving me the bracelet?"

"It's mine. I don't want to give it to Iris. She

has other ways to remember Aunt Dandy. She doesn't need the bracelet."

"Well, she has the saddle, but Violet wants the saddle. Iris said she'll give Violet the saddle if she can have the bracelet. She won't have anything to remember Aunt Dandy by if you don't give her the bracelet."

"If I give it to Iris, then I have nothing. How is that fair? Why do Iris's feelings matter but not mine?" J.R. was being a tad manipulative seeing as how she didn't have the bracelet. Regardless, it still hurt that Flora cared more about what everyone else wanted or needed more than what J.R. wanted and needed.

"Honey, there has to be something else you could want. I'll give you anything. I have things that belonged to Dandelion. They're yours. Just let Iris have the bracelet so she'll do what I'm asking of her."

That was the real issue here. Flora wanted something from all of them. She wanted them to put themselves back on display for the world to see whether they wanted to be seen that way or not. Just like when she was "Queen Mother," bossing them around when they had no way to escape. This wasn't about her sisters' wants and needs, once again, it was all about Flora's wants. Period.

"I'm not performing and I am not giving Iris

the bracelet. I'm sorry if that causes some kind of chain reaction where none of us perform, but that's just the way it is. You're going to have to be satisfied with all eyes being on you and you alone." J.R. stood up. "You love being the center of attention, so I'll assume you'll get over it sooner rather than later."

"Jasmine Rose, do not walk out that door."

J.R. stopped in the doorway. "I'm sorry, Mom. I'll understand if you don't want to stay here with me any longer. I'm sure you need to figure out what to do with everyone else because of my decision. Feel free to leave as soon as possible."

Tessa stood outside Flora's room, holding the dog. Tears welled up in her eyes. "Why are you fighting with Grandma? I don't want them to leave. Why do you always chase everyone away?"

"I'm not—"

Tessa wasn't buying it. She cut her off. "Yes, you are. You told her to leave as soon as possible. You were being mean. I could tell." She stepped around her mother and went to give the dog to her grandma on the bed.

"Don't be mad at your mom," Flora said, taking Zinni back. "I'm not going anywhere. If there's one thing I learned over the last couple months, it is that I have some work to do to make things right. I made some progress with your Aunt Maggie, Aunt Violet, and Aunt Iris, but I have to stay so I can do the same with your mom. She probably has a good reason to be upset with me."

Tessa threw her arms around Flora's neck. "I don't want you to leave. I'm glad you're staying. I wish you could stay forever."

Forever was a little much. J.R. wasn't sure which emotion she was feeling the most—frustration or regret. She didn't want Tessa to be in the middle of any family conflict. She hated that there was a conflict for her to be in at all. That didn't change the fact that there were some deep-seated resentments she had been holding on to for what felt like her entire adult life.

J.R. came back in the room. She folded her arms across her chest. She didn't like it being two against one. "I'm not making Grandma leave. If she wants to stay longer, she can. I just know that Grandma needs to talk to your aunts again because she isn't going to be able to give them what they asked for."

Tessa pepped up. "I can show you how to text them, Grandma, so you don't have to leave."

Flora cupped the little girl's cheek. "You are so sweet, honey. I really do want to stay and find out why your mom is so unhappy with me. If we figure that out, maybe I won't have to text your aunts with bad news at all."

How was she supposed to explain to Tessa or her mother that she was still mad that she had to put her dreams on hold so she could do what was best for the family? She had wanted to quit the Belles when she finished high school. Her dream had been to go away for college, but Flora and Dandy wanted them to travel more and train harder. That meant J.R. had to stay close to home. She could only enroll in community college, taking one or two classes a semester. She had spent six years being a Belle instead of putting all her effort toward her real passion, which was science.

Of course, as soon as her sisters wanted to stop after Willow shot Maggie with the arrow, they stopped. It didn't matter when it had been J.R. wanting to quit. She had to wait for everyone else to come to that decision. As soon as they were done, she had applied to transfer to the University of Texas in Austin and she had planned to finish her degree in less than two years. That was when she met Chad and got pregnant with Tessa. It had taken her another three years to get her degree.

J.R. had gotten her degree and a divorce in the same year. She had been twenty-seven, alone with a two-year-old, and struggling to find work. Flora hadn't been there to help. Neither had her sisters. They had all gone their own ways, had been busy living their own lives. That was a sting that didn't fade with time.

"I don't think there's enough time left in my lifetime for me to help you understand, Mom."

Flora tipped her chin. "It would be nice if you would at least try."

"You can try, Mom," Tessa said sternly. It was clear that Tessa was connected to Flora after their short time together. It didn't matter to the ten-year-old that Flora hadn't been around when she was a baby, it only mattered that she wanted to be around now. There was no way that J.R. could take that away from her. She didn't want to raise a child who thought she didn't need anyone because her mother made her grow up without anyone.

J.R. took a cleansing breath. "I will try. Not right this minute," she clarified because she could not have this conversation without a chance to clear her head a bit. "But I promise that I will try."

"I think she needs a hug. Should we both give her a hug?" Flora asked Tessa.

This was not what J.R. needed. She held her hands up defensively. "I'm fine. You don't have to."

They didn't listen. She was quickly engulfed in a double hug. "We love you, Jasmine Rose. Don't we, Tessa?"

"We do when you're not so mad." J.R. ignored the fact that her child had to qualify it like that.

"You know what makes your mom less mad?" Flora asked as she released her from the hug. "I think spending some time with Mr. Hunter makes her less mad. Did she seem happy when you went on your hayride?"

"Most of the time," Tessa said, ending her half of the double hug. "He invited us to a bonfire tonight and Mom said maybe. She should have said yes."

"We still have a lot to do today. We might be too tired to go to a bonfire." Tessa's stomach rumbled. "Did you hear that? You need to eat some lunch. We all do. Come on, you two. Let's see what Hunter bought us to make for lunch."

"Did someone say lunch?" Big E already had the refrigerator open. "Who wants a sandwich? We've got turkey and ham."

Gran was up and in the cabinet. "I'll get the plates. Flora, can you get some chips out of the pantry?"

Somehow, J.R. had gone from single mom doing everything by herself to someone with a whole army of people helping her out. She knew she shouldn't get used to this, but she also knew she should enjoy it while she had it.

AFTER LUNCH, J.R. and Tessa ended up going shopping for clothes by themselves. Flora had decided to stay back, most likely to strategize with Denny and Big E about how she could convince J.R. to give her the bracelet. Little did they know that there was nothing they could say that would make the bracelet appear. A stabbing guilt kept sneaking up on J.R. throughout the day. How could she lose Aunt Dandy's charm bracelet?

"Can I invite Addie over for the bonfire?" Tessa asked as they made their way out of the store, carrying several bags of new clothes and other necessities. "We'll have more fun if we're together."

It felt good to have a few more things checked off her to-do list, so J.R. said yes to the bonfire and a sleepover. They called Hilde to get the okay, and picked up Addie on their way back to the ranch. Happy Tessa meant a less unhappy J.R.

The two girls ran into the Grand Dixie and Tessa immediately started showing her friend around. Flora, Denny, and Big E were sitting with their heads together on the couches in the family room section of the lodge.

"Tessa brought home a friend from the store?" Flora asked, uncrossing and crossing her legs.

"We picked her up on our way back. Addie is my neighbor's little girl. They want to do the bonfire tonight and have a sleepover. What kind of trouble have you three been getting into?"

Big E leaned back in his seat on the leather couch. "Nothing you need to worry about...*yet*."

That was exactly why she was worried now.

"And this is my grandma, great-grandma, and great-great-uncle. They are old but pretty cool," Tessa said before she skipped away again.

"I know she was not referring to me when she said the thing about you two being old," Flora said, running her fingers under her eyes as if that would smooth out any wrinkles.

"When you're as old as I am, you stop being offended by being called old and take the cool part as a real compliment," Gran said.

J.R. needed to contact Hunter about coming to the bonfire. She texted him.

Tessa is bringing a friend to the bonfire. What time does it start?

In typical Hunter fashion, he texted her back right away.

7. I could come pick you up at 6:45 and walk you over.

Like a date? she replied, hitting Send before she could take it back.

I would love to call it a date. How about you?

J.R. paced in front of the stone fireplace, staring at his message. He would *love* to call it a date. She hadn't been on a date in over eleven years. She wasn't sure she wanted to put that kind of pressure on herself and this evening. At the same time, the thought of going on a date with Hunter gave her butterflies in her stomach.

"Are you alright, Jasmine?" Gran asked. "You're staring at your phone like it's about to tell you something terrible."

She stopped her pacing and slipped her phone in her pocket, leaving him unanswered. "I'm taking the girls to the bonfire with Hunter tonight. Did y'all want to come with?"

"Yes," Big E said at the same time Flora said, "No."

The three of them exchanged looks and seemed to be having a silent conversation. Gran hadn't responded to J.R. but chimed in after a few glances between her and Big E. "I think we're a yes. Yes is the way to go."

"You two more than anyone need to be a no," Flora said. "This is exactly what I was talking about. She's got this."

J.R. wasn't following. "Got this? Got what?"

"You're right. I change my vote to no," Gran said.

"Why is this the weirdest conversation I've ever been in?" J.R. asked. "It's a simple question. Do you want to come to the bonfire? Big E can come and you and Mom can stay here. It really doesn't matter."

"No, we'll all stay here, sweetheart," Flora said. "You have a good time with Hunter."

"It's not a date. He thought Tessa would enjoy it, so he invited us. All of us."

Gran's brow furrowed. "What's wrong with it being a date?"

"Are you not coming because you think it's a date?"

"Are you freaking out and pacing around this room because you think it *is* a date?" Gran challenged.

J.R. sat down in one of two cowhide armchairs in the room. "Maybe."

They all laughed at the ridiculousness of it. She was a thirty-five-year-old woman who shouldn't be fretting like a teenager over a bonfire date.

Gran's smile was warm and not at all judgmental. "There's nothing to worry about. Like your mom said, you got this."

J.R. took her phone out of her pocket and typed a message back.

A date sounds nice.

CHAPTER FOURTEEN

THERE WAS THAT word again. Hunter was never sure how to feel when J.R. used the word *nice*. This seemed like one of those times it was a good thing, though. She wanted to call this a date, so a date it would be.

Hunter's plan to be himself and let the chips fall where they may was working pretty darn well. He was walking on air as he headed up the stairs to shower before this big date.

"What's got you looking over the moon?" his mom asked as they passed in the hall. She was carrying a laundry basket of dirty clothes.

"I have a date tonight." His smile felt permanent.

"All that worrying you've been doing seems to be for nothing if you have a date already."

"You were right, Mom. All I had to do was embrace my niceness and she's coming around."

His mom did a fist pump. "There's nothing a mom loves to hear more than those four little words—*you were right, Mom*. Have fun on your date, Hunter."

"Hunter has a date?" Cody popped his head out of his bedroom door.

Hunter jogged a little faster toward the bathroom. He didn't want to lose it to Cody. "Shouldn't you be at the lodge working?"

"I only work a half day on Saturdays. Did you forget?"

"I don't have your schedule memorized. I have my own life to worry about. Unlike you, who is clearly obsessed with me. I know you wish you were as cool and good-looking as your younger brother, but someone in the family has to be the ugly duckling and that just so happens to be you."

Cody could take the roasting. He thumbed his nose. "The ugly duckling turns into the majestic swan, little brother. All you'll be is a duck! Hope your date doesn't think you're a lame one!"

Hunter let him have the last word, closing the bathroom door without looking back to even acknowledge that he was speaking. Nothing was bringing him down today. He had a date with J.R. Blackwell and he was going to make the most of it.

HUNTER WAS STANDING outside the front door of the Grand Dixie promptly at six forty-five. He wanted to make a good impression by being on time. He knocked on the door and Big E answered.

"Don't you clean up nicely. Maybe you'll get it right after all." The old man swung the door open wider. "Come on in, J.R. is still getting ready."

Hunter did as he was told. He stepped inside and followed Big E to the kitchen, where Flora and Denny were sitting with Tessa and her friend.

"This is Mr. Hunter," Tessa said to her friend, gesturing toward Hunter. "He's the one who rescued us from the storm the other night and brought us here. Mr. Hunter, this is Addie."

Tessa's friend could have been Tessa's twin, but their coloring was totally different. Addie had jet-black hair instead of blond and brown eyes instead of blue. They both had their hair braided and sparkles on their cheeks.

"Hi, Addie. It's nice to meet you."

"My dad says you're one of the best bull riders he's ever seen ride."

"That's very nice of him. Tell him I said thank you."

"Can you take a selfie with me so I can send it to him?" she asked, taking a phone out of the bag she had strapped across her chest.

Hunter came over to stand behind her. She held out her phone and took a couple pictures.

"Are you famous or something?" Tessa asked. Her face was all scrunched up in confusion.

Her friend answered before Hunter could tell her he wasn't. "He was a famous bull rider. He used to be in all the PBR tours. My dad said he had to retire, but he was the best to come out of this part of Texas in a long time."

"That's cool. My grandma was famous, too. She's getting put in the Cowgirl Hall of Fame soon. She could do tricks on horses."

"I wasn't the only famous one, you know. Your—"

"Mom." J.R.'s tone was sharp and startled everyone. "I think your dog needs to go out. She's making that weird barking noise in your room."

Hunter couldn't take his eyes off J.R. once they found her. She had on jeans and a fuzzy dark blue sweater. Her hair was down and she must have spent some time curling it. His fingers tingled, wanting to run through it. At work, she didn't wear a lot of makeup, but tonight she had done a little more to her eyes to make them stand out. Her lips were lightly glossed and he wanted to tip her chin, and kiss them. Everything made her seem softer. It was exactly how he pictured she'd look if they ever went out on a date.

"Are we ready to go to the bonfire?" she asked, her gaze shifting from Hunter to the girls at the table.

"We're ready," Tessa said, tugging her friend out of her seat.

"Great. Shall we go?" She looked to Hunter, who was still frozen and staring.

He forced himself to snap out of his stupor. "We should go."

"Have a good time," Denny said. Big E waved.

Hunter placed his hand on the small of J.R.'s back. "You look beautiful, by the way. I love what you did with your hair."

"The girls wanted to play beauty shop. I did their hair and my mom did mine." J.R. ducked her head. "She went a little overboard per usual."

"No, I love it."

She lifted her face to him. Her cheeks were a little pinker than they were a minute ago. "Thanks."

"Have fun, kids," Flora said, coming out of her room with Zinni in her arms. "Doesn't she look beautiful tonight, Hunter?"

"Mom, stop."

"I was just telling her how much I like her hair this way. She gave you all the credit," Hunter said, trying to ease the tension.

"I used to do all the girls' hair when they were young. I could tease and curl big Texas hair with the best of them."

Hunter found Flora amusing. She needed positive affirmation all the time. "You are a woman of many talents."

J.R. tugged on his arm. "One of them being not knowing how to let people leave when they've been trying to do so for several minutes. Goodbye, y'all."

Hunter and J.R. led the way to the main lodge as the two girls trailed behind them, giggling and gossiping. J.R. was quiet again, but this time it was a much more comfortable silence.

"Did you get your shopping done this afternoon?" he asked, taking hold of her hand to get her attention.

She glanced down at their linked hands but didn't pull away. "I did. I've learned that ten-year-olds in today's world are not like me when I was ten. My daughter walked me into the cosmetic section today and asked me to buy her wrinkle cream. Of course, it had some fancy name, but it was essentially wrinkle cream."

"I was wondering how she was going to handle those fine lines I noticed on the hayride today," Hunter joked.

J.R. leaned in to playfully bump him. "I wrongly assumed it was my mother's influence because that woman has been pushing creams on my sisters and me for as long as I can remember, but apparently everyone on TikTok says it's the best."

"Mom, when can I get a phone?" Tessa called out from behind them.

J.R. didn't turn around, she simply looked up

at the sky and replied, "When you're working full-time as a doctor and your office needs to get ahold of you."

"Mom! For real. Everyone has one except for me."

"You'll thank me one day for not being like everyone else's mom."

Tessa's grumbling wasn't loud enough for Hunter to make it out, but he was pretty sure she didn't agree.

"My dad would give you a parenting medal of honor for your stance on phones," he said, giving J.R.'s hand a squeeze. "He believes they are the root of all evil."

"It's a blessing and a curse. The internet is a wild place. Tessa doesn't have a phone, but that doesn't mean she doesn't have any technology. She has a tablet and borrows my phone all the time when we're at home. I monitor it, but as you might have guessed, other parents do not. Hence, I have a child with baby skin trying to buy glycolic night serum."

"Do I want to know what that is?"

J.R. laughed. "*I* don't even know what it is!"

"Then, I'm in good company," he replied, meaning it in every way possible.

The smell of smoke was in the air. The R&R bonfires were the best. On the west side of the main lodge there was a sixteen-foot circled seating area around the large fire pit. The stone-stacked wall of the fire pit was made from rocks they'd unearthed from the property years ago. His dad was all about using the materials the land provided. Hunter remembered being a teenager and helping his brothers put together the benches that surrounded the pit for the guests to sit on. He and Cody had carved their initials under a couple of them to mark them as theirs.

Savannah had a table of goodies for the guests to make s'mores or roast hot dogs. Tessa and her friend were all about the sweet stuff. J.R. stuck a marshmallow on a stick for herself and then slid one on the stick he was holding.

One of the teens who worked on the ranch sat tuning his guitar. "Please tell me we're not going to sing campfire songs," J.R. said as they took a seat by the fire.

"Savannah plans the best bonfires. That means campfire songs for sure." He held his marshmallow near the flames. The fire crackled and popped. "Are you not a singer, Ms. Blackwell?"

"You do not want to hear me sing. I don't even sing in the car when I'm alone because I ruin the song for myself."

Hunter pressed his fist to his lips. He loved that she could be a little self-deprecating. Sometimes at work, she took herself much too seriously. It was nice to see her let her guard down.

He leaned forward to get a second opinion of her singing talents. "Tessa, have you ever heard your mom sing? Is it really that bad?"

Tessa pressed her lips together to suppress a smile. She nodded. "It's worse."

"Worse?" J.R.'s eyes widened at her daughter's critique. "Ouch. Now, I'm for sure not singing."

Hunter hadn't been paying attention to his marshmallow. It had caught on fire and needed to be blown out. "Good thing I like them extra crispy," he said, carefully taking it off the stick and shoving the whole burnt sugar glob into his mouth.

His three companions giggled. J.R. reached up and wiped a little bit that was left behind on his upper lip. The touch was so intimate it made his heart skip a beat. He wanted to lean in for a kiss right then and there. He would bet her lips tasted better than any marshmallow.

Savannah walked over to them and put her hand on Hunter's shoulder. "Glad to see y'all are having a good time. We're about to start the sing-along. Do you have any requests?"

"J.R. claims she can't sing. Are there any songs that won't require her to carry a tune?"

Savannah's forehead scrunched. "I don't think there's any song that doesn't require a tune, but this is a judgment-free bonfire. You are welcome to sing as off-key as you need to."

"Can we sing a Taylor Swift song?" Addie asked.

"How about Olivia Rodrigo?" Tessa added.

"I will see what my guitar-playing friend knows by those two ladies," Savannah promised. "What about you, Hunter? I know how much you love the classics. Maybe you can lead us in a sing-along of 'She'll Be Coming 'Round the Mountain'?"

J.R. tipped her head to the side. She couldn't hide her smile. "Yes, Hunter, will you lead us in that one?"

"You're going to sing that one with me. You won't be able to stop yourself. That song is too catchy."

He had been right. Once the campfire songs got started, J.R. couldn't help but sing along. None of the tunes required much range, so her tone issues went unnoticed. The guitar player knew one Taylor Swift song, so Addie and Tessa were happy. They sang it at the top of their lungs like they were at a concert instead of a bonfire.

Hunter didn't want the night to end. Yet, there was only so much wood to burn and so many songs to sing. They stayed there, though, until they were the last ones remaining.

"Can we say good-night to Bubba before we go back to the lodge?" Tessa asked.

Hunter was up for extending this evening any way he could. He hoped J.R. felt the same. "I'd be happy to take you to say hi to the little guy if that's all right with your mom."

She checked her watch. It was probably past the girls' bedtime. He feared she was going to say no. "We can go see Bubba, but then I need to get you two in bed."

Hunter silently thanked the powers that be. He took her hand in his and led them to the barn where they kept the goats. During the day, the goats were outside in a pen. At night, for their safety, they were kept in the barn. Goats were notorious light sleepers. Hunter knew that Bubba would be easy to rouse. He had to use the flashlight on his phone to find the light switch in the barn.

The overhead fluorescents hummed to life, flickering just a bit before lighting up the entire space. All thirty-some goats at the R&R were huddled together in two large pens. They sprang to life as soon as they realized someone was there to pay attention to them.

"There's Bubba." Tessa pointed. "Hey, Bubba. Come meet Addie."

Bubba hopped around, bleating like a champ. His little pink tongue poked in and out of his mouth.

"Just a warning—they might think we're here to feed them, so be prepared to have some of them get a little friendly." Hunter opened the door to Bubba's pen and let the girls go in.

Several of the goats did just as Hunter predicted and came running over, looking for a late-night snack. Addie and Tessa giggled but held their arms up defensively in front of their bodies, dodging the hungry animals. Tessa led the way to Bubba and showed Addie that it was safe to pet him on top of his head. It was obvious Bubba already trusted Tessa. He ate up all her attention.

"Thanks for tonight," J.R. said as they watched the girls play with the goat. "For the whole day, really. You brought us groceries, took us on a hayride, fed me toasted marshmallows, made me sing terrible campfire songs, and last but not least, made Tessa the happiest she's been in a long time."

"It was my pleasure." If she would let him, he would do this for her every day. "I have had a lot of fun today as well. I can't believe you know all the words to 'Chicken Fried' by Zac Brown Band. That was impressive."

J.R. tipped her head and raised a finger. "Like my mother, I am a woman of many talents. Singing on key is not one of them but knowing the words is."

"I can't wait to learn more about your talents. I would say we could take Tessa and Addie horseback riding tomorrow, but I got the feeling today that horses maybe aren't your thing."

A deep crease formed between J.R.'s eyebrows. "Not my thing?"

"During the hayride, I asked about riding horses and you clammed up on me. Trust me, I know a lot of people who have had a bad experience on a horse and never want to get on one again. I would totally understand if that was going on with you."

J.R. stared at him for a minute before she doubled over in laughter. "You think I'm afraid of riding?"

Hunter was going to put Everett in a headlock until he begged for mercy tomorrow for leading him to think that was the problem. "I don't know. You got all weird. I thought maybe you were offended that I asked you because it wasn't one of your many talents."

J.R. caught her breath. "I can ride a horse. I can probably ride a horse better than you, cowboy."

Competitive J.R. was in the barn. "Better than me… You know that I used to ride bulls for a living, right?"

"You mean you used to hold on for dear life for eight seconds? That is not the same thing as riding a horse and you know it."

Those were fighting words. "I guess we're

going to have to go on a second date. Horseback riding tomorrow. Would you prefer a morning ride or an afternoon one?"

"I'd love a morning ride," she said with a wistful smile. "That's my favorite time of day on a horse."

"Little girls or no little girls?" He was happy to have them join if that was what she wanted. There was a part of him that hoped she would say no little girls, though.

J.R.'s gaze traveled to the girls playing with Bubba. "I think we deserve a child-free date. I've got three babysitters at my beck and call, might as well put them to use."

Hunter shoved his hands in his pockets so he didn't make a fool of himself by throwing them up in the air in celebration. He was getting J.R. all to himself tomorrow morning and he couldn't wait.

CHAPTER FIFTEEN

BIG E AND GRAN were already chatting over coffee when J.R. got up the next morning to go horseback riding with Hunter. Her mother was still fast asleep and probably would be the last one up.

"Good morning, you two," she said, pouring herself a cup from the coffeepot.

"Someone's up bright and early with a very big smile on her face, looking like she's ready to go somewhere," Gran noted. Her long gray hair, that was usually pulled back in a braid, was brushed out. She looked so cute in her pajamas, wrapped up in her robe. Morning Denny was the most relaxed Denny of them all.

"I'm meeting Hunter to take some horses out on the trails this morning. I figured you two and mom could handle making the girls some breakfast when they finally roll out of bed. They had a late night, and I bet they'll sleep in."

"A second date so soon?" Big E sounded impressed.

"Hunter thought I was afraid of horses, so I need to show him I am quite capable on horseback."

Gran set her mug on the table. "The boy doesn't know what you can do on a horse?"

J.R. shook her head. "No one in Brighton knows what I *used to* be able to do on a horse, and I'd like to keep it that way."

"No one?" Gran was incredulous. "What about Tessa? She knows about the Belles. Right?"

"Tessa Jean is not aware that I was a trick rider. She knows that I grew up around horses. She knows that Mom and my sisters did some fancy riding. She doesn't really understand what the Blackwell Belles were. I like it that way. Hence the reason we have the rule that we don't talk about the Belles."

"You should be proud of what you used to do. You were one of the most talented riders out there," Gran argued.

"Tessa would probably think you were cool," Big E added.

J.R. didn't need her daughter to think she was cool. The only thing she needed everyone in Brighton to know was that she knew how to breed the best bucking bulls in Texas. Anything having to do with the Blackwell Belles would only be an unwanted distraction.

"I would prefer that Tessa thinks it's cool that

I have a college degree and understand things about bull DNA that very few other people do. I am trying to show her that there is more to life than being entertainment for someone else. That she can be a doctor or a lawyer or an astronaut. I don't want her to have any limits."

Gran folded her hands in front of her on the table. She cocked her head ever so slightly. "So, if she wanted, she could be a trick rider like her mother, her aunts, and her Hall of Fame grandmother and great-aunt?"

"I see what you did there." She had to give her gran credit for finding that little loophole in the point J.R. was trying to make. "If after being presented with all the options she has before her, she wanted to be a trick rider, I—" it pained her to say it "—would let her."

Gran picked up her coffee and took a sip, never breaking eye contact. She set the mug down and said, "Good to know."

J.R. hadn't expected this little conversation to go sideways so fast. She had woken up in a good mood for the first time in a long time, and she wanted that feeling to last a little bit longer. "I have a date. You two are good with helping me out with the girls this morning if they get hungry before I get back?"

"We're here to help, remember?" Gran said.

J.R. remembered. She hoped she didn't regret taking them up on their offer.

HUNTER WAS WAITING for her at the stables. He had on his dark-washed jeans and a gray T-shirt. His hat was black like his belt and his boots. His belt buckle had a silver longhorn on it. He looked so good, it made her knees weak as she made her way over to him.

"Good morning, Ms. Blackwell. You're lookin' lovely this morning. You must have slept well." He tipped his hat up so she could get a good look at his handsome face. He had chosen not to shave this morning and the stubble on that jaw of his had her heart hammering in her chest.

"I did. It must have been all that fresh air I got yesterday. How about you, did you have sweet dreams?" she asked, coming to a stop in front of him.

"I slept hard last night. No dreams to report, but I'm hoping my day with you is going to be filled with more good stuff than any dream could give me."

"Well, we'll see how that works out for you."

His smirk was as flirtatious as his words. "I can't wait. Shall we get going?"

Hunter had two horses saddled up and ready to go. One of them was a gorgeous brown-and-white paint like the one she had been telling

Tessa about yesterday. "Who is this pretty girl?" J.R. stroked the horse's neck as its tail swung freely.

"That is Lone Star. She is my mom's favorite. I had a feeling you might like her, too."

He paid attention. He listened. He made an effort to do nice things over and over again. Hunter had to be too good to be true. It scared her so much to think she could let herself fall for him only to end up disappointed like she had been with Chad.

He isn't Chad. She had to keep reminding herself. Hunter shouldn't be judged on another man's mistakes or shortcomings. She certainly wouldn't want him to do the same to her. Something told her Hunter had plenty of exes to compare her to. A man didn't look like he did and win on the circuit the way he did and not have a plethora of female fans hoping to get some time with him.

J.R. mounted Lone Star effortlessly. Hunter took notice.

"You definitely know your way around a horse," he said with a chuckle. "This is going to be fun."

They steered their horses down toward the start of the trail. The sun was peeking up over the hills, spreading its morning light across the fields and through the big oak trees lining this part of the property. J.R. loved the quiet of a morning ride. The animals and birds were just waking up. The noisy crickets that spent the night chirping were silent this time of day. She especially loved that there was a slight chill to the morning air. Everything about it was comforting.

"So tell the truth, how many dates have you had on these trails over the years?" she asked, breaking that comfortable silence.

They rode side by side. Hunter glanced over at her. "That's what you want to talk about?"

"I'm just curious. We don't have to dwell on it."

"Well, I'm not going to lie even though the truth might not make me look very good," he said. "I was a teenage boy who grew up on a dude ranch. My brothers and I used to work these trails during the summers when all the families from the city would come for a week or two. Nothing impresses a city girl more than a boy on a horse. I have had many dates on these trails, but they were all nothing more than short-term summer flings. You are the first date I've had out here that I hope won't ever get categorized as short-term or a fling."

That was a mighty good answer for someone who had probably kissed more girls on this trail than she could imagine. She couldn't help but wonder if she could get added to that long list.

"If it helps, I do not do flings."

"Noted."

"What about all the women you must have dated while you were riding bulls? No one ever got an invite to the family ranch?"

Hunter fell silent.

She turned to see what was wrong. He was staring straight ahead with a somber look on his face. "What? Am I being too nosy?"

"I didn't realize this was going to be a deep dive into my past romances. I thought we were out here to see if there was potential for a present one."

J.R.'s trust issues were crashing this date. She swallowed hard. "I didn't mean to come at you so hard right out of the gate. I was married to a rodeo cowboy who dreamed about being as famous as you. He ended up being way more interested in the attention he got from fans than he was in his wife and daughter. It makes me gun-shy about relationships, especially when someone comes from that same world."

"I have been in that world, but I am currently very much in the same world that you are in. You see me every day, J.R. Do I talk about going on a million dates or get distracted by every pretty woman I see?"

"No," she admitted. Hunter never talked about other women. He was nice to everyone, but he never seemed overly flirtatious or gave special attention to anyone. If she really thought about it, the only person he seemed to treat differently was her. She often caught him staring at her when they were both in the office at the same time. He did extra-nice things like bring her coffee. He didn't do that for anyone else.

He halted his horse. She pulled on Lone Star's reins and turned her around so they were facing one another. "There's no black book filled with names of groupies who followed me on tour. There are no stories to tell about bringing women to meet my family. I have never brought anyone home to meet my family until you and Tessa needed a place to stay. You are the first woman I care about and wanted to be here."

J.R. didn't know what to say to that. She suddenly felt very warm, her face flushed. Was Hunter Robbins in love with her? How had she missed that? It felt strange and wonderful at the same time. J.R. had almost forgotten what it was like to be that important to someone. Her troublesome trust issues had made her doubt Hunter's affection all this time.

She turned Lone Star back around, giving her a gentle squeeze with her legs to cue her to move forward. They followed the trail down and around a small patch of trees.

"My brothers and I used to saddle horses and

race each other out here. We didn't have a care in the world. I think that's how I became a thrill junkie. Being the youngest, I would do anything to keep up with them. Even when I was scared to death when the horse would be galloping at top speed. There was no way I would back down. I wasn't going to look weak."

"Caring about your personal safety does not make you weak. If you ignored all those warning alarms, you'd be reckless."

"Sometimes being reckless is fun."

"I don't know about that. I am a big believer in having a plan."

"Fair enough. Where do you see yourself in five to ten years? What's the next big thing for J.R. Blackwell?"

"That is a good question." There were a few things J.R. hoped to accomplish in the next few years. Having dreams for the future was tough, though, when the present was full of so many challenges. "The ultimate goal for me is that I would love to have my own breeding business someday. I don't know that Walter and Jed would ever turn Bucking Wonders over to someone else, but I would do it if they asked. I would also be happy starting fresh with something that was all mine."

"Interesting. It is truly your passion. I love that."

"I'm good at it. I know we've been teasing and trash-talking the last couple days about the bulls going to auction, but I really believe I know what I'm doing. I have worked so hard to learn from others in the business and made my own mistakes that I could learn from. I believe that I am ready to prove myself."

Hunter coaxed his horse into speeding up so they were side by side again. "You're the smartest person in the business that I know. I don't think you have to do much to prove you belong there."

"Thank you for saying that."

"It's true. When I hear you talking about the science behind which bull and which cow should be mated, I listen. I know that Jed does, too."

J.R. could only hope that was true. Jed was a tough one. He had an old-school mentality when it came to breeding. She felt like she had to jump through hoops to get him to see things her way most of the time.

Hunter pulled her from her thoughts. "Besides working, what else do you see yourself doing down the road? In ten years, Tessa will be all grown up and out of the house."

"Wow, way to make me feel old. I can't imagine Tessa not living with me. I don't know. When you're in this phase of parenting and you're doing it on your own, it's hard to see a light at the end of the tunnel when all the responsibility won't be yours and yours alone."

"You've never thought about getting married again, having more kids?"

"Honestly? I haven't. It seems so out of the realm of possibility that I never bothered to give it a thought."

There was silence again. As much as he didn't want to elaborate on his past, she wasn't sure she wanted to speculate too much about her future. She so badly wanted to ask him how he felt. Hunter had never been married, didn't have kids. These were things that he surely could want in his future. She had no idea if they were things she could give him if she was the person he wanted. That made things much more complicated. She was too afraid to dig any deeper.

"Let's take the horses to the creek over there. I may have stolen some goodies from the dining hall for us to share."

Food was always a good idea when conversation was stalled. It was a lot easier for J.R. to say less when there was food in her mouth. Hunter led them off trail and tied the horses to a tree. He didn't pack a blanket for them to sit on, but he did have a very nice assortment of pastries and doughnuts.

They settled down in the grass and munched on the sweets. It was going to be another beautiful day. The storm that had clobbered her house this week seemed to usher in nothing but blue skies. There wasn't a cloud for miles in every direction.

"Do you miss bull riding? We talk about bulls every day and how they're going to perform when they get out there in the arena, does it ever make you want to be back in it?"

"All the time. It was my whole life. I thought I was going to be riding bulls until I was old and gray."

"Not many guys last that long, you know. It's not an old man's sport."

Hunter took off his hat and wiped his brow. "I know. I guess I just thought I had a few more years. Never in a million years, did I think I'd be sidelined before I was thirty."

It was the first time she had seen the faintest bit of sadness in him. Hunter was like today's weather—full sunshine. There never seemed to be a cloud in his sky.

"No chance you'd ever go back? I could tell your mom is against the idea. Is that why you wouldn't or were the injuries too bad?"

"They were bad, but there are guys in the PBR who had worse and are still riding. Did you ever do anything just to make your mom or dad happy?"

J.R. wanted to say welcome to her life. That

was exactly what she had done her entire childhood and early adulthood. "I am familiar with doing that."

"I feel like I owe them. So I do what I know makes them happy. All I can do is make the best of what I got. I still get to be around bulls. I get to go to shows. I get to contribute to the sport, make it better in some ways."

"Can I tell you something?"

He set his hat back on his head and squinted. "I'm not gonna lie, after everything we've talked about today, I'm a little nervous to say yes."

He made her laugh. She didn't mean to be so scary. "When you first came to work for us, I used to get so frustrated with you because you were literally the happiest person I have ever met in my entire life."

"And that frustrated you?"

J.R. broke off a piece of the vanilla-frosted doughnut in her lap. "It did. I couldn't understand how a person could be so happy all the time. Maybe it was because I struggle so much to find joy. It was infuriating to think there could be people in the world who were allowed to take happiness for granted. I thought you were just handed it by the truckload."

"You thought I never struggled to be happy?"

"You, my friend, are very good at making lemonade out of lemons. So good that I didn't know you were aware that there were lemons in your lemonade."

Hunter pulled at the grass and stared off into the distance. "When you're lying in a bed of lemons, your body broken in more ways than you thought possible, your spirit broken in ways you don't ever want to think about again, you have to decide if you're gonna make some darn lemonade or let the lemons have you." He turned and looked her right in the eye. "I chose the lemonade because the alternative would have led to a very dark place for me and for my family."

J.R. couldn't let that linger in the air between them. She tossed her food aside and lunged forward, wrapping her arms around his shoulders and burying her face in the crook of his neck. "I see now that it's not as easy for you as I thought it was. I am so proud of you for choosing the light. I would be sad not to have known you."

Hunter's arms roped around her waist and squeezed her tight. "Me, too," he whispered.

They held each other, neither one wanting to let go. J.R. would never again judge him for his sunny disposition. Hunter had been to hell and back. He deserved all the sunshine the world had to offer.

When she finally let him go, he was quick to turn his head and wipe his face. He didn't need to be embarrassed for having more than one emotion. She stood up and brushed the grass and crumbs off her jeans. She held out a hand for him. “Let’s keep riding. I haven’t even shown you what I can do on a horse yet.”

“Let’s go, cowgirl. Show me what you got,” he said, accepting her hand up.

She wouldn’t be able to reveal all her secret talents, but she could show off a little. Hunter was teaching her that happiness was a choice you could make every day. It wasn’t something that she had to wait around for; she could stop focusing on the woes of her past and start embracing the moments in her present.

CHAPTER SIXTEEN

J.R. BLACKWELL KNEW how to ride a horse. She had Lone Star flying through the fields. Had someone else seen her out there, they would have assumed J.R. and Lone Star had been riding together for years. She communicated so well with the horse, getting her to turn and spin with no trouble. J.R. gave the horse all the credit, but he had to admit her riding skills were more advanced than his.

"Why don't you ride anymore? You're a natural?" he asked as they walked the horses into the stable for untacking.

"Honestly, I forgot how fun it was." Her tone was wistful.

"You know when your house is fixed and you move back in, you're welcome to come to the ranch and ride anytime you want."

"That's very sweet of you. I might just take you up on that."

Hunter handed over the horses to Davis, one of the ranch hands. The guests were beginning to move about the property. There were scheduled trail rides coming up and plenty of activities for them to participate in from clay shooting to cattle roping. It was a good day for fishing or going on a long hike.

Pony rides were popular with the kids on the ranch. "Tessa told me she's never been on a horse. Maybe next time we can set her up on a pony." It seemed like a safe suggestion given that J.R. didn't have a real hang-up about horses like previously thought. "You might want to invite your mom. She was very excited about getting Tessa on a horse."

J.R. shuddered. "My mother would love it if everyone followed in her footsteps. She dreams of having a whole army of mini-Floras."

"I am familiar with coming from a family that wants the children to take over the family business generation after generation. I am fortunate that I've got three brothers who were all interested in ranching. It takes some of the pressure off and, other times, makes me feel guilty about doing something else."

"Oh, I don't feel guilty at all," J.R. said unequivocally.

"I'm not super familiar with the world of trick riding, but I can't believe none of your sisters got into it if your mom and your aunt were so popular."

"Hunter!" Savannah came running from the main lodge. "Thank goodness I found you. Can I ask a huge favor?"

He had a sinking feeling that this favor was going to be the end of his date. It wasn't like Savannah to be rattled, however. "What do you need, Sav?"

"We had two guys call in sick today and I've done all the shuffling of staff that I can. We need someone to lead a hiking group in an hour. Any chance I can bribe you to be that person for me today?"

Disappointed that he had to cut his time with J.R. short, he knew the right thing to do was to pitch in and help. "Sure. I got it covered."

"Thank you!" Savannah's whole body relaxed, and she gave him a hug. "You are the best brother-in-law in the whole wide world." She turned to J.R., pointing at Hunter. "This guy is gold star. If you have any sense, you will take a chance on this one. There are few better than him. Trust me," she said before taking off running back to the lodge.

Hunter appreciated the support, but still made light of her exuberance. "You can take that with a grain of salt considering she thinks Everett is the best. Her judgment is questionable."

J.R. shook her head. "I don't know. I think she

might be on to something. You are a good guy. I had a really nice time with you this morning."

"Me, too. Maybe we need to do this dating thing more often. It seems to be working."

"Let's not get too ahead of yourself, big guy," she said, giving him a pat on the chest. There was a playfulness in her eyes. "You might not want to date me after I get promoted and become your boss."

"Can I get in trouble if I require you to date me when I become your boss?" he teased back.

She gave an exaggerated nod. "You would for sure get fired for that."

"It might be worth it for a few more dates." He wanted to kiss her, prove to her that all joking aside, they could be good together.

He stepped closer, but she took a step back. Her expression turned serious. "I know we kid around about it, but the job is number one for me. You know that, right?"

The hope that had been building inside him all morning deflated like a balloon with a leak. She had been very clear about what she wanted in her future. She hadn't ruled love out, but her career aspirations were solidly in place. If given a choice between getting Jed's job and exploring this relationship, there was no doubt they would not pick the same thing. Hunter was just glad he was still in the running.

OVER THE COURSE of the next week and a half, J.R. was laser focused on bringing attention to all the reasons prospective buyers should take a look at Buckwild. Hunter, on the other hand, had a more diverse agenda. He split his time between marketing Sweetwater's Revenge to everyone in the bull riding community and marketing himself to J.R.

By the Tuesday before Thanksgiving, he wasn't sure on which he was making more headway.

He had done his best to put into words what made Sweetwater's Revenge the bull to buy. He didn't have a background in marketing, but he reached out to people he worked with when he toured with the PBR and asked them to spread the word. Unlike J.R. and her knowledge of genetics, Hunter only had his reputation as a champion rider to convince buyers he knew a champion bull when he saw one.

On the personal front, Hunter had managed to convince J.R. to drive with him to work so her family could use her car, a more manageable mode of transportation than the RV, while she was at Bucking Wonders. It was his sneaky way of getting a few extra minutes alone with her every day. Over the weekend, he had got her to go horseback riding again. She had even let Tessa take a riding lesson.

He hadn't gotten that kiss yet, but he felt like he was getting close.

He sat across from her right now, imagining he could find the nerve to sweep her up in his arms and show her how he felt about her with actions instead of words.

"I appreciate you giving me a few minutes of your time, Beau," J.R. said to one of the many contacts she'd been calling all day. She was relentless and single-minded when they were at work. "Did you get a chance to review the information I sent you last week about the bull we're going to have at auction on Saturday?"

Her half-eaten sandwich sat on the paper it had been wrapped in when he brought it to her during the lunch break she hadn't taken. It was the second day she had worked through lunch.

She threw a balled-up napkin at him, hitting him in the chest.

"What was that for?" he whispered.

Stop, she mouthed. "That's right. Buckwild. He's the son of Wild-n-Out and Pearl, who comes from a line I know is close to your heart."

Stop what? he mouthed back.

She glared at him. *Staring at me*, she replied silently.

He was doing it again. She had caught him watching her a few times over the last couple days. He couldn't help it. He needed to study her, to figure out what made her tick so he could convince her to add him to that future she saw for herself.

"That's great," she said to the man on the phone. "I just wanted to see if you had any questions I could answer for you. I know you like to do your homework before an auction like this. I'm happy to help if I can."

"Sorry," Hunter said quietly when she glanced his way again. He shifted his attention to his emails. He had one from Randy. The subject line read: Come to Austin or I'm coming to Brighton.

Hunter clicked on it only to find there was nothing else. The subject line was the whole message. He hit Reply and sent an actual message, inviting him to come to the auction on Saturday since it was being held in Austin. As a joke, he added a link to a website that outlined the perfect ab workout, noting that he might want to focus on that in the meantime if he truly aspired to be the rider Hunter once was.

Randy was going to love that. The two of them had always had a competitive relationship. They spent the early part of their careers taking turns one-upping each other until Hunter rose in the ranks and became the star.

That familiar ache appeared in his shoulder. Sometimes he thought it was his guardian angel's way of reminding him that bull riding was off-limits. This invisible force had one job—catch Hunter getting nostalgic about riding and send shooting pain down his arm so he remembered why he didn't ride.

"That's a serious face. Is everything okay?" J.R. pulled him from his thoughts.

He hadn't noticed she'd hung up with Beau. "Finally, you're off the phone."

"That doesn't answer my question," she said, undeterred.

Hunter hit Send on his email. There was no reason not to tell the truth. "Old injury acting up, that's all."

"I have some pain relievers in my purse. Do you want some?"

It was unsurprising she was prepared for anything given what he had seen her take out of her purse the other day. He loved that she wanted to help. "Nah, I'll be fine. When I used to ride, this kind of stuff was how I knew I was working hard."

"That's not how it works in this job. There should be no physical pain."

"How are the follow-up calls going?"

Her satisfied smile answered him before her words. "They're going well."

Jed walked in without knocking. He motioned for both of them to follow him to the reception area. "We have a problem."

Hunter and J.R. exchanged nervous looks as they rose from their chairs. On the floor in front of Pam's desk was a stack of boxes. The mailman had really gotten a workout today.

"We're four days away from the auction. Walter says he's been contacted nonstop and has gotten a lot of positive feedback. Interest is high. I think the bucking bull community knows we're doing all the right things and they're going to turn up and pay out."

That sounded far from a problem.

"I've been hearing similar things. What's wrong?" J.R. asked.

"The printer sent the catalog for the auction and instead of them being put together like we ordered, we've got this." He reached in one of the boxes and pulled out a stack of uncollated catalog pages. "There's no way, with Thanksgiving in two days, we can ship these back and get assembled ones returned to us on time."

Hunter knew where this was headed. Walter had worked remotely today from his daughter's house in Dallas. Jed and Pam had a houseful of family waiting on them. Lou and the ranch hands had been sent home already. The only ones left were J.R. and Hunter.

Jed at least had the decency to look chagrined. "I know it's the last day of work before you take off for the holiday, but we really need your help."

"Who's ready to start stapling?" Pam asked, waving a long-reach stapler in the air.

With twenty-six pages in the catalog, they needed to fold thirteen full-sized pages together into one booklet. Stapling was the last thing they needed to worry about. J.R. started by separating the glossy pages into piles on the floor. Hunter cleared off the table they had in the reception area that housed the coffee maker and extra office supplies so it could be used to house the completed booklets. Then began the tedious process of putting two hundred catalogs together.

J.R. texted her mom that she was going to be late. Very late. Hunter texted his mom the same, so she knew not to wait on him for dinner.

"Who would have thought I would be happy my mom was in town to watch Tessa for me? Two weeks ago, I would have told you snow in July would be more likely than my mom living with me and watching Tessa so I can work late."

"Flora really stepped up. I saw you two actually laughing the other day when we took Tessa to riding lessons. I'd say you're starting to warm up to her and her sequins and hair spray."

J.R. let out a bark of laughter. "She loves sequins and hair spray more than she loves me and my sisters. I'm sure of it."

"Oh, come on now. She loves you. I can tell." He wanted to say he could tell because he loved

J.R., too. The fear that being too real could cause her to run away and leave him to put together these catalogs all by himself made him bite his tongue.

"Gran and Big E seem to be having a positive influence on her. Those two are so family-focused, it's a little overwhelming at times. Did you hear Big E tell the story about spending four months searching for the son he didn't know he had a few years back?"

"I must have missed that one. I heard about the time he got his ranch forewoman to help him trick his grandsons into coming home to run his ranch. The guy lacks a few boundaries."

"Yeah, you could say that. He told me he had a son he didn't know he had and that guy had five daughters who were actually raised by their mother and stepfather. Only they didn't know he was their stepfather. No one told them until one of them went to get her birth certificate so she could get her marriage license. That's when she found out her dad wasn't her dad. Her birth father was some guy with the last name Blackwell. His mother hadn't told Big E she was pregnant and raised him on her own but gave him Big E's last name. The granddaughter who was supposed to get married ended up pulling a runaway bride with the help of…you guessed it… Big E. Then he has some guy who works for him drive her to his ranch in Falcon Creek and the two of them end up falling in love. Big E goes searching for her daddy slash his long-lost son for four months so he could be at his daughter's wedding and be reunited with his whole family. You can't make this stuff up."

Hunter chuckled. "He makes my family history seem kind of boring. I need a long-lost relative to come and tell me I'm really related to royalty in some small country in Europe or something and they need me to take over the throne."

"King Hunter Robbins." She curtsied in dramatic fashion. "Your Majesty."

He stepped closer to her. His heart thumping against his rib cage. "Would you be willing to come to my kingdom with me if it meant you could be queen?"

"As queen, would I get to breed bucking bulls and sell them?"

"You could do anything you wanted. You would be queen." He reached up and brushed some hair off her cheek. He kept his hand there, holding her face as he began to lean in and finally kiss those lips.

A banging on the door caused them to jump apart and his heart started bucking like a bull in his chest. "Who in the world would be showing up here at this hour?"

Hunter opened the door to find his whole family standing outside. His brother Cody was holding pizza boxes and his mom handed Hunter a case of soda.

"We're here to help. Put us to work after y'all get some food," his dad said, patting him on the shoulder.

Savannah and Cora hugged J.R. and offered to take over production of the catalogs while she got something to eat. With the help of all seven of them, the whole gang was caravanning back to the R&R in less than an hour.

J.R. leaned her head against the passenger's seat headrest. "Your family was a lifesaver tonight."

Hunter was grateful for their help, although a bit disappointed in their timing. If they had only shown up two minutes later, he would have known what it was like to kiss J.R. right now.

"They are the best."

"Being around them makes me wonder what it would be like if my sisters and I were close. I feel like my estrangement from them hurts Tessa. She could have four more people in her life loving on her."

Hunter reached over and put his hand on hers. "It's never too late. If Big E has taught us anything, it's that you can reconnect with people anytime no matter the circumstance or distance that stand in your way."

"My mom is trying to get us to all come to her induction ceremony next month. It would be the first time we were together in twelve years."

"There you go. That sounds like your chance to get the ball rolling."

"Small problem. There are some conditions my sisters have put on this little get-together in order for it to happen. One being my sister Iris wants my Aunt Dandy's charm bracelet that was given to me. She won't give my sister Violet Aunt Dandy's saddle until she gets it. The saddle is Violet's condition for coming to the ceremony. Maggie wants Violet's pet bull. That's a whole big thing."

"That's what you'd call a *small* problem?" Hunter felt like he was caught in one of Big E's family webs of drama.

"I lost the bracelet. I can't do my part to make this reunion happen even if I wanted to."

Hunter tried his best to be positive. "Maybe once you can get back in your house, you'll be able to find it. It's got to be somewhere, right?"

"Mr. Half-Full. I wish I could be so optimistic. This time, I'm not sitting here with an empty glass, I don't even have a glass."

He gave her hand a reassuring squeeze. "I'll help you find it. I will get my whole family to help you find it if I have to. If you want to reunite with your sisters, I'll do whatever it takes to make that happen for you."

J.R. placed her other hand on top of his. She had to clear her throat. "You have no idea what that means to me."

Hunter pulled up outside the Grand Dixie and shut off his truck so he could walk her to the door. A little piece of him hoped maybe they'd be able to share a kiss good-night.

J.R. held his hand all the way to the front stoop. "Thanks for the ride. Please tell everyone thanks from me one more time—for the help with the catalogs and for dinner."

"I will." Their fingers were laced and he didn't want to let her go. "I'll see you tomorrow even though we don't have to go to work? We could take the horses out in the morning."

"I'd like that."

They were chest to chest. The space between them was just a sliver. He began to dip his head as she lifted her face to his. "I'll meet you at the stables at our normal time?" he asked in almost a whisper.

"Sounds good." Their lips were almost touching. The anticipation of this moment was almost too much. Hunter could feel it from the top of his head to the tips of his toes. He started to close his eyes, ready to enjoy this moment wholeheartedly.

The door to the lodge flew open and a strange man stood in the doorway. “I thought I heard someone out here. Happy Thanksgiving, baby girl!”

J.R. stepped back and let go of Hunter’s hand. The instant absence of her was worse than the pain he got in his shoulder. She wrapped her arms around the man’s neck. “Dad!”

CHAPTER SEVENTEEN

"WHAT ARE YOU doing here? When did you get here? How?" J.R. had a million questions, but she started with those.

"I figured if your mom and grandmother were going to stay here for the holiday, I might as well come join them! It's been too long, sweetheart."

It had been almost a year since she had seen him last. He had been in Austin on business right before Christmas and made the drive to Brighton to deliver Christmas presents for Tessa. He looked the same. His hair maybe a little more gray than the last time. People used to comment on what a beautiful couple her parents made. Her mom had always been over-the-top with the glam and her dad was ruggedly handsome.

"I didn't see a car when we pulled up. How did you get here?"

"Your mom had some friends in Flame driving down to Austin for Thanksgiving and asked them if I could tag along. She came and picked me up in the city while you were at work."

It was a good thing she had ridden with Hunter to work today so her mom had a car at her disposal. "I'm really glad you're here."

Hunter cleared his throat, getting their attention. A minute ago she thought he was finally going to kiss her and then, she had forgotten he was even there.

"Dad, this is Hunter. Hunter, this is my dad. Hunter is—"

"The man I have to thank for taking care of my family in their time of need." Her dad stuck out his hand. "It's nice to meet you, young man."

Hunter shook his hand. "It's nice to meet you, too, sir. I've heard a lot about you from your daughter, your wife, your mother, and your uncle. They're an informative bunch."

"Don't I know it. I have heard a lot about you from them as well." Barlow realized he was standing in the way of them coming inside and pivoted to make room for them. "Come on in, you two. Everyone has been waiting for you to get back from work."

J.R. looked to Hunter. They had just finished working an eleven-hour day. She didn't want to assume he wanted to stay. "Did you want to come in? If you want to go home and wind down for the night, I would totally understand."

"I don't want to impose. If you'd rather catch up with your dad without me around," he replied, misconstruing her offer to leave as more of a request.

"I don't want you to go." She tugged on his jacket. "I'd love for you to stay. I just meant I'd understand if you wanted to go. You were planning to go. I didn't want to make you change your plans."

He leaned closer, so close that she could feel his breath on her cheek. It caused her own breathing to hitch. "I'll stay."

She swallowed hard and wet her bottom lip with her tongue. She was very excited her dad was here, but she wished he would have opened that door a minute later than he did. Kissing Hunter was proving to be a challenge. A challenge she was beginning to desperately want to accomplish.

Her attention was stolen away again, this time by something that sounded a little bit like a combination of the weird noise that her mother's dog made and bleating. J.R. stepped into the lodge to find a tiny black-and-white goat chasing her mother's dog around the pool table.

"What is Bubba doing in here?"

"Let me explain," Flora said, getting off the sectional.

"He's in love with Zinni, Mom," Tessa explained for her. "He loves her so much that Grandma and Grandpa helped me sneak her out of the pen so they could be together."

"We were going to bring him back to the barn later tonight," Flora added. "He's not going to spend the night. He's a goat. A very cute goat, but still…a goat."

"Does anyone in my family know that Bubba is not in the pen?" Hunter asked until he realized he knew the answer to that question. "They were all at work with us, so no."

"Nobody was around. We looked for Jack Jr., asked for Cody in the main lodge. We even tried to find Savannah, but they were all gone. The nice boy who was putting the goats in the barn for the night, let us take Bubba for a walk. I told him we'd be right back."

J.R. scrubbed her face with both hands. Only her mother would steal a goat from some poor teenaged ranch hand. "We need to take Bubba back to the barn, Tessa. He isn't supposed to leave his pen or the barn."

"Mooooom," she started to whine. "He's Zinni's best friend. Look at them."

The dog and the goat were playing, taking turns trying to pounce on one another. It was adorable. "Honey, you can bring Zinni to see Bubba tomorrow. He can't stay here."

"I'll take Bubba back to the barn," Hunter offered. "You enjoy your night with your family. I'll see you tomorrow for our morning ride."

"Thanks. I'm sorry for the goat-napping or I

guess we could refer to it as kidnapping. He is a kid."

"Sorry, Hunter. Grandparents aren't as good at saying no as parents. You'll understand some day!" Flora said, scooping up Zinni and petting Bubba on the head. "Say bye-bye to your friend. We can visit him tomorrow."

Hunter picked up the goat. He said his good-byes to the rest of the family as J.R. walked him to the door. She watched as he walked to his truck, wishing they could have had one moment alone to finish what they had started back at the office and tried to finish on the doorstep a few minutes ago.

He waved from inside the truck and drove away. She missed him and he had only just left. Hunter was doing the impossible, he was making her believe this could be something real. He could potentially be part of a future she hadn't dared to dream possible until now.

She blew out a breath and went back inside to catch up with her dad and find out what other trouble the family had gotten themselves into today. Two weeks ago, it had been her and Tessa. Today, she had a lodge full of family. Maybe Hunter was right, maybe it wasn't too late to reconcile their differences. She could have a big, happy family, too.

"So besides stealing goats and surprising me

with special guests, what else has been going on here while I was at work?" she asked, joining everyone in the sitting area. She sat down next to Tessa, who snuggled up to her right away. Apparently, she was already forgiven for sending Bubba back to his barn.

"We were watching videos," Tessa said. "Did you know Grandma has a YouTube channel? She has all these videos of her doing her horse tricks. She even has videos of you doing tricks!"

"Me?"

"How come you didn't tell me that you and your sisters used to be trick riders like Grandma? Mom, you were awesome!"

It felt like all the blood drained from her face. Thank goodness Hunter had left when he did. J.R. stared at her mother in disbelief. She had been very clear that Tessa did not know about her riding and that she wanted to keep it that way. The agreement from Day One had been no talking about the Belles.

"We had a deal."

"I didn't talk about it. I showed her some videos."

"Mom…" J.R. was not going to play this game of semantics. Flora knew exactly what she was doing.

"Mom." Tessa put her hand on J.R.'s cheek

to get her attention. "You were really awesome. Can you teach me to do that stuff?"

This was the moment J.R. had been dreading. She didn't want Tessa to know because she didn't want that life for her daughter. She also didn't want to relive those days. "That stuff takes a lot of practice, honey. You rode on a pony for the first time last weekend."

"Your mom and her sisters used to practice for hours every day," Barlow said, clearly unaware that this subject was taboo. "They didn't get to watch TV or play with their friends. To be as good as they were, they had to work."

"You didn't get to play with your friends?"

The truth was they didn't even have friends. How could they make and keep friends when they were busy performing all the time? "My sisters were my friends," she said around the lump slowly growing in her throat. "My sisters were my only friends when we were in the Belles."

"You girls were just like me and Dandelion," her mom said. "We had each other, a built-in best friend."

Tessa sat up straight and raised her finger like an idea had just popped in her head. "Maybe if you and Mr. Hunter get married, I can get a sister to do trick riding with."

This was all too much. J.R. was about to have a panic attack. She got up off the couch, rubbing her sweating hands on her jeans. "I'm not feeling very good. It's been a super long day and I have to get up early to meet Hunter for a ride in the morning. I think I am going to go to bed."

Before anyone could say anything to stop her, she flew across the room to her bedroom and closed the door. She slid down the other side and held her pounding head in her hands. This family had a way of playing with her emotions. One minute she had been so grateful for their presence, and the next, she wished they never had come to Brighton. There was so much baggage she'd never unpacked. How silly she had been to think it would be easy to let her parents and her sisters back in her life. If her parents, grandmother, and great-uncle could wreak this much havoc, what would her sisters do?

She wasn't sure she wanted to find out anymore.

MORNING CAME AND Hunter was waiting for her with both horses tacked and ready to ride.

"How's the family? Did you guys have fun catching up last night?"

Mr. Half-Full had no idea how the Blackwells rolled. She certainly wasn't going to mention that Tessa was hoping they'd get married and start having babies for her to be best friends with. That little nugget was never going to be shared if she could help it.

"I went to bed early. It had been such a long day, you know."

"Oh," he said, adjusting his cowboy hat. "I hope you and your dad get some time together today then. He seemed happy to see you."

"My dad and mom were separated not too long ago and my mom went to live with my sister and got herself a boyfriend. I think it was his wake-up call that he needs people in his life more than he thought he did."

"Boy, everyone in your family seems to need that reminder, huh? Too bad Big E can't go around and spread his family-first mentality to everyone." Hunter paused. "Wait, he kind of is doing that, isn't he?"

"I think that's exactly what he's doing. My grandmother is his partner in crime, and I still haven't figured out why they are letting my mom tag along."

"It's not a crime to want to see your family be happy. Remember when you told me you wouldn't call your family big and happy? Obviously, your gran would like that to change."

"All I know is that I would like to take Lone Star for a ride and not think about my family for a little while."

Hunter was smart enough not to argue with

that. They mounted their horses and took off down the trail. A ride on horseback was exactly what J.R. needed. Fresh air, sun on her face. Her emotional batteries had needed this recharge after last night.

The dew-drenched grass sparkled in the morning sun. It wouldn't take long for the Texas sun to dry it up. A breeze rustled the leaves on the trees lining one side of the trail on this part of the property. In other parts of the world, the trees had changed colors and the leaves had fallen. Down south, there were only two seasons—blazing hot summer and less hot not-summer.

"Penny for your thoughts," Hunter said as they made the turn by the lake where the guests could do their catch-and-release fishing. "Are thoughts still a penny or has inflation driven up the price on those, too?"

J.R. laughed despite her gloomy mood. "You are so weird sometimes."

"Is weird better or worse than nice? I need to know so I don't blow this."

She shook her head at him. "I'm not sure. You're lucky you're cute. It counters the niceness and weirdness well."

"Ah, so you're one of those women who only loves me because I'm handsome. I see."

The L-word threw her for a second. She knew he was kidding around, but with everything that was going on in her brain, it tripped her up. Was she falling in love with him? Should she? Wasn't she giving Tessa this false hope that they were going to get married and have babies? She was thirty-five years old. J.R. wasn't sure she wanted to have another baby. Why was she thinking about babies? They hadn't even kissed yet.

"J.R." Hunter snapped her out of her spiral. "Are you okay?"

She wasn't okay. She was more overwhelmed than she had ever been. The yearling auction should have been the only thing keeping her up at night. Being successful at her job was her number one goal in life. Yet, here she was wondering if she was in love and dealing with a lodge full of family she didn't ask to visit. A family that wanted her to think about a past she had worked so hard to bury. A past that she had feared would make that goal of being successful in her job harder to attain.

"Do you want to come on a canter with us?" she asked, coaxing Lone Star into a trot. A faster ride meant she'd have to concentrate harder on what she was doing, and right now, J.R. needed to narrow her focus.

She didn't hear Hunter answer. She encouraged Lone Star to go faster and the only sound to be heard was hooves hitting the dirt. Before she knew it, J.R. had Lone Star galloping. The wind hit her face and blew her hair back. It felt like she was leaving the world and all her worries behind.

A weather-battered signpost loomed up ahead. J.R. tried and failed to slow the horse down, blowing right past it and off the path. She grabbed a piece of Lone Star's mane with one hand while giving short, sharp tugs on the reins with the other. J.R.'s heart was racing as fast as the horse, but her head was clear. When Lone Star wouldn't slow, she shortened her reins and used one rein to steer the horse in a circle. Thankfully because they had veered off trail and into a field, she had the room to do so. Since horses couldn't gallop at full speed in a circle, Lone Star had to slow down.

J.R. patted Lone Star on the neck. The horse had to be tired after all that. "Did you need that as much as I did? Is something bugging you, too?"

Hunter appeared, concern etched all over his face. "Are you trying to give me a heart attack? What was that? I thought we were going on a quiet morning ride and you're out here running the Kentucky Derby."

"Sorry. I didn't mean to get her going like that."

"You scared me half to death when you went off the trail. I thought…ugh. Never mind." Hunter turned his horse around and headed back to the designated path.

J.R. followed after him. "I said I'm sorry. I didn't mean to run off on you or scare you."

"Maybe I should be the one apologizing for scaring you," he said over his shoulder.

Confused, J.R. trotted next to him. "What does that mean? When did you scare me?"

His gaze stayed fixed straight ahead. "I think I scare you all the time."

Now that the adrenaline was wearing off, all the muddled emotions came rushing back. She didn't need to ask him what he meant by that. He did scare her. Hunter made her like him and that gave him power she didn't want anyone to have over her.

CHAPTER EIGHTEEN

PUSH, PULL. Run to, run away. Wall up, wall down. J.R. was the queen of mixed messages. The truth was that she didn't know what she wanted. That made it challenging for Hunter. How was he to know how to reassure her that he was here to make certain she got what she wanted?

"Somebody was looking for you," Carlos, one of the ranch hands, said when they returned to the stables.

"One of my brothers or one of the guests?" Hunter asked for clarification.

"He was with Cody. I told them you were out on a ride. They said to tell you they would wait for you in the main lodge."

J.R. handed Lone Star's reins to Carlos. "It's your turn for a surprise visitor, huh?"

"Guess so. Do you want to have some breakfast with me or do you need to head back to your family?"

She toed the dirt. "I should probably go back.

Thanks for riding with me. I didn't mean to ruin it at the end."

"You didn't ruin it. I wish you would tell me what was going on inside that head of yours. It might make it easier for me to not say things that cause you to run away."

Her blue eyes were full of remorse. He knew trust wasn't something she could give freely. She needed time, time to see that he was trustworthy.

"I'll see you later? Maybe you can join us for dinner," she said. The invite was appreciated and a sign that she wasn't planning to stay away for good.

"Text me the plans and I'll be there."

She gave him a small smile and they went their separate ways. He needed to find Cody and his visitor. There was only one person he could think of who would be looking for him the day before Thanksgiving.

"So they come out of the chute and this bull has wings. The airtime is wild. He barely touches the ground and boom!" Randy smacked his hands together in dramatic fashion. "He's back up and he's perpendicular to the ground. The kid doesn't know what's happening. It's been less than two seconds and he is already on the ground. One of the pickup men comes over to get him out of there, but he won't move. He's curled up in the fetal position and they can't get him out."

Cody said what Hunter was thinking. "Sounds like that guy should not be riding. That's dangerous for him and for the pickup men."

"They're letting anyone ride these days. Is that it?"

Randy and Cody both turned at the sound of Hunter's voice. A wide grin spread across his old friend's face. "There's the man I've been looking for."

Hunter opened his arms and Randy gave him a manly bear hug. "I thought I told you I'd see you when I'm in Austin this weekend."

"I didn't want to wait until Saturday. Plus, I heard you're only auctioning off the young ones. They won't even have riders. What fun is that?"

"I'm not in the business for fun anymore. I'm all about creating the next generation of champion bulls. It's serious stuff."

Randy side-eyed Cody. "Boring," he said in a sing-song voice.

"My little brother can't mess around with the big bulls, Wilder. All that metal in his body probably makes him too heavy to be a good rider anyways."

That was all the excuse Randy needed to wrestle Hunter and attempt to lift him off the ground. "He doesn't feel too heavy to me," he panted as they roughhoused in the front lobby.

"Hey, hey, hey! This is not a playground,"

Hunter's mom scolded them as she came out of the dining hall. "We have people coming in and out for breakfast. Hunter, you may not work here, but you still represent this family when you are on this ranch."

"Sorry, Mrs. Robbins. It was my fault."

His mom hadn't noticed who it was that Hunter was roughhousing with until he turned around. "Randall Wilder, is that you?"

"It is. I was back in the area and figured it was time for a check-in with this guy. He looks great. Whatever you did to nurse him back to health seemed to have worked really well."

Mom had never been a big fan of Randy's. He was loud and obnoxious. He was also the one who convinced Hunter to sneak out when they were sixteen, steal his father's car, and drive the two of them to Waco for a rodeo that they did not have permission to go to. He was also the guy who started the fight at the bar in Tulsa that landed them both in jail after a big win five years ago.

"I have my boy back in one piece and I plan to keep him that way."

"That's what good moms do, Mrs. Robbins." Randy pinched Hunter's cheek. "He's your baby."

Hunter swatted his hand away. "Did you eat before you drove down here or do I need to feed your skinny butt?"

"You're jealous of my rock-hard abs, aren't you?" Randy patted his stomach. He was the perfect size for riding bulls. He was five foot seven and weighed around a hundred and forty pounds. The only thing Hunter had been jealous of was that he'd had to relearn how to ride after his growth spurt after high school and Randy hadn't.

"Dream on." Hunter moved to punch him in the gut, but Randy jumped out of reach.

Before they could start tussling again, his mother snapped, "Hunter, that's enough."

He didn't need to be told a third time. He put his hands up to placate her.

Randy tried to be serious but couldn't keep himself from giggling. He threw his arm around Hunter's shoulders. "I'm starving. I knew you'd feed me. Why do you think I showed up this early?"

It was almost nine, not exactly the crack of dawn. "Glad I could motivate you to get out of bed before noon."

"Hey, it's not like I had a hot date with a pretty lady and needed to be up before the sun," Randy teased.

Hunter glared at Cody, knowing he was most likely the gossip. His brother laughed. "How else was I supposed to explain why you were up so early horseback riding on your day off?"

Randy nudged him. "Let's go get some food and you can tell me all about her."

Hanging out with Randy was like putting on an old pair of jeans—easy, comfortable. The guy never changed. He was older. There were a few more wrinkles around his eyes and his hairline was starting to recede, but he still had the same sense of humor as that twelve-year-old kid Hunter had met when they were in the juniors.

They loaded up their breakfast plates at the buffet and sat down at one of the smaller tables in the corner for some privacy. Randy added some sugar and cream to his coffee. He had twice as much food in front of him as Hunter did. He was small, but he had the appetite of a prize-winning bull.

"Tell me about the girl."

Hunter smoothed his napkin on his lap and raised a disapproving brow. "She's not a girl, she's a woman, thank you very much."

"Sorry, I forget we're in our thirties. Tell me about the woman you're dating."

Dating someone and having hung out on the ranch a few times felt like two very different things. He wasn't sure J.R. would classify them as dating.

"It's very new. The dating part is new; we've known each other for over a year now. We work together at Bucking Wonders. She's a single mom to a really awesome little girl. They're staying here on the property while her house is under construction. We're taking it slow. Spending a little time together outside of the office to see if this could be something more."

"Slow? Since when does Hunter Robbins do anything slow? You don't even walk slow. If she works for a bull breeder, she's got to know you as a rider. Does that not help you win the women over anymore?"

"I'm doing just fine winning her over." Hunter needed to get off the subject of J.R. fast. The best way to do that was to ask Randy to talk about Randy. "What about you? Catch me up on what's been happening on tour."

Randy talked on and on, only stopping long enough to shovel some eggs and bacon in his mouth. He made it sound like he was living his best life. He had plenty of stories to tell about some of the bulls he'd drawn and the terrible judges he'd had to deal with lately.

"I held on all eight seconds on a bull that scored a forty-five and they only gave me an eighty-two total? Can you believe that?"

"Sounds like you were robbed. Or your core strength needs some work so your rhythm is better."

Randy poked a sausage link and pointed the forkful of meat at Hunter. "Don't you start with me again about that. My training has been better than ever. Speaking of training, you really do look good, man. You must have been lifting weights, putting some muscle back on."

After the accident, Hunter was out of commission for a good six months. He had lost a lot of weight and had to work hard to gain it back in the form of muscle once he was able. Randy wasn't mentioning it to boost Hunter's self-esteem, though.

"I feel good. Better than I have in a long time."

"Better as in as good as you felt when you used to ride?"

Hunter sighed. He knew that was where they were headed. "I can't ride, Randy."

"Can't or won't?"

"Both."

"Won't because you don't want to or because your mom doesn't want you to?"

"It's not just my mom. My accident and recovery impacted my entire family. I can't do that to them again."

"Then don't get trampled by a bull again."

Hunter shot him a look. "That's what I'm doing by not riding."

"Oh, come on, you've ridden hundreds of bulls and one of them got you good. Gettin' beat up is what bull riding is all about. What are the chances you'd ever get an injury that serious again? I hate to see fear keep you from doing what you love, man."

"That's not it," Hunter said, shaking his head.

"Come to the training facility with me on Friday. Get on the barrel drop. See if your body even remembers what to do. Maybe we could even get you on a training bull."

"Randy, I haven't been on a bull in two years. My body is held together by screws in some places. I can't show up and ride."

"You could if you wanted to. Davis Hill was trampled by a bull that put a hole in his chest. Doctors had to bring him back from the dead three times during his surgery. He made a comeback and rode again. If he can do it, so can you."

Davis Hill never won anything after he returned to riding. What was the point of making a comeback if there wasn't the possibility of any of the glory? Hunter didn't want to retire a second time with nothing new to add to his accomplishments. Though there was something enticing about the idea of making it big again. What a story it would be if he came out of retirement and won the next national championship. He was getting way ahead of himself.

"We're supposed to spend the night in Austin before the auction on Saturday. If I can carve out some time for you, I might come give you a few pointers. That's all I'm promising you."

"I'll take it," he said, grinning over his cup of steaming hot coffee.

Hunter noticed his mother by the doors to the dining hall. She had been watching them, he was sure of it. She knew, like he did, that Randy hadn't come all this way to say hi. She was right to be suspicious and to worry that Randy could be persuasive. He always had been.

"What are you doing for Thanksgiving?" Hunter asked.

"Not celebrating it this year. My parents are visiting my sister in Phoenix. They asked me to cat sit, which means I need to check in every other day and make sure the animal has water and a clean litter box."

Randy's parents still lived between Brighton and Austin in a dusty little town called Daisy. That was how he got the nickname the Duke of Daisy in the bull riding world.

"Well, then you have to come back here and eat dinner with us. You can't not celebrate Thanksgiving."

Randy's eyes widened. "For real? You sure your mom would be okay with that?"

Hunter glanced back at the entrance. His mom was gone. She would understand that he couldn't let his friend be alone on the holiday. She was the one who made him that way.

"She would be more than okay with it. You know her—the more, the merrier."

"Any chance that means I'm going to meet this new girlfriend of yours?"

Hunter hadn't thought about that. J.R. and her whole family were joining them for Thanksgiving dinner and he'd forgotten when he extended the invite. He would have to seat Randy as far from J.R. as possible. "She will also be at dinner, but do not call her my girlfriend." He leveled his gaze. "And do not embarrass me."

"I would never embarrass you." Randy chuckled as he finished the last of his breakfast. "Not on purpose, at least."

J.R. would tell him it was his own fault. Being too nice had its consequences. Hunter already regretted opening himself up to this one.

Once they finished breakfast, Randy was off to check on his parents' cat. He repeated how grateful he was for the invite to Thanksgiving and how much he looked forward to not embarrassing Hunter in front of the woman who was not his girlfriend.

Cody and his mom were standing at the reception desk when Hunter came back inside the lodge.

"That was nice of Randall to come check in on you. Is he in the area to spend the holiday with his family?" his mom asked as she polished the counter with a rag.

"His parents are out of town actually. I invited him to come back tomorrow for Thanksgiving, so he didn't have to spend it alone."

"Oh, that was nice of you."

"He probably showed up here today, knowing that Hunter would invite him to come tomorrow," Cody said. "The Duke of Daisy is always thinking one step ahead. Mom thought he was here to talk to you about coming out of retirement."

Hunter wasn't going to lie, so he said nothing. His mom didn't need him to say anything, though. She knew she was right.

"But you told him you're happy doing what you're doing now." Her polishing got more aggressive. She lifted the little bell guests could ring to get someone's attention and scrubbed under it like it was filthy. "That there would be no reason for you to go back to a sport where you risk serious injury every day."

"I am happy at my job. I also miss riding. I know that you don't want to hear that, but it's true."

She set the bell down with a clatter. "You almost died, Hunter. That bull tried to smash your head in."

"It didn't, though. They have safety precautions for a reason."

"Safety precautions," she said with a snort. "If you took all the money that your father and I have spent over the years at hospitals and orthopedics and physical therapists, we would have enough to buy a second ranch. The doctors should have named a wing after you at the hospital here in town alone."

"I made ten times that when I was winning championships."

She threw the rag on the ground. Her face flush with her anger, which was so unlike her. "I don't care about the money. I care about you."

"I know you do. I don't know why you're getting all worked up. I didn't tell Randy that I'm going to try to go back to riding. I invited him to Thanksgiving. That's it."

His mother took a deep breath and wiped her forehead with the back of her hand. "I need to go check with your father about the turkeys for tomorrow. You boys stay out of trouble."

When she left, Cody pressed his lips together and leaned down to pick up her rag. "She won't ever be okay with you getting on a bull. You know that, right?"

Hunter sighed. "I know."

"I get it, though. It was a cool life. You made a lot of money. You had people who loved you, cheering for you all the time. It's hard to give that up."

It wasn't the money or the adoration. Though both were nice. It was the challenge. It was the thrill. Hunter had fallen in love with bull riding when he was a little kid and his dad took him to his first rodeo. That next Christmas, his parents gave him a wooden rocking bull instead of a rocking horse. Hunter dreamed of nothing else after that, and his parents encouraged him every step of the way. It made him sad that his injury caused his parents to hate bull riding when they had been his biggest supporters.

"You have no idea."

CHAPTER NINETEEN

"WHAT IF I took lessons?" Tessa was stuck on the idea that she should be trick riding, and it was driving J.R. up the wall. She hadn't stopped talking about it since she saw the Blackwell Belles on video.

"I don't know if anyone within fifty miles of here gives trick riding lessons, Tessa. You would have to start with regular horse riding lessons. You need to be more than comfortable on a horse before you can even think about doing tricks on one."

"Can you sign me up for that then?"

J.R. slipped the oven mitt over her hand. She had baked a strawberry rhubarb pie to take to Thanksgiving meal at Hunter's because she couldn't bear to come empty-handed. "Horse riding lessons are expensive. I'll have to look into it. We have a lot going on with the house and with Christmas coming up."

"You could get them for me for Christmas!"

"We could all chip in and give her lessons

for Christmas," Gran said from the dining room where she was playing cards with Big E.

"I would pay for a week of lessons," Big E said, staring intently at his cards.

"We could do a whole month," her dad said from the other side of the lodge where he was watching the Thanksgiving parade in New York City on the television with her mom. Zinni was snuggled up in between them.

Flora had to chime in. "I bet Hunter would let you give her lessons for free here at the ranch. You could teach her better than anyone else could."

Great idea, J.R. wanted to scream. Maybe she could quit her job, dedicate her life to making her daughter a famous trick rider, force Tessa to perform until she was twenty-four years old or until she hated her mother's guts for listening to everyone who told her that she should do this.

"Y'all are *super* helpful."

Her tone hit its mark. Gran set her hand of cards down. "Listen here, Jasmine Rose, you're the one who said that you wanted Tessa to feel like she had a say in what she wants to do with her life. Yet, here you are trying to steer her away from something just because you didn't like it. That doesn't seem fair."

"Don't say she didn't like it. She loved riding," Flora said, getting up from the couch and making her way to the kitchen. "You loved riding. You can't tell me that you didn't. I wouldn't have had you girls do it if you didn't want to do it."

J.R. set the piping hot pie on the stove top and pulled the oven mitts off. "Is that really how you remember it?"

"When you were three years old, you used to watch me and Dandelion perform and go on and on about how you were going to do that one day. You couldn't wait to get on a horse."

"I do remember you loving horses," her dad said.

"I might have loved horses. Maybe I thought it was cool when I was *three*, but I clearly remember telling you when I was seventeen that I wanted to go to college after high school. That I wasn't sure that I wanted to be in the Belles anymore, and you told me it was the Belles or nothing."

Flora defended herself, refusing to admit that she was the one who made all the decisions when they were younger. "You weren't sure. That is exactly what you told me. Why would I break up the Belles when things were going so well? Because you were confused about what you wanted to do? You would have made it harder for your sisters to be successful on the circuit if you dropped out. We decided together that you would take classes at the community college as a compromise."

"I can't talk about this anymore." J.R. washed her hands and took a breath, hoping it would calm her down. They had different recollections of what happened.

"Does that mean I can have horse riding lessons?" Tessa asked, oblivious to the family drama that had been unfolding since Friday night.

"We will talk about that later, Tessa. Can you please let it go for right now?"

"Grandma had a really good idea. Can I ask Mr. Hunter if we can do lessons here for free?"

"We are not asking Hunter for anything. We are going to eat with his family, be on our best behavior, and thank them for their hospitality. That's it." J.R. could not imagine asking for anything more from Hunter. He had done enough for her, for Tessa. "Why don't you get ready to go over there."

The Robbins family did Thanksgiving together in the afternoon so they could all pitch in and serve Thanksgiving dinner to the guests later in the evening. Tessa and J.R. usually went to the Langleys' for the holidays. Hilde didn't have room for the entire Blackwell crew, so it was a good thing Mrs. Robbins had invited them.

"I don't understand how you girls remember things so differently from the way I do," Flora said when Tessa left the room. "I am really proud of everything you accomplished as a group. I remember all the laughter and the way you had each other's backs. You used to support one another, rely on one another. I thought we had an amazing family, but you all act like I was some kind of tyrant."

"You were the one who wanted to be called Queen," J.R. reminded her.

Flora flinched as if J.R. had jabbed her. "You know I didn't like it when you called me that."

"You didn't like it when I called you Queen Mother. It made you feel too old."

"You remember all the bad things. Don't you ever think about the good?"

"I remember all of it, Mom. What frustrates me is that you have such a selective memory. You forget how you made me feel like I had one path and that it didn't matter what I wanted."

Flora's chin began to tremble and she fingered the pendant on her necklace. "It hurts me to hear you say that."

It wasn't on her agenda to make her mom cry on Thanksgiving. There was nothing she could say that would make it better. She had spoken the truth and the truth hurt.

Barlow shut off the television and joined them in the kitchen. "Today is not the day to air out all our grievances. Can we try to enjoy spending the holiday together since we don't get the chance to do this very often?"

"I'm going to get ready to go," Flora said, wiping under her eye. Barlow gave her a kiss on the cheek and whispered in her ear. She nodded and went to her room.

Her father's sigh told her he was disappointed.

"She lives in a fantasyland, Dad."

He bent over and rested his forearms on the kitchen island. "I know you have issues with your mother. All of your sisters do. She ran this family a little bit like a tyrant when you were younger. When you have five daughters, with five big personalities, you sometimes have to run it that way or there's chaos."

"If it wasn't for you, she never would have let me take a class or two at the community college. She would have set me back more years than she did."

"Jasmine, stop." He stood to his full height. "I get it. You're holding on to these resentments so tight. When are you going to take a minute to look around and think about how your mother might have helped you get where you're at now?"

J.R. folded her arms across her chest. It wasn't often that her dad got firm with her. He was always the one keeping the peace.

"A tree falling on my house got me here."

He frowned at her badly timed joke. "You

know that's not what I'm talking about. You are tenacious. You know who else is like that? Your mother. She's also the one who nurtured your love of animals. That love led you to choose animal sciences as your area of study. Your experience being a part of rodeos probably helps you with developing relationships with your customers. You know how to talk to people in the business because you were in the business. There are positives to growing up the way you did. Don't deny it."

"Like I told Mom, I remember everything, the good *and* the bad."

"But you focus on the bad and you use it to keep your mom at arm's length."

He wasn't wrong. It was much easier to push her away because of the things that J.R. held against her than to appreciate the things that weren't so bad.

"Can I add my two cents?" Big E had been unusually quiet throughout this whole thing. Even if she wanted him to keep his two cents to himself, she knew he was going to give them. Her nonresponse was all he needed to continue. "Take it from an old man who almost waited too long to be there for the people he loved because I either thought I knew better than they did or was hurt by something foolish they did or said. Push people away long enough and they'll leave you alone. You'll get what you thought you wanted, but what you'll really get is loneliness. You'll get regrets. You'll get stuck with a lot of should've, could've, would'ves. You deserve better than that, Jasmine. I hope you know that."

Now she was the one with the trembling chin. She didn't want to cry. They were due at Hunter's parents' house and she did not need to be falling apart at the seams. She sniffled and swallowed down the emotion that was trying its best to bubble to the top.

"We all need to get ready to go to Thanksgiving. I'm walking over there in ten minutes with or without y'all," she said, disappearing into her own room.

JULIE ROBBINS WAS the sweetest. She greeted them at the door with the warmest smile and the biggest hug. J.R. had handed the pie off to Hunter, who claimed strawberry rhubarb pie was his favorite.

"Please come in," Julie said, leading them all down the hall to the great room. The aroma of fresh baked cornbread and roasting turkey made J.R.'s mouth water. "Make yourselves comfortable. Hunter, can you get everyone something to drink, sweetheart?"

"We've got mulled wine, water, soda, some of those flavored sparkling waters as well," Hunter said. "Barlow, my friend, brought some of Kentucky's finest bourbon—can I get you one? Big E?"

Both her dad and her great-uncle took him up on that offer. Savannah hopped up and helped the ladies get themselves something to sip on. The Robbins had a massive home. With the size of their family, they needed one. Hunter and Cody lived in the main house with their parents. Everett and Savannah and Jack Jr. and his family had their own cottages on the property.

The great room was open to the kitchen. One wall was floor-to-ceiling stone. An enormous bison head was mounted above the fireplace that was situated in the middle of it. They had plenty of seating. There were two full-sized couches facing one another and two wingback chairs at one end and two oversized leather chairs with ottomans at the other end. The thick wooden ceiling beams and borders gave it a rustic feel. The floors were hardwood and covered in a cream-colored rug that lightened up the space.

Jackson came out of the kitchen holding a platter of appetizers. He offered some to J.R. and Tessa first. Tessa took a cracker with cheese and surprised J.R. by remembering her manners.

"Thank you. You have a really nice house," she said.

"You are very welcome and thank you. This

house has been in our family for a long time, so I'm glad you like it."

"Your great-great-grandparents used to raise goats like Bubba."

Jackson reared back a bit in surprise. "You're right. How did you know that?"

"Mr. Everett told us on the hayride," she answered plainly.

"Did you hear that, Ev? Someone actually listens to you talking on the hayrides." Jack Jr. came over to sample the appetizers.

Everett sat a little straighter. "A lot of people listen. I am an amazing storyteller."

"Says the guy who storytells to a captive audience on a hayride," the man sitting across from him on the other couch said.

"Who invited this guy again?" Everett looked to Hunter.

Hunter placed his hand on the small of J.R.'s back. "J.R., this is my friend, Randy Wilder. Randy, this is J.R., her daughter, Tessa, her mom and dad, Flora and Barlow, and her grandmother Denny, and Big E, her great-uncle."

"Randy Wilder as in the Duke of Daisy?" J.R. knew the name but not the face. "I saw you ride at the Stockyards Showcase up in Fort Worth earlier this year."

"I like her already, Hunter," Randy said, getting to his feet. He offered his hand and J.R. shook it.

"It's nice to meet you. I hear you're stuck working with this guy now that he doesn't come to work with me every day."

"It's hard, but someone has to do it."

Hunter rolled his eyes. "She loves it. She used to work in this super tiny office all by herself and now she gets to share that same tiny office with me. It's a dream come true, I'm sure."

Hunter's family made room for J.R.'s family, and everyone fell into easy conversation. Big E and Barlow chatted up Jackson and Jack Jr. Denny and Flora offered to help Julie and Cora in the kitchen while Savannah asked Tessa to help her with something in the dining room. Everett and Cody got up to mix some drinks, so J.R. sat down with Hunter and Randy.

Before they knew it, it was time to head into the dining room for the meal. The farmhouse table took up the entire room. There must have been three leaves put into it so all sixteen of them, including Cora and Jack Jr.'s two-year-old, Nico, could fit around it. Julie had the table decked out for the holiday with pumpkins that doubled as flowerpots and an assortment of colorful gourds and unlit candles scattered down the center. Each place setting had a charger plate, dinner plate, and a little pumpkin holding a place card with someone's name on it.

"I helped put the pumpkins on the plates," Tessa whispered.

They had seated J.R. next to Hunter on one side and Tessa on the other. The rest of J.R.'s family was sprinkled two by two between the Robbinses. Once the food was placed, practically every inch of the table was covered. All of the traditional favorites were served. Large bowls of cornbread stuffing and mashed potatoes were passed around. The green bean casserole that was topped in Texas pecans and french fried onions was a big hit.

"The turkey is absolutely delicious," Flora complimented. "I don't think I've ever had one this good."

"Not many of us Blackwells are known for our culinary skills," Gran admitted. "At my ranch, we trust most of the cooking duties to my great-grandson. We don't know what we're going to do when he goes to college. The rest of us are hopeless."

"We might not cook, but the Blackwells can eat," Big E said, loading some more of those green beans onto his plate.

"Blackwells?" Randy's brow furrowed. "Why do I know that name?"

"I own a ranch out in Montana," Big E replied, so certain that had to be it. "It's a guest ranch in Falcon Creek, nestled in the Rocky Mountains, near the Absaroka Range. We were featured in a movie once. You probably heard about it if you've ever competed in any of the PBR events in Bozeman or Billings."

"No, I'm not thinking about a ranch. This was a bunch of girls. Wasn't there a troupe of horse riding showgirls with that name who used to perform at the state fair and at the rodeos?"

"The Blackwell Belles," Flora said and J.R. wanted to bolt from the table. If she could leave the state right now, she would. "That was us. We used to travel all over Texas and the surrounding states."

Hunter was totally unaware of what was about to be revealed. He proudly shared, "Flora was a trick rider for years. She and her sister are getting inducted into the Cowgirl Hall of Fame next month."

J.R.'s stomach clenched. She knew exactly where this conversation was headed and there was no stopping it. As the Robbinses all congratulated Flora on her upcoming honor, Randy pointed at J.R. It wasn't her mom or Aunt Dandy that he recognized.

"You're the girl who used to do that dancing thing with the bull. What was that bull's name? Fernando? Fer—"

"Ferdinand. His name is Ferdinand," Flora said. "He's still alive, you know. He lives up north with my daughter Violet. Although, he could be moving to Oklahoma soon."

Hunter turned his head. His eyebrows squished together and he tugged on his ear. "What are they talking about?"

CHAPTER TWENTY

HUNTER WAS SO CONFUSED. J.R. was mute. Randy started asking all of these questions, but Flora was the only one who answered.

"Didn't you do the acrobatics on the horses, too? I remember thinking, how do they not end up falling off or getting dragged in the dirt?"

"It's all about the straps."

"Which one of you did the fire stunts? Those were really cool."

"Jasmine's sisters Magnolia and Willow did the fire stunts. The rings of fire."

"Jasmine Rose. Oh my gosh, that was your name." Randy's mouth was agape. "All of you have flower names, wasn't that the gimmick?"

"It wasn't a gimmick. Those were their real names. It was a family tradition. My name is Flora, my sister's name was Dandelion. When I had my girls, it was a given that they would all have floral names."

"Hold on." Hunter needed them to stop for a second. He needed to hear from one person, and she was sitting like a stone statue next to him. "You were a trick rider? All of your sisters were trick riders? You said no one followed in your mom's footsteps. You said you didn't ride."

"We don't ride," she said, staring down at her plate and pushing around the food with her fork. "None of us ride anymore. No one performs for a living as an adult like my mom and aunt did."

She knew that wasn't what he had been asking when they were talking about it on the hayride. This was why she shut down on him that day. She wasn't mad at him, she was hiding something. Something huge.

"How did you not know she was a Belle?" Randy stared at him incredulously. "The Blackwell Belles were very popular. They were all over the place when we were teenagers. Come on, five girls, all those pink sequins and spandex."

Hunter shook his head. He didn't remember ever seeing that.

"Oh, yeah," Everett said. "I think we saw them once in Arlington. Did someone shoot arrows?"

Flora nodded. "My daughter Willow did, yes. She was very good at it until—"

"The guys you work with must give you so much grief about your experience in the arena with a bull, Jasmine Rose," Randy teased. "She used to do this trick where she danced with the bull. She would ride a horse around him and he would do these little dance moves. I can't even explain it. I just remember thinking it was hilarious. They used to put that bull in a tutu. I kid you not."

"Ferdinand was a good sport," Flora said. "He let us dress him up all the time. I think he liked it."

"We watched some videos the other day. My grandma has a YouTube channel. We can show you, Mr. Hunter," Tessa offered up so innocently.

"Yes! We have to watch that," Randy said. "I need to see that bull in the tutu."

J.R.'s face was bright red. She kept poking at her plate but seemed to have lost her appetite. The conversation shifted when J.R.'s grandmother asked how his mom made the cornbread stuffing. Hunter put his hand on J.R.'s thigh, silently begging her to just look at him.

After everyone stuffed themselves with turkey, the desserts were brought to the table. Pecan pie bars, brownies cut and decorated in the shape of a turkey, pumpkin cheesecake, and J.R.'s strawberry rhubarb pie were all on the menu.

No one left the table hungry except for maybe J.R. who took a piece of cheesecake but barely ate it. When everyone was done, Hunter's dad announced that the men would be clearing the table and doing the dishes. He suggested the women grab a drink so they could go sit and relax for a bit.

Getting J.R. alone so they could talk about this revelation was going to be harder than he thought. Cleaning the mountain of dishes that had been created in the preparing and eating of this meal seemed insurmountable.

Hunter volunteered for the job of clearing the table. When he saw J.R. excuse herself to use the bathroom, he snuck down the hall to wait for her. She yelped when she came out to find him standing there.

Her hand flew to her chest. "You scared me."

"Are you okay? I have a feeling that you weren't a big fan of our dinner conversation."

She still wouldn't look him in the eye. "I'm sorry I lied to you. I'm sure you're mad. If you want us to leave, we can leave."

Hunter put both hands on her arms to get her attention. "I am not mad at you. I'm confused, but I'm not mad. If you didn't tell me something, I'm sure there's a reason for it. Come here."

He pulled her in for a hug. She melted against him and pressed her face against his chest.

"It's so embarrassing."

"There's nothing to be embarrassed about. I can't wait to see what you used to do."

That was what finally prompted her to look up

at him. Her eyes were red as if she had been crying. "Your friend sure thought it was hilarious."

"I'm sorry about Randy. He gets so carried away sometimes. I don't think he realized how he was making you feel, going on like that."

She ducked her head again. "He's right about how people would give me grief if they knew. Why do you think I go by J.R. instead of Jasmine? I don't want to make it easier for anyone else to make the connection."

"I haven't seen what you do with this bull, but I don't think anyone at Bucking Wonders would give you a hard time."

"How are you not mad at me?"

Hunter placed his hand under her chin and lifted her face to his. "Because I care about you. I could see how talking about it made you feel. If it makes you feel this bad about yourself, why would I be mad you didn't want to talk about it? Of course, you wouldn't."

Without a second's notice, she lifted up on her tiptoes and planted a kiss right on his lips. The kiss caught him off guard but luckily lasted long enough for him to show her what he could do. J.R. kissed like she did everything else—she was the best. She seemed to be trying to make up for all those times they almost kissed and got interrupted.

Hunter wrapped one arm around her waist

and held her face with his other hand. She had both palms flat on his chest and he worried she could feel his heart beating fast. She had thought being a trick rider was embarrassing? How about freaking out over a first kiss?

The embarrassment faded fast, though. All Hunter could think was how lucky he was. This was the moment he had been waiting for and it was worth every second. Her lips were soft and sweet. He didn't ever want to stop kissing her.

But all good things must come to an end as his father always said. She pulled away first. Both of them were breathing heavy when all was said and done. Her cheeks were pink and given the fact that his felt warm, he guessed his were the same color.

"You just made this the best Thanksgiving I have ever had," he said, moving his hand from her cheek to take hold of one of hers. "We should make that a new holiday tradition."

Her lips twisted, fighting the smile that wanted to form there. "You want a Thanksgiving kiss every year?"

"From you? Yes."

She dropped her forehead to his chest. "I don't know what I'm doing, but I'm glad I did that."

That was a huge relief. Hunter never knew what to expect from J.R. They didn't think alike, which was what made her so interesting but also unpredictable. It was nice to hear that she felt the same way he did about that kiss.

"I need to get back to the dishes or my brothers are going to come looking for me. Will you please spend the next half hour convincing yourself that everything is going to be okay and that there is absolutely nothing to be embarrassed about? This house, these people, this is a safe space. You got that?"

She peeked up at him with those baby blues, and for the first time he saw trust in them. "I got it."

He gave her a kiss on the forehead before letting her go. Earning her trust was almost better than kissing her. It had been the mission from the start and he finally felt like he had accomplished it.

The men finished cleaning up and joined the ladies in the great room. No one had forgotten about the Blackwell Belles much to J.R.'s dismay.

As much as Hunter wanted to see what she could do, he also didn't want to make her miserable. He decided to give her an out. "I don't think we should watch the videos unless it's okay with J.R. I know I wouldn't want y'all pulling up old videos of me riding bulls."

"What? You love watching yourself riding bulls," Cody said, taking a seat next to Big E.

"I like watching my videos by myself. When

I watch them with you, I have to listen to you critique me. That part isn't so fun."

"Come on, Mom. Can we please watch your videos? You are so awesome in the ones we'll show, okay?" Tessa begged.

Hunter knew that J.R. was not going to say no to Tessa.

"Let's put them on," J.R. said, sounding more sure than Hunter had expected. "Y'all can have your fun, but then we never speak of the Belles again. Deal?"

"Never?" Randy wasn't on board with that.

Hunter gave him an elbow to the ribs. "Never. You got that?"

Everyone agreed that there would be no talk about it after they watched some of the videos. Flora was thrilled to narrate.

"Let's see. Go to the one that's labelled Dallas 2005," she directed Jack Jr., who had the remote control and was navigating the smart TV. "That's one of the best ones. Jasmine Rose was fifteen and she had just learned to do the Suicide Drag. You have to see it to believe it."

Hunter was completely enthralled. There was a lot of pink sequins and spandex, and the horses had glitter on their hindquarters, but the tricks these girls could pull off between the ages of nine and fifteen were incredible. It was J.R. who stole the show, though. The grace she showed as she hung from the side of a galloping horse was amazing.

"Stop and go to the one called El Paso 2010," Flora said before the first video was over. "Jasmine Rose really shows off her vaulting skills on that one. It's dangerous yet so beautiful."

Jack Jr. found the one she was referring to and hit Play. Hunter had no idea that seeing J.R. riding a horse could somehow make him fall more in love with her, but that was what was happening. Sitting in his parents' great room, surrounded by his entire family and some of hers, he fell hard.

She was absolutely spectacular. The skill, the concentration, the fearlessness she had to possess to do the things she did were so impressive. Hunter could watch her do this stuff all day and it would never cease to amaze him.

"That's Magnolia. She was also very talented. This was the trick she and Jasmine did together." The pride in Flora's voice was clear. Hunter reached over and squeezed J.R.'s hand. He hoped she had picked up on that like he had.

"Oh my gosh, Mom. That is so cool." Tessa couldn't sit, she was on her feet, mesmerized by what she was watching. "You have got to teach me how to do that."

"That's Violet," Flora said. "She was the least confident of my girls, but she's going to be performing a brand-new juggling trick at my induction. Wait until you see her, Jasmine. There's going to be fire. She finally overcame her fear. I am so proud of her."

"Violet and fire? I can't wait to see that," J.R. replied.

"You can stop it and we'll go to another one," Flora said to Jack Jr.

"Wait, we need to see the bull," Randy complained. "Which one has Jasmine dancing with the bull?"

"I don't remember which one would have that. Most of these feature the girls in action, not Ferdinand."

Hunter didn't miss the way J.R. reacted to what her mom said. It was a mixture of surprise and confusion quickly followed by disbelief and then something he hadn't seen her give her mom the entire time she had been in Brighton—she looked at her with gratitude and respect.

"Go to the one that says Oklahoma City 2009," J.R. told Jack Jr. "That was the state fair, wasn't it, Mom?"

Flora turned and flashed J.R. the biggest smile. "That was the one where you girls did the big entrance to that Beyoncé song."

"We were a bunch of single ladies, weren't we?" J.R.'s lips curled upward into a grin of her own. It was Hunter's second-favorite moment of the day. The kiss was still winning by a mile, but seeing J.R. embrace something that she thought was so embarrassing an hour ago was right up there.

After a few more videos, someone suggested they all play a game before they had to get ready to go to the lodge to serve dinner. Cody picked Pictionary and no one objected.

Hunter followed Flora into the kitchen to get a drink before the game play began. "That was pretty amazing stuff. I'm going to have to go to your channel and watch the videos of you next time."

"My girls were way more talented than I ever was. I had the pizzazz, though."

"I bet you did," he said with a chuckle. "I mean, you still do."

"Thanks," she said, giving him a wink.

"And thank you for not showing the bull tricks. I could tell J.R. appreciated it."

"Well, better to disappoint your friend than my daughter. I've learned that much so far."

"I don't know what caused your falling out, but I do know that it may take J.R. time to sort through things, but she always does in the end."

Flora pressed her lips together and reached up, giving his arm a squeeze. "Thank you for saying that. I hope you're right."

"I am," he said, placing his hand over hers and giving it a pat.

The two families played a very competitive game of Pictionary. The Robbins family won the first round but the Blackwells plus Randy came back in round two. There was so much laughter, Hunter almost moved that moment to his second favorite of the night. Still not as good as the kiss, but good nonetheless.

When the Blackwells said their goodbyes, Hunter told his parents he would meet them at the lodge after he walked their guests to the Grand Dixie. He wanted every second he could get with his new girlfriend. J.R. let him hold her hand and so did Tessa.

"What was your favorite part of Thanksgiving?" he asked Tessa as she swung their arms back and forth.

"Um, I think it was dessert."

"Dessert?" J.R.'s face scrunched up in surprise.

"I know your mom and my mom made some good stuff, but that can't be your favorite part," Hunter argued.

"No, not dessert." The little girl tipped her head and placed a finger on her chin. "Oh, I know! Beating you in Pictionary!"

"Oh, wow. Well, I beat you one time. Maybe that was my favorite part of Thanksgiving." It wasn't but he had to play along.

"No, I know what your favorite part was," Tessa said, causing him to trip over his own two feet.

J.R. giggled as he righted himself. "Are you okay?"

He nodded. "I'm fine. Watch out for the invisible trip hazards on this walking path. Sometimes they just jump out at you. You were saying, Miss Tessa? What do you think was my favorite part of Thanksgiving?"

Had she seen them kissing? His eyes had been closed for the whole kiss, it was very possible that anyone could have seen them. During the moment, the only two people who existed were him and J.R., but that wasn't reality.

"It was watching my mom flying in on that horse holding the American flag with Beyoncé playing in the background. That was so cool, Mom. We should put that on TikTok and tag Beyoncé."

"I have no idea what that means, but maybe you can show me later and I can decide if that's a good idea or not."

When they got to the Grand Dixie, Hunter said his goodbyes to everyone except J.R. who stayed outside with him.

"Please tell your family one more time that I said thank you. That was the best Thanksgiving meal I have ever had in my thirty-five years on this planet."

"My mom will love that."

She laced her fingers with his and lifted their hands between them, palm to palm. "And thank you for helping me get over myself. I needed that more than you know."

"You're welcome. I was happy to help. It was my favorite part of Thanksgiving."

Her smile finally reached her eyes. "I thought it was watching me on that horse in Oklahoma."

He leaned in closer, so close that their noses brushed against each other. "You know that wasn't my favorite part. What was your favorite?"

"I think you know," she said when her lips were nothing but a breath away from his.

Hunter felt like he had magnets in his chest that were drawn to her in a way that he'd never experienced before. "I'm hoping it was the same as mine."

"What if it's right now?" she asked and he accepted the challenge, pressing his lips to hers and creating a tie in his mind for the best Thanksgiving moment ever.

CHAPTER TWENTY-ONE

THERE MUST HAVE been some magic in Hunter Robbins's kisses. J.R. walked into the Grand Dixie feeling at peace in so many ways. The inner turbulence that had been driving her to keep people at a distance was finally quelled. Not only did he make her believe she could trust someone like him, Hunter had done the unimaginable—he had helped her see that her past was not some mark of shame.

Her dad was waiting for her and wrapped her in a hug. "Hunter's family is great, sweetheart. Thank you for inviting us to come with you."

"I'm glad you're here, Dad. I'm glad everyone is here."

The rest of the family must have retreated to their rooms. The common space was empty besides J.R. and Barlow.

"It meant a lot to your mom that you shared the Belles with them."

Seeing how excited Tessa was and the awe on Hunter's face while they watched the videos made it worth the comments from Hunter's friend, Randy. The Duke of Daisy responded exactly how J.R. expected men in the bull riding profession to. It was all a joke to him.

"It was nice of Mom to not indulge Randy with the clips of Ferdinand."

"She's not always as oblivious as you expect her to be."

Flora exited her room with Zinni on her leash. "I'm going to take her out to do her business." She noticed they were both staring at her. "What? What did I do wrong this time?"

J.R. felt bad that she assumed the worst. Given how she had been treating her mom these last couple of weeks, it shouldn't have been surprising that she expected J.R. to be mad at her about something.

"You didn't do anything wrong, honey," Barlow reassured her. "Take your dog out and then come cuddle with me on the couch. All that turkey I ate is starting to make me sleepy."

Flora relaxed and Zinni let out one of her strange gurgling noises. That dog never made dog noises. She grunted, groaned, chirped, and choked, but she rarely barked.

Tessa slipped out of her room. "Can we take Zinni to go see Bubba? I bet he's missing her. They have to see each other on Thanksgiving."

When that child wasn't asking to take trick

riding lessons, she was obsessing over that goat. "I can take them if you're okay with Zinni going to the barn," J.R. offered.

"It's fine. I can walk them both over there," Flora said.

"All three of you could take Zinni to visit her boyfriend," Barlow suggested. "I'll take my nap like the other old folks here must have."

Flora looked to J.R. for the okay. Maybe a trip to the barn would be good for them. "Let's make it a mother/daughter, mother/daughter adventure," J.R. said.

Her mother's smile said more than any words could.

They walked Zinni to the barn. The ranch was deserted since all the guests spending the holiday here were in the dining hall enjoying a feast. The goats were outside in their pen. Some of them were munching on feed that was left out for them in black grain bowls in the corner. A couple were standing on top of the goat house in the back while others wandered inside it. A big brown-and-white one was sunbathing on the ramp that led to the roof. Bubba was off to the side by the water tank.

Zinni made a noise that was a mix between a howl and a snort. It was like some kind of mating call because Bubba's ears perked up and he made a beeline for the gate.

"Happy Thanksgiving, Bubba!" Tessa said in greeting. She unlatched the gate door and her little friend pranced over to her.

"Bring him out over here," J.R. said, opening the smaller, empty pen next door. "Then he can play with Zinni."

Tessa scooped Bubba up and carried him into the neighboring pen. Flora brought Zinni in so they could play. It was such a funny friendship, but perfect in its own way.

"Tessa sure loves that goat," Flora said.

"She does."

"I'm sorry," they both said at the same time.

J.R. wasn't planning on giving an apology and she in no way thought one was coming her way.

"What are you sorry about?" Flora asked.

"You first."

Flora wrung her hands. "I can't until I know what you were going to say."

"I can't until I know what you're going to say."

"Your father is right, you are too stubborn just like me," Flora huffed. "I was going to say I'm sorry for not being more sensitive to your feelings. I tend to look at things one way—my way. But I know that it's not how everyone views our shared experiences. I need to get better at accepting that my perception is not the reality, it's simply how I view the world through my lens."

She was admitting that there might be two

ways to look at a situation. It was the same realization that J.R. had come to. She had been looking back at the Belles with distorted glasses on. Her mom had been looking at them through her rose-colored ones. A bit of what both of them remembered could be the truth.

"I'm sorry I've been so hard on you. I realized this afternoon that a lot of what you do comes from a place of pride. I also watched those videos and saw five sisters having fun." It had been a long time since she had thought about the camaraderie she had felt between her and her siblings. Maybe she had blocked it out to make it easier to walk away.

"You girls had a lot of fun. Sometimes at my expense if you remember."

J.R. had a distinct memory of her and her sisters making a game of hiding their mom's favorite hat every time they stayed at a hotel. They did tend to gang up on her.

"I let myself forget that we used to laugh a lot, and that you listened to some of my ideas. I realized that when we were watching the video from the show in El Paso. I came to you with that idea for the trick with me and Maggie. She didn't think you would let us try it, but you did."

"You had good ideas, Jasmine Rose. You were the oldest. I was proud of you when you wanted to take on the leadership role."

She hadn't been a very good leader since the Belles broke up. She had let everyone go their own way. She wasn't being a good role model for making family a priority. "I also need to apologize because I haven't been totally honest with you."

"About what?"

"I told you I didn't want to give Iris the charm bracelet, but the truth is I don't know where it is. I don't want to be the reason why the other girls don't perform. If you want me to talk to Iris about the charm bracelet, I will."

"What about a charm bracelet?" Tessa wiped her hands on her pants and she stood up from a crouch.

"I was telling Grandma that I misplaced my aunt's charm bracelet. I thought it was in my room, but it's not there."

Tessa's expression changed. She bit her lip and pulled at the collar of her shirt. "Are you talking about the one with the horse and the flowers?"

J.R. tipped her head. "Yes. Tessa Jean, do you know where my charm bracelet is?"

"Maybe," she squeaked.

"Where is it?" J.R. moved closer. She wasn't mad. It was actually a relief to know it wasn't missing but rather stolen by a ten-year-old sneak.

"It's in the drawer of my nightstand. I took it just to look at it one day, but I got nervous when you came up to my room and I hid it in the drawer. I meant to put it back, but I forgot about it."

J.R. sighed with relief. Tessa's nightstand had water damage, but the contents should be intact. "Thank you for telling me and not keeping it a secret. That bracelet is special."

"It's more than just Aunt Dandy's memories. It tells the story of the Belles, doesn't it?" Tessa guessed correctly now that she knew more about what J.R. and her sisters used to do.

"It does. The charms represent things we did or accomplished when we were a team."

"You were so lucky to do all that with your sisters. You should wear the bracelet more so you don't forget how awesome you guys were."

Flora let out a laugh. "She's a smart one."

"My sister Iris wants the bracelet, and I'm going to give it to her. I should be able to remember without it now that I have you to remind me." J.R. threw her arm around her daughter's shoulders. "Do you think you can handle that?"

"I can do that."

"Even when you're mad at me because I won't let you wear makeup?"

Tessa squinted up at her. "How come you got to wear makeup when you were my age, but I can't?"

"Because I'm your mom and this glamma was

mine," J.R. said, thumbing over her shoulder at Flora.

"Oh, I like that!" Flora fluffed her hair. "How come I never thought of that name before? No more Grandma for me, I want to be called Glamma from now on."

J.R. and Tessa giggled at her new nickname, although it fit her perfectly. It was clear that J.R. would have to make more of an effort moving forward to keep family in Tessa's life. The way her little girl lit up in the last few weeks was something that she couldn't let go because of old resentments that simply didn't matter anymore.

"What trick do you think your mom should work on when she performs with her sisters at your glamma's induction?" Flora asked Tessa.

"Oh, hold on. I will give you the bracelet to give to Iris, but I am not performing. There isn't one trick I saw on those videos that I could pull off today."

"You'll have to practice. Maybe while you're giving Tessa riding lessons, you can work on your tricks?"

"How about this—if my bull sells for the most in Saturday's auction and I get the promotion, I will consider spending a little time relearning one very simple trick for the show."

Flora clapped her hands together and attacked J.R. with a hug. "Thank you! I know you'll choose something amazing. We're going to have to fix your hair, though. It needs styling, maybe some highlights? What do you think, Tessa?"

J.R. could only laugh as the two of them dissected her hair and her makeup. Typical Flora, only hearing what she wanted to hear. J.R. was sticking to her wait and see mantra since it had been working so far. The auction would be the deciding factor.

FRIDAY, J.R. AND HUNTER drove to Austin to prepare for the auction. There was a reception scheduled at the hotel bar near the venue where they were staying overnight. It was the last chance for the two of them to shake some hands and encourage the big buyers to put their money on the right bull.

The right bull being Buckwild.

"Jed sent me the spreadsheet with the RSVPs for tonight's reception. Looks like the heavy hitters are going to be there," she said, glancing over the list.

"Perfect. I will make sure to thrill them with my stories of Sweetwater's Revenge in the practice arena."

"You can do that, but it may fall flat once they hear about the family history of Buckwild and how he was specifically bred to carry his family's best traits."

"I'm sure you will make an impression. You always do." Hunter lifted her hand to his lips. He hadn't stopped touching her since they got in the truck. He had a hand on her leg or held her hand. He brushed her hair off her shoulder. It was obvious that those Thanksgiving kisses had had the same effect on him that they did on her.

"We need to play it cool in Austin. I don't think we should announce anything until after the auction." She didn't want Jed or Walter to think either one of them was distracted by this new office romance.

"I will do whatever you say but know that it is going to kill me not to hold you in my arms every second we are in the same room together."

J.R. touched her cheek, trying to hide how hard he made her smile. She didn't want it to go to his head that she was completely enamored by him.

She did her best to switch into work mode. She reviewed the day's agenda. Today, they needed to get checked in, place some promotional materials in and around the hotel, and deliver the rest of the promo package to the arena where the auction would be taking place tomorrow. They both needed to be focused on the job, not each other.

"I promised Randy that I would stop by his training facility later this afternoon. I'll have time, won't I?" Hunter asked.

"I don't see why not. Once we finish with the promo, we should have a few hours to kill before the reception." She was relieved that he didn't ask her to come to the training facility with him because she wasn't the biggest fan of one Mr. Randy Wilder.

"I won't be gone long, I promise."

"You do what you need to do," she said, trying to be supportive.

When they got to the hotel, they worked together to unload the truck before checking into their separate rooms. J.R. pushed one of the luggage carts into the lobby.

"Look who made it," a voice said.

J.R. peeked around the cart to find Tyson Quinley standing in front of the reception desk in his three-piece suit and ten-gallon hat. He owned one of the highest rated bulls on the circuit these days, Kick Back. It was nice to have a champion on his team, but he was looking for some new blood. She knew he was going to be spending a lot of money tomorrow. He was there with another man she didn't recognize.

"Good to see you, Tyson." She stuck out her hand and he shook it. "Y'all settling in okay?"

"Oh my goodness, this is her, isn't it?" the other man said. He was a bit too gleeful for her liking.

"This is her. Ms. Jasmine Rose Blackwell herself." The use of her full name took her aback.

"Will you be auctioning off any bulls in tutus tomorrow?" the man said, failing to hold back his laughter.

She cleared her throat as her brows pinched together. "Excuse me?"

"We saw the video online this morning. You sure know how to pick 'em."

J.R.'s mind was whirling. Her mouth went dry. She had no idea how, why they were talking about this.

"Did you check in?" Hunter's voice broke through the stream of chaotic thoughts that were spinning in her head. "Oh, hey there, Tyson."

"If it isn't Hunter Robbins. Hunter was the best rider to come out of that small town. Bucking Wonders was smart to hire you to promote their stock," Tyson told his friend. "If anyone knows a champion bull, it's him."

"Which bull should we be on the lookout for? Who's your pick to be the next Kick Back?" Tyson's friend asked.

J.R. was about to have a full panic attack. This had to be some kind of nightmare. This could not be real life.

"I'm a big fan of Sweetwater's Revenge. He's got that look in his eye that tells me he can't wait to get a rider on his back and do everything in his power to get that rider off."

"I love it," the friend said. "What about Ms. Blackwell?"

J.R. couldn't speak if she wanted to keep breathing. Hunter hadn't noticed she was about to pass out. "She's backing Buckwild."

"Does he come with glitter?" Tyson's friend asked before howling with laughter. "Or is that extra?"

That was all J.R. could listen to. She managed to spit out, "Excuse me for a minute." She bolted out of the reception area and searched for the public bathroom. Once inside, she locked herself in a stall and let herself fall apart.

This was no dream. This was a living nightmare. Everything she had done to make sure this moment didn't happen was for naught. There was only one reason this was happening. There could only be one and he was standing out there laughing with the men who just belittled everything she was trying to accomplish in her career.

She never should have trusted Hunter.

CHAPTER TWENTY-TWO

HUNTER WAS BAFFLED by what happened in the lobby of the hotel. This was his first time helping with an event like this and he felt like he was doing it alone. J.R. had disappeared. He had texted her three times and gotten no reply.

He checked in and texted her that he was taking all their stuff up to his room and that she could meet him there. Another fifteen minutes went by and there was no reply from her. He was just about to go looking for her when there was a knock on his door.

J.R. didn't say a word as she pushed past him and pulled her bag off the luggage rack. He all but jumped in front of her when she turned back around.

"What is going on? Why are you not talking to me?"

Her face was red and so were the whites of her eyes. He would have thought she'd been crying if she didn't look so lethal at the moment. "Get out of my way."

"Not until you tell me what happened? What did I do?"

"Ha!" Her laugh was more maniacal than it was humored. "Like you don't know."

"Forgive me, but I do not know. Can you please tell me why you look like you want to run me over with a two-thousand-pound bull?"

"Oh, why would you be worried about that? The only bulls I associate with wouldn't hurt a fly. In fact, they're more likely to want to dance with you than run you over. Maybe they even have glitter on their hindquarters."

The glitter comment made him pause. That was the same weird comment that Tyson Quinley's associate had used when they were talking in the lobby. "Why are we talking about glitter-bombed bulls? Did that guy with Tyson say something to you before I came in?"

J.R. set her bag down and pulled out her phone. She tapped around and then handed it to him. "It's all over any social media having to do with the event."

Hunter scrolled through her feed. There was a video of her from a Belles performance linked in the comments on one of the marketing posts about the auction. Replies to that all pointed out that J.R. Blackwell was Jasmine Rose Blackwell who used to dance with a bull named Ferdinand.

"I don't know who did this, but we'll shut it

down. We can delete the posts and put new ones up that don't accept comments."

"You don't know who did this? Really? I trusted you, Hunter. I let you and your family watch those videos. You told me that it was a safe place. That I didn't need to worry or be embarrassed."

His heart sank. Never in a million years would anyone in his family do this to her. It was hard not to be offended that she assumed they would. "My brothers would not post this. I did not post this. These videos are on the internet, J.R. Your mom has them all out there for the world to see. Anyone could have stumbled upon it."

"Are you really going to blame my mom?"

"I'm not blaming anyone. I'm trying to defend my family who you're trying to blame for this. Why are you so afraid of accepting who you were? Why do you have to hide?"

J.R. snatched her phone out of his hand and picked her overnight bag back up. "I'm going. I don't want to be here."

"I swear to you that no one in my family had anything to do with this. My brothers would be more likely to post videos of me not lasting eight seconds than they would be to post anything about you."

"I never said it was your brothers, but there was someone at your family's Thanksgiving who was very interested in my act with the bull. He also found it hilarious that I was in this business with that kind of a background. There was one person who you just happened to invite to Thanksgiving, who just happened to recognize me. So many coincidences right before the auction, wouldn't you say?"

What was she accusing him of exactly? Plotting this entire thing for days? Hunter was not going to simply stand there and let her accuse him of something he didn't do.

"I hate to break it to you, but no one I know cares if you get this job or not. There's no big conspiracy against you." He moved aside and she pulled open the door.

With her back to him, she said in a tone as cold as ice, "Please call the front desk and have them bring the promo materials for the hotel to my room. You can oversee taking the other stuff to the arena. We don't need to do any of that together. At the reception, you will not talk to me. You will tell everyone Sweetwater's Revenge is the bull to beat. I will get a ride to the arena tomorrow and back to Brighton with Jed and Pam. When I get back, my family and I will check out of the ranch, and I would appreciate it if you did not show your face until we're gone."

So that was it? She wouldn't even listen to anything he had to say? She didn't want him to help her figure out how to fix it. She just wanted to wipe him out of her life?

J.R. let the door close behind her. Hunter raked a hand through his hair. There was one person in town who might do something like this. It was a good thing they had plans to meet up because Mr. Randy Wilder had a lot of explaining to do, and it had better be good.

HUNTER'S FORMER RIDING team had a newly remodeled training facility on the northeastern side of the city. Hunter used to train there when he was part of the PBR. It should have felt like coming home, but everything was tainted by what Randy had done.

"Hunter Robbins, as I live and breathe!" Ulysses Hightower was a stout man with a pockmarked face. He was one of the wranglers here at the facility.

"How's it going, Ulysses? Long time, no see." Hunter gave the man a one-armed hug.

"I heard a rumor you might be coming in, but I didn't want to get my hopes up. We miss you around here."

"That's kind of you to say. I've been missing being here— I can promise you that." It was strange to be back and not be the champion. His picture used to be on the wall in the reception area. Only active members of the riding team were up there. He noticed Randy's picture right away.

"I think there are some people working out on the drop barrel. I assume you still know your way around and can find them?"

Hunter grinned. "Sure, I can find my way."

There were different spaces for different needs. The front space looked like a typical gym. There were machines for strength training and plenty of free weights. It smelled like sweat and foam mats. No one was there, so it was quiet. The next area housed the drop barrels. This was where riders could warm up or work on their technique without needing a whole team to manage the bulls. Lastly, there was the practice arena. When needed, they could get in a ride on some practice bulls. They weren't exactly as tough as the ones they rode in competition, but they could give riders some live action.

Randy was in the drop barrel room with a couple other guys. His eyes lit up when he saw Hunter come in.

"Look who it is, boys! The former champ is back in the house." Everyone stopped what they were doing to greet Hunter.

He couldn't deny that it felt good to receive such a warm reception. It was hard not to feel like somebody when he was in a place like this. Hunter caught up with the other guys for a few minutes until it was time to ask for a minute alone with Randy.

"Let's get you out in the arena. I want you to feel that dirt under your boots and tell me you don't want to get back in here full-time," Randy said.

"I know I told you I'd come watch you ride and give you some pointers, but I need to talk to you about something real quick."

Randy's head drew back. "What do you need to talk about?"

"Did you post videos of J.R. on social media and maybe encourage other people to comment on posts about the auction tagging those videos?" Hunter already knew the answer, but he wanted to hear Randy admit it.

"Your brother told me that you're up for a promotion at work and that you're competing against Miss Pretty in Pink for it. He said that if the bull you picked went for more money than the one she picked, the job was yours."

Hunter didn't like his nickname for J.R. It was demeaning and dismissive of her true talents. "First, don't call her that. Second, you thought I needed your help to win the competition, so you felt the need to throw her under the bus?"

Randy fidgeted with the hat on his head. "Oh, come on. It was funny. Did she tell you to come yell at me? Is she mad that I simply pointed out to the bucking bull community something that could easily be found with one quick internet search?"

"That's the thing, no one was searching for it until you pointed it out. She works extra hard to be taken seriously in this world and you just made it a heck of a lot more difficult for no reason."

He blew out a long, hard breath. "I didn't mean any harm. It was a joke."

"It was a joke that ruined my relationship, man."

Randy looked genuinely shocked. "You've got to be kidding me. What do you want me to do? You want me to call her and apologize. I'll explain you had nothing to do with it. I'm goofy, a prankster, a fool. That's got to be easy for her to believe."

Hunter shook his head. He didn't know what Randy could do to make things better. Having any contact with J.R. would definitely make it worse. Her biggest fear had come true and it was all his fault because he didn't think about Randy and his impulsiveness.

"I just needed to know why you did it. I don't know if she'll listen to me. I spent my afternoon deleting posts and comments. She didn't care. Still won't talk to me."

"Sounds like she's being unfair. I think she's jealous that you are more famous than she is.

It's not your fault that your fame helps you out more than hers does."

"I don't even care about the job promotion. I believe she deserves it. But she wouldn't let me take my name out of the running because she thought that was me showing a lack of faith in her."

"If you don't want the job, why don't you just quit?"

Hunter elbowed Randy in the rib. "Because I still need to do something with my life."

"You can do anything."

"I don't want to do anything. I want—" He stopped himself from finishing that sentence. He couldn't admit that he wanted to get back on a bull. It was reckless and stupid to want that.

Randy put a hand on his shoulder. "You want to ride. Say it."

Hunter frowned. "My parents would—"

"Stop worrying about everyone else! Stop worrying about your mom, stop worrying about J.R. Start thinking about what Hunter wants. I'm giving you permission to do what you want."

This was not the kind of temptation he needed on a day when he was feeling out of control. He was frustrated and not even sure who he should be most frustrated with. Randy? The friend of Tyson's? J.R.? Himself?

"How about you get on a bull and I'll share my opinions? Let's start there," Hunter suggested.

"You got it, boss."

Randy got the crew together and they had a practice bull ready for him in no time. Hunter felt like he was back in it just watching them prepare. Everything about this place was calling to him. What was the point of working at Bucking Wonders if J.R. hated him? There was no way he could go back. It didn't even matter if she got the promotion or he did. He couldn't work for her and she'd never work for him.

His whole world felt like it was spiraling out of control all because she didn't want to be famous. At least, not for dancing with a bull. That was the big difference between the two of them. Hunter wanted to dance. He wanted to dance bad.

He watched as Randy entered the chute. He wrapped the bull strap tightly around his riding hand. Everyone got set. The pickup men were in position. They opened the chute and the timer started. He needed to hold on for eight seconds. Randy was out of rhythm from the start. He tried to get himself back in sync, but the one-ton bull had other ideas. He twisted and bucked and Randy was down before the eight seconds were up.

The pickup man on the right got the bull's attention and led him away from where Randy was on the ground, while the other one swooped in to help him up and out of there.

"It's your hips, man. You're too tight. You need to lean back more when he does those kicks."

"I was. I couldn't lean back any farther than I did. This wasn't my first time riding, Hunter."

To be a good bull rider, a man had to be a little bit cocky and have a whole bunch of confidence. Those things also made it difficult to give constructive criticism to a bull rider.

"You asked me to watch you and give you feedback. If you don't want it, I won't give it."

Randy scoffed. "Fine. I need to lean back more. Load him up again," he told the wranglers.

The second time, Randy stayed on for a fraction longer. He hit the dirt with his fist in frustration before the pickup man got to him.

Hunter attempted to give him some coaching again. The third time, Randy was too in his head and didn't last more than a couple seconds before he was flying off the back.

"You got to—" Hunter started.

"I swear if you tell me to lean back, I will lose it."

"You need to take a break. You're mad and that's not a good state to be in when you're riding."

"You wouldn't last a second on that bull. They

pulled up the toughest practice bull we have in this place. It's ridiculous," Randy complained.

"I could ride that thing all day. There's no way that's the toughest bull in this place. I wouldn't even score him in the forties."

Randy didn't take too kindly to Hunter's comments. "You've chosen to sit out. I know you want to blame your mom for why you won't ride, but we all know it's because you're scared. Don't come here and tell me that you could ride this bull better and that he's not even that challenging when deep down you're too chicken to get back in the arena."

Maybe it was because he had been having a bad day since he got to Austin. Maybe it was because Randy was mostly to blame for that bad day because of his need to be the funny man. Maybe it was because the accusation hit a little too close to reality.

Hunter asked for a helmet and some gloves. Today was the day he was going to prove to himself that nothing could keep him from being who he wanted to be, and he wanted to be on the back of a bull.

CHAPTER TWENTY-THREE

"WILD-N-OUT IS, in my opinion, one of the all-time greats."

"Agreed," J.R. said, her attention going to the entrance one more time. She had been talking to prospective buyers for the last hour. For hours, she had prepared herself to see Hunter, and then he didn't have the nerve to show up. Jed had been asking about it all night.

"I like the way you think, J.R. I would love to talk to you more about how you choose the cows. I have been considering breeding Golden Bullseye, but I need someone to consult with me on who would make the perfect match."

"I would love to talk to you about it. We broker deals all the time. Why don't you email me a good time to get in touch and we'll set something up."

Golden Bullseye's owner shook her hand and was off to talk to someone else. J.R. checked her phone. No messages. No calls. What was he trying to prove by not showing up? Was this his way of trying to make it up to her? If he didn't come and talk up Sweetwater's Revenge, maybe that would give her a fighting chance?

There was nothing he could do to counteract the damage that had been done by his friend. She had noticed that someone had gone on all the Bucking Wonders social media pages and deleted any comments that had to do with Ferdinand. He had been a busy bee earlier in the afternoon, but now he was just off the grid.

"No word from Hunter?" Jed asked for the umpteenth time.

"No. He hasn't responded to your texts?"

"Nothing. They say delivered but none say read. Maybe his phone is dead. I'm not sure if I should do more than reach out to him."

J.R. was sure that it was nothing. She truly believed this was his messed-up way of trying to make amends.

"If you hear from him, let me know," Jed said, concern etched on his face. "I'm going to head up to my room. I'll see you in the morning?"

"Yes, sir."

The cocktail reception served its purpose. They were able to hobnob with several of the big spenders in town looking for a yearling. J.R. was pleasantly surprised that more people didn't mention that they saw the video and that they realized now who she was.

She waited until everyone had left and the bartender made the last call. Hunter wasn't coming, and she was fine with it. She would perhaps give him grief for it tomorrow when she saw him at the auction. If he would even let her talk to him. She could admit that she had been more than a little harsh.

The deeper she dove into what happened, the more she could tell that it had been purely Randy's doing. She could also tell that what he posted fell right in line with all the other ridiculous things Randy posted from his social media accounts. He fancied himself a funny guy who roasted his friends and his enemies. She could tell that the original post he made had been in jest, a gentle ribbing. It was other internet trolls who took that and made it seem worse.

If the video clip of her dancing with Ferdinand kept people from acknowledging her science was sound, that was their loss. If Hunter ended up getting the promotion over her, that was Bucking Wonders' loss. J.R. was not going to let herself play victim to her past. Hunter had said one thing that really stuck with her—why was she so afraid of accepting who she was? It was actually a good question. Maybe people would make a big deal out of it, but after her bulls started winning, would it matter anymore?

Perhaps embracing her past could help her instead of hurt her. She could prove to the bull riding world that thanks to her history, she knew what made a bull like Ferdinand docile and could weed out those traits.

J.R. went to bed after checking her phone a thousand times. Finally, she decided to send a message, just in case he wasn't calling her because he was simply doing as she had asked.

Let me know you're ok.

She woke up Saturday morning with that text delivered but left unread. She figured he was mad that she had accused him. Maybe he turned off his phone and went home. She considered calling the ranch but decided against it. She didn't want to needlessly worry anyone if he ended up being at the auction.

Jed and Pam gave J.R. a ride to the arena. Everything was set up exactly as they had planned. The catalogs were ready to be distributed to the spectators and buyers who showed up. No one would know that J.R. and Hunter (and his entire family) had worked overtime to get those catalogs together. She tried not to think about how that was the night he almost kissed her for the first time.

Hunter was a no-show at the auction. J.R. still fluctuated between being angry and being concerned. If he was intentionally not attending because he thought that was going to change the outcome somehow, she was mad. The fear that something had happened to him made her worried.

She finally caved and called her dad. He picked up on the third ring.

"Aren't you at the big auction?" he asked.

"I am, but Hunter is not. Any chance you could check to see if he went back to the ranch last night?"

"Why would he come back to the ranch? You guys have been working on this thing for so long. This is the big day. He wouldn't miss it."

The knot in her stomach tightened. He was right, Hunter would not miss it. "I have to call you back." She opened up the browser on her phone to find the number to the main lodge just as Sweetwater's Revenge went up for bidding. Even without a final push by Hunter, that bull was going to go for a good price, she just knew it.

She dialed the main lodge. It was ringing at the same time it was announced that Sweetwater's Revenge sold to Tyson Quinley for $9,500. That was the highest bid thus far. It was one of the highest bids in Bucking Wonders history.

"R&R Dude Ranch, how may I help you?" the voice on the other end of the call asked.

"Is this Cody?"

"No, I'm sorry, this is Howard. Can I be of assistance?"

"Is Cody around? Are there any Robbinses in the general vicinity of where you are that you could put on the phone?"

"Um, hold on a second. I think I saw Savannah go into the dining hall. Can you hold?"

"Sure." J.R. tapped her foot. She felt like she was about to jump out of her own skin.

Buckwild was up next. He was released out of the chute with the dummy on his back. The young bull kicked and turned. He twisted and kicked some more until the dummy went flying off. He was a powerful son of a gun. If people were smart, they would snatch him up. He was going to be a moneymaker.

"Hello, this is Savannah. How can I help you?"

"Savannah, this is J.R. I was wondering if anyone at the ranch has heard from Hunter. He didn't show up at the auction this morning. No one has seen him since yesterday early afternoon. I'm starting to get a little worried. Okay, a lot worried."

"Oh, J.R. I figured you knew," Savannah said in a voice that did not give J.R. comfort. "There was an accident. Hunter is in the hospital. I don't remember which one. I can text Everett. Mom and Dad and the boys all went up there last night."

J.R.'s heart stopped and she thought for a second

that she might pass out. She meant to say thank you, but absolutely nothing would come out of her mouth. If she tried, it would most likely be a scream.

She ran out of the arena without even telling anyone where she was going. She needed to find out what hospital he was at, so she just started calling hospitals in Austin. While on hold with the third one, someone called her on the other line from an unfamiliar number but one that had a Brighton area code. She answered it.

"Hey, J.R., it's Everett. Savannah said you were looking for Hunter. We're all here at St. David's. He's been in surgery for about two hours, so I don't know if you want to come now or maybe in a couple hours. They said it could take up to four hours and then he'll be in recovery."

"I'm coming now," she said without hesitation. "What happened?"

"I can explain when you get here." He gave her the information she needed to find them once she got to the hospital.

St. David's was in the heart of the city. Her rideshare driver dropped her off right at the main entrance. She ran in and followed the directions to the surgical wing that Everett had given her. The whole Robbins family was sitting in the blue waiting room chairs.

Julie saw her first and stood up. "You made it.

He told me not to call you. I'm sorry I listened. You must have been frantic."

It was a punch in the gut to hear that he had asked them not to call her. Was that because he didn't want her here or because he didn't think she would want to be there? He was a fool if he believed the latter.

"What happened?"

"Robo Bro decided that he was ready to come out of retirement. After two years of not riding, he thought he could just get back on a bull and not get hurt," Jack Jr. explained.

"I can't believe he didn't try something a little less dangerous first," Cody said. "Do a barrel drop. Don't get on a live animal that can kick you in the face."

"Did it kick him in the face?" J.R. was horrified at what kind of trauma that could have been.

Julie wrapped the light cardigan she had on around herself. "No, it didn't kick him in the face. It got him good on the leg. Broke his femur."

"He'll be down and out for the next four to six months," Jackson said, holding a cup of coffee in his hands. "He's going to hate that."

"That's what he gets for being reckless," Everett said, getting up out of his chair. "I knew he was going to do something like this. As soon as I heard Randy was coming for Thanksgiving."

"Don't go blaming Randy," Jackson said. "Your

brother makes his own decisions. No one put the man on that bull other than himself."

"Did he say why he didn't want you to call me?" J.R. asked Julie as the boys continued to bemoan what a boneheaded decision it was for Hunter to try to ride.

She gave J.R. a sad smile. "He said you were upset with him and that he had really made a mess of things. He said we shouldn't expect you and your family to be at the ranch when we got back."

It broke her heart to think he didn't think she would care what happened to him. "Why didn't he have you call Jed or Walter? No one knew why he wasn't at the auction."

"Well, he was pretty out of it yesterday. They had him sedated. This morning, he told me he would reach out after the surgery. He didn't want to be a distraction given what a big day it was."

J.R. felt the tears sliding down her face. "Well, not knowing if he was alive or dead was a pretty big distraction."

She didn't know why she was crying. He was alive and would recover. There was just so much emotion that she had been pushing down that it all came bubbling to the surface now that she knew he was okay.

Julie drew her into a hug. "Oh, sweetheart. I

shouldn't have listened to that boy. I should have called you. I'm sorry he worried you so much."

A nurse came out and checked the chart she was holding. "Hunter Robbins?"

Julie raised her hand. "That's us over here."

The nurse smiled and came over to give them an update. He was out of surgery. Everything had gone well. They inserted a metal rod in his leg. He was going to be in recovery for a while and when he woke up, they would be moving him to a room and that was where they would be able to visit with him.

"Time to get some food," Cody said, getting to his feet. "No reason to sit here while he's sleeping. Let's get some lunch."

Everett came over to him and slapped him on the back. "Is that all you do is think about filling your stomach?"

"Someone's got to think about it. It doesn't feed itself."

"There's an In-N-Out across the street. I'm buying," Jackson said, tossing his coffee in the nearest garbage can.

"Come with us?" Julie asked J.R.

Being with family was nice, so she agreed to tag along.

The two women trailed behind the men. Julie linked arms with J.R. "On a scale from one to ten, how mad are you at him?"

"Today? Three. Only because I'm mad at him for not letting you call me. Yesterday, it was probably a ten. What about you? You must be furious."

His mom nodded her head. "Oh, on a scale of one to ten, I am still about a twenty, but yesterday, I was a hundred, so my temper has cooled quite a bit."

"He knew how you felt about him riding. He had a fire burning in him, though. I know it was hard for him to resist. Something tells me that our little fight yesterday didn't help him make rational decisions."

"Hunter feels big. That's the only way I can describe it. He does his best to contain his feelings most of the time, but I can tell you they are filling every inch of that big ol' body of his. The bad part about that is he will do things without thinking because the feeling is in charge. The good thing about it is that no one will love you more or harder than that man."

J.R. felt the tears pricking at the corners of her eyes again.

Cody turned around and walked backward. "Hey, how did the auction go? Did your yearlings sell?"

"I was only there for Hunter's. Sweetwater's Revenge sold for $9,500. That's going to be hard to beat." J.R. realized she didn't even care. She was so mad at him yesterday because she thought the world was going to end because his bull might sell for more than hers. In reality, the only time she really felt like the world was ending was when she heard he was in the hospital. Hunter was so much more important to her than any job could ever be.

"Good thing he did well. Maybe he'll make it at this job after all. One thing's for sure, there will be no more bull riding."

"Amen to that," Julie said.

After lunch, they learned Hunter had been moved into a patient room. His parents visited him first. It only took a few minutes before Jackson appeared and motioned for J.R. to come back. "He was surprised to hear you were waiting. I told him if he swore to never get on another bull, I would trade places with you. He swore up and down that his bull riding days are over, so here I am. Room 345."

J.R. thanked him for giving up his time for her. She followed the signs on the wall that led her to the right room. She could hear Julie talking to him as she pushed open the door.

"Only time will tell," she said. She turned and smiled at J.R. "I'm going to go find the nurse and ask about an extra pillow. You two need a little privacy."

Julie reached out and touched J.R.'s hand as

she walked by her. J.R. smiled in return. Hunter was lying in bed with his leg wrapped in a complicated brace.

"I can't believe you're here."

"Tessa wanted me to come. She has a new bull joke for you," she said, taking the seat his mom had just vacated.

"Lay it on me."

"Why was the cowboy always broke?"

"Oh, man, I think I know this one. Why was the cowboy always broke?"

"Because he kept getting bucked off his bull."

Hunter laughed, then cringed. He gripped his side. "I have to be careful with the laughing."

"Okay. No more jokes for you."

His expression turned serious. "I was afraid you wouldn't, but I hoped you would come."

"So, it's true."

His brow furrowed. "What's true?"

"You went through all these dramatics just to get me back. That's what Cody thinks."

Hunter snorted a laugh and moaned at the same time. "Is that right?"

"Careful," she scolded him.

"He thinks I let a one-ton animal step on my femur just so you'd feel bad and take me back?"

"That's what everyone is thinking actually."

"Did it work?"

J.R. took hold of his hand. She hated seeing

the tubes and the bruises, but she was glad to be there with him. “It sure did.”

He closed his eyes and squeezed her hand. “Well, thank goodness because it would have really stunk if I did all this for nothing.” He opened his eyes back up and she could see the humor was masking some real hurt.

“I’m sorry I was so mad yesterday. I attacked you because I didn’t know how to handle the fear of losing everything I had been working for, but you know what I realized today?” Hunter shook his head ever so slightly. “I would give it all up… for you. Ask me where I see myself in ten years.”

He swallowed so hard his Adam’s apple bobbed up and down. “Where do you see yourself in ten years?”

“I see myself taking morning horseback rides with you and driving to work together. I see us cheering the loudest for Tessa when she graduates from college. I see us snuggled up on the couch, watching movies. I see a life with you. That’s what I see.”

Hunter had tears in his eyes. “Wow, I sure hope this is not some hallucination I am having because of all the drugs they gave me for the pain.”

They both laughed. “This is for real, I promise.”

He took a deep breath. “I’ve been in love with

you for a long time, J.R. I'm glad you finally caught up."

She was in love with this foolish, loving, amazing man. She didn't need time to tell her that it was going to work out.

"So, what happened at the auction?" Hunter asked. "Am I going to be working for you or are you going to be working for me?"

J.R. scrolled through her contacts and dialed Pam. J.R. had been texting her updates since she had gotten to the hospital. It was time to get an update from Pam.

"How are things going? Is he awake yet?"

"I'm awake," Hunter replied since J.R. had it on speakerphone.

"We're wondering how things fell out at the auction. How much did Buckwild sell for?" J.R. had already accepted that Hunter's bull sold for more.

"Let me check with Jed. Hold on."

"How much did Sweetwater's Revenge sell for?" Hunter whispered to J.R.

"$9,500."

His eyes nearly bulged from his head. "What?"

"Don't rub it in too much. I'll get over it, but it's still going to sting."

Pam came back on the line. "Buckwild sold to Beau Johnson for $9,800, which is the most we have ever sold a bull for. Congratulations, J.R.!"

She couldn't believe it. She had won.

"I knew you would beat me," Hunter said with a proud grin on his face. "Congratulations."

J.R. thanked Pam and hung up the phone. She leaned over and kissed Hunter. "I did it."

"You did it."

"I love you, Hunter Robbins."

"I love you, too."

"But I can't wait to have my own office again."

Hunter laughed so hard it hurt.

EPILOGUE

"THE HOUSE LOOKS GREAT, HONEY." Flora and Barlow gave J.R. a family hug. "Your father and I look forward to coming to visit more often." It had taken a few weeks, but J.R.'s house was finally livable again. There was still work to be done in Tessa's room, but the new roof had been installed.

"I'm going to wait until you move back to the ranch. Something tells me that's going to be pretty soon," Big E said as he opened the door to the RV. They had a long drive back to Flame.

"You're always welcome to stay at the ranch, whether we live there or not," Hunter said from his wheelchair. Tessa had locked the wheels and was holding herself up on the handle like it was some kind of gymnastics apparatus.

"If we live on the ranch, can I get free horseback riding lessons?" she asked.

"You already get free lessons," J.R. reminded her. "I'm your instructor. I don't charge myself."

"Can I get my own horse?"

"No," J.R. said at the same time Hunter said, "We can talk about it."

"I guess you should talk about it," Denny said, handing her bag to Big E.

"Why are you handing this to me? What do I look like?" She was always so bossy. Sometimes he was sure she had forgotten that she was the younger sister. She wasn't supposed to be in charge.

"You look like a guy who can put that in the RV for me so I can hug my granddaughter and great-granddaughter goodbye."

Had it been for any other reason he would have refused. He tossed it inside while his sister hugged Tessa and then J.R. "The next family reunion, I expect to see your face," Denny said firmly.

J.R. had developed a new fondness for family. "I'll be there, Gran. You just tell me when."

"We'll all be seeing each other again in less than a month. Don't forget," Flora said as if the woman talked about anything other than her induction ceremony. "December 21."

"I got it, Mom," J.R. assured her. "I'm not going to forget. I have practice five days a week between now and then so I can perform at this thing." His great-niece had finally agreed to being part of the reunion performance.

"You're going to be amazing. I have no doubts."

"Do you guys have everything?" Hunter asked. He seemed a bit anxious to get them out of there. Of course, the man had just gotten out of the hospital and was looking forward to spending time with his new girlfriend. Big E really couldn't blame him.

"I think so." Zinni swished from side to side in her carrier that hung from Flora's arm as she looked around to make sure. "Oh, I need the bracelet. I know Iris is going to be thrilled. I feel bad that it's the only thing that you had of Aunt Dandy's. If you want to come to Flame and look through the things I have, you're welcome to."

"Uh, well. I was thinking. I'll give you the bracelet if you can find me Aunt Dandy's old hat. You know the one with the flowers embroidered on it, one for each one of us girls? I think that's a fair trade."

This was new. J.R. hadn't been adding any contingencies to this thing until now. She was just like the rest of them. Big E should have known.

"Honey, I think Willow has Aunt Dandy's hat."

"Perfect, you talk to her and if she agrees then I will give you the bracelet."

Flora looked at Barlow, who looked at Denny, who shrugged. "The woman has a right to strike a deal just like the other ones did. We're heading up to see Willow next anyways. We'll talk to her about the hat. Don't you worry about that."

"Say goodbye to Bubba for Zinni," Flora told Tessa. "She's going to miss him big-time."

"I will, Glamma."

"All aboard. We've got places to be and one last grandniece to harass," Big E joked.

"Well, if anyone can convince Willow that family is the most important thing, it's you, Uncle Elias." That was one of the nicest things J.R. had said to him since he'd arrived.

"I appreciate that, Jasmine. I mean, she can't be a tougher nut to crack than you were."

"Thanks?" J.R.'s face scrunched up.

"Great! Now he's jinxed us for sure," Denny shouted from inside the RV.

"Only time will tell!" J.R. shouted back.

Wasn't that the truth? Time would tell and it wouldn't be long either because December 21 was right around the corner.

* * * * *

Next month, the final installment of The Blackwell Belles miniseries from author Cari Lynn Webb and Harlequin Heartwarming is coming!

Visit www.Harlequin.com for more great romances in this miniseries!

Enjoyed your book?

Try the perfect subscription for Romance readers and get more great books like this delivered right to your door.

See why over 10+ million readers have tried Harlequin Reader Service.

Start with a Free Welcome Collection with free books and a gift—valued over $20.

Choose any series in print or ebook.
See website for details and order today:

TryReaderService.com/subscriptions

RSBPA24R